ELLE JACKSON

A Blues Singer to Redeem Him

(H) HARLEQUIN®
HISTORICAL™

Recycling programs
for this product may
not exist in your area.

ISBN-13: 978-1-335-40736-8

A Blues Singer to Redeem Him

This edition published by arrangement with Harlequin Books S.A.

For questions and comments about the quality of this book,
please contact us at CustomerService@Harlequin.com.

Harlequin Enterprises ULC
22 Adelaide St. West, 40th Floor
Toronto, Ontario M5H 4E3, Canada
www.Harlequin.com

Printed in U.S.A.

Elle Jackson writes everything from historical romance to science fiction and fantasy romance. A Midwest girl at heart, Elle was raised in Kansas City, Kansas. She credits her desire to become an educator to her mother, who taught for more than thirty years. Elle has a doctorate in educational leadership, a master of fine arts in writing popular fiction and a master of arts in teaching. Working in urban, richly diverse schools, Elle has transitioned into writing stories about the beauty in diversity. She thanks her husband, son and toddler daughter for keeping her grounded in reality when she goes too far into her imagined worlds.

A Blues Singer to Redeem Him
is Elle Jackson's debut title
for Harlequin Historical.

Look out for more books from Elle Jackson
coming soon.

Visit the Author Profile page
at Harlequin.com.

Mikal—the one who makes it all possible.

Prologue

May 31, 1921, Greenwood, Oklahoma
Evelyn

Evelyn Laroque had never smelled human flesh burn. The metallic stench hung heavy in the air as she and her family packed to flee Greenwood. Her father and mother, Mr. and Dr. Laroque, had heard from one of their friends in the Tulsa Police Department about the mob headed for Greenwood.

Evelyn's fearless mother trembled with terror. Watching as her mother's hands shook, Evelyn blinked back warm tears. Her mother dropped several garments to the floor before they actually made it into the bag she was packing. The smoke from the fires seeped into their two-story home like the smells from a barbeque.

Evelyn followed her mother from the kitchen to the living room, stepping over large bags filled with her mother's medical books, her dad's collection of pocket watches, the jewelry her grandmother had handed down to her mother, that Evelyn had used to play dress-up as a child. The black bags stood out against the gray couch, the light oak floors, and paisley-patterned red-and-beige carpet.

"Why do we have to leave?"

Evelyn stood under the arched opening separating the dining room from the living room, intentionally blocking her mother's way. She tried desperately not to yell, but she could no longer feign indifference to her mother's resolve to flee. Her mother had been flitting about since she'd gotten the phone call. As soon as the first gunshots rang out, her mother's demeanor had completely changed.

"Evelyn Anne Laroque, go to your room and pack. We don't have much time, so only take the things you need." Her mother's voice quivered.

"No, Momma. I'm not going. If the police know about what's happening, why aren't they stopping it?"

Evelyn couldn't understand what her mother was doing. Her mother hadn't backed down from a fight *ever*. Now Evelyn couldn't reconcile the woman she saw, hands shaking, packing only the essentials, with the woman who'd fought to become a doctor when the entire world had said she wasn't smart enough, wasn't good enough.

How could her mother leave Greenwood so willingly? Their custom-made artistic white house with navy shutters was their dream home, a home that contained some of their best memories—Evelyn's seveneenth birthday, the first time she'd told her parents about her dream to become a singer and the first date she'd been allowed to go on with Jimmy Martin, a future dentist.

In her mother's study, Evelyn could see the destruction from the window. Their house sat high on a hill that overlooked Greenwood. Tulsa was flat, but her parents had bought the only lot that offered a view of the city.

Black clouds of suffocating smoke billowed up from the raging fire that ate through the entire town. The mob led by the Ku Klux Klan had opened the gates of hell and were burning everything the residents of Greenwood had. Hate had clawed its way into Tulsa and erupted on the affluent Black section known as Black Wall Street.

Evelyn's father had been silent throughout Evelyn's protest. He quietly pulled pictures that couldn't be replaced from the walls and stuffed them unceremoniously into a bag. Evelyn looked at him for a moment. What had he and her mother been like when they were Evelyn's age? Was she the crazy one for wanting to stay and fight?

Evelyn's mother went upstairs. Evelyn followed her. Her normally charismatic mother pulled clothes frantically from the drawers and took Evelyn's favorite paintings from the walls. Beads of sweat dripped down her forehead. Her mother even packed Evelyn's favorite gramophone records. She had many, but her mother knew Evelyn's favorites were always on top.

Looking around one last time, Evelyn's mother grabbed Evelyn's arm and pulled her back down the stairs and out of the house. Her father threw as many bags as he could carry into their Nash Touring before returning to their home to get the rest. The smoke smothered Evelyn. She coughed, choking on the particles in the air that might be the remains of burned bodies—her friends and neighbors' burned bodies. The thought made her retch.

Her mother opened the passenger door of their brand-new car and got in, pulling Evelyn after her. The future, no longer certain, clenched scorching hands around Evelyn's throat and she coughed uncontrollably. She could barely breathe, but she couldn't shake the feeling that her family owed it to the rest of Greenwood to stay and help.

"I'm not leaving without my friends, Momma. I can't. What about the rest of our family? We have to help them."

Dr. Laroque always had a stern expression. It was her normal everyday look. But today she had been more than stern throughout Evelyn's objection to their abrupt retreat. By the time news had spread about the Black boy who'd been accused of attacking a White girl in an elevator Downtown, Evelyn's mother had already had them packing.

"We told everyone we could, baby. Our family and friends are doing exactly what we're doing right now—

the only thing we can do. We have to get out of here before they kill us all." Tears slid down Evelyn's mother's face, cresting over high cheekbones. Her dad used his thumb to wipe them away.

They'd only been in Greenwood a short time. Leaving Louisiana had seemed like the right thing to do. Evelyn and her older brother, Carmichael, her dad and her mother, had only come a year ago. They'd traveled a long way so her mother could practice medicine in a town where Black people could be successful.

Carmichael had left Greenwood six months ago to move to Kansas City. Evelyn hoped to go stay with him as soon as she finished school to finally take a chance at singing the blues. Evelyn wanted to follow in the footsteps of her Aunt Shirleen, who sang in the same nightclubs as Mamie Smith. Now all that seemed foolish.

The car jerked as her father shifted and accelerated too fast. The moon shone brightly in the sky, casting a spotlight on the destruction of their hometown. Evelyn stopped fighting and allowed the tears to fall.

Her heart started to beat normally as they neared the border of the town. Her father had slowed to make the turn to leave Greenwood when blinding bright lights barreled down toward them. Another set of lights headed straight for them. They were trapped.

Chapter One

Five years later, August 1926
Lorenzo

Lorenzo De Luca stared up at the massive estate. The red brick stood out against the backdrop of a starry night sky. This home had been built as an homage to his family's native country of Italy. Generations of De Lucas had lived in this house.

The windows loomed like eyes to the soul, reflecting a childhood of happy memories now clouded with the blood of all who'd lost their lives because of his family. His mind went to Holly briefly, before he shook his head to clear his thoughts.

The only reason he'd come was to see his *madre*. She'd been his saving grace as a child. It was her strength that he'd pulled on to stay committed to not falling into the family business.

Lorenzo stepped onto the porch and sighed deeply. It had been months since the last time he'd been home—if he could still call it that.

His thoughts floated back to that night—the final family meeting he'd attended. The memory carried him back.

He could still hear the way the wineglasses had clanged and the moonshine had sloshed in mugs gripped by the callused hands of the De Luca family. A memory of the centuries-old table with all the important members of the family business around it stung especially deep. The young children who hadn't been old enough to hear the gory details of the family's work had played in the court-yard of the mansion that day.

Lorenzo had unbuttoned the top button of his dress shirt and cleared his throat. That had been his almost impercep-tible signal that the meeting needed to start immediately.

After a few more pats on the back and kisses on the cheek, Lorenzo's father, Alonzo "No Hope" De Luca, had said, "All right, everybody sit down, already."

Lorenzo had grown up running the halls of this mansion that had seemed full of ghosts to a child. At that meeting, he'd stood next in line to run the De Luca family. Ghosts should've been afraid of *him*.

The room had grown quiet and everyone had taken their seats. There'd been an obvious hierarchy.

The most important and dangerous members of the fam-ily sat toward the middle of the table. They were the cen-tral players in the business. Lorenzo's grandfather's seat was left empty out of respect. His grandfather was serv-ing two consecutive life sentences for the murders of the Ricci family bosses. He hadn't acted alone of course, but he wasn't a rat. Being the oldest, his grandfather had taken the fall for the younger bosses, as was expected.

"We need to get down to business. I'm getting old, and the time has come to prepare to hand over the reins to the next Don. I'm honored that my son, Lorenzo, will be tak-ing on a more active role in the family."

Alonzo had turned and kissed Lorenzo on both cheeks. Everyone around the table had erupted in cheers. Lorenzo's jaw had tightened. The thought of having to take on the burden of his family had sat heavily on his chest, making it hard for him to breathe.

The wallpaper in striking golds, blacks and whites had seemed to close in around him. He'd hoped the smile he'd practiced so well wouldn't betray the roiling emotions he'd hidden inside. He'd been able to hold himself in check so far, but the closer he got to being an actual boss, the more he'd feared what he had to tell his father.

Seeming to notice Lorenzo's discomfort, Alonzo had said, "All right, let's settle down. There's a lot to go over and the change won't happen overnight. I'm just excited that my son, in all his brilliance, along with his cousins, will be leading our family into a new era."

Lorenzo hadn't been able to breathe. He'd unbuttoned another button on his dress shirt. Sweat had slicked his skin. Dragging his hands through his hair, he'd closed his eyes and rested his head against the back of his chair.

The old chairs had been brought over from Italy when the house had been built, a hundred years ago. They'd been restored a couple of times and were now adorned in black and embellished with gold. He'd briefly considered throwing the relic through the stained-glass window.

"Can I talk to you…in private?" His voice had been but a whisper in the large room.

Alonzo had looked at his son, concern etched in his features. He'd nodded. "Discuss the issues we're having with the new city officials. When we get back, I want to hear options for handling it."

Lorenzo's father had led him to the library, down the hall from the meeting room.

As soon as the door had closed behind them, Lorenzo had turned to his father and said, "I can't do this." His voice had come out stronger in the small room than he'd expected.

"What did you say?" His father's voice, though tempered, had been laced with venom.

Lorenzo had lifted his head and met his father's glare. "I said, I can't do this. I won't continue to be a part of this business. I wouldn't even *call* the intentional murdering of people a business."

"It's called a family," Alonzo had said. "And if you can't be a part of the business, then you aren't a part of this family either. Think about what you're saying and tread carefully."

Lorenzo had walked closer to his father to make sure he got his point across. "Then I guess I won't be a member of the family. I'm finally realizing the cost of being in this family. It's too great."

"Don't forget what the De Luca name has done for you and continues to do for you." His father's voice had risen.

Lorenzo walked to the door. With his hand on the handle, he said, "That's the problem. How can I call myself a boss, someone to be respected, when I stand on the backs of the De Lucas? I won't continue to benefit from this…" Lorenzo motioned to the expensive furniture in the room "…this family any longer."

He'd opened the door and walked out. The sound of glass shattering behind him as he'd fled the room hadn't surprised him. His father's temper was legendary.

"Lorenzo, where are you going?" His father's voice had thundered.

"Don't worry, Father. I won't be back."

Lorenzo had let the door slam in his wake.

The memories flooded in as Lorenzo stood outside the front door to the home he'd once loved. The night air yanked Lorenzo from his reverie. He couldn't focus on his last conversation with his father. He had to move forward and try to stay connected to the only member of his family who still spoke to him—his mother.

Before he could knock, the heavy door swung open. "Lorenzo, my sweet boy. I was worried you'd changed your mind about coming. Why are you standing out here?"

Lorenzo's mother stood in a gray floor-length flowing

gown covered with black lace and beading. Her intricately coiled hair was pinned up away from her face, the inky black strands shining against a crystal headband embellished with equally dark feathers. She reached out and pulled him into a hug.

Lorenzo took a deep breath. She smelled of expensive perfume and flowers, as she always did. As a child, he would hide his face in her neck as she held him tight. He'd often been running from his father, who'd thought discipline was synonymous with heavy fists and yelling.

Lorenzo had grown up thinking his father hated him, but when he'd gotten old enough to join the family meetings, he'd realized his father had been trying to prepare him for a life of violence. His father had wanted Lorenzo to be someone everyone else feared. His father had wanted him to be the strongest De Luca there ever was.

"I've missed you, Mamma."

Lorenzo pulled back. In one night, he'd gone from seeing his mother and father just about every single day to not seeing either of them for months. He still talked to his mother on the telephone daily, but it wasn't the same.

He missed her soft smile and kind eyes. He missed her home cooking that always made him feel like a child again. Even with hired help, his mother relished being able to cook authentic Italian meals for the entire family. Lorenzo had always thought she should rely more on the maids when it came to preparing meals, but it was one of the few things that made her happy in a world filled with imminent danger.

His mother moved out of the doorway and gestured for him to come in.

The butler appeared in the hallway. "Can I take your jacket, Mr. De Luca?" The tall man stood statuesque in a black tuxedo.

"No, Alan, I'm not staying long. And please don't call me Mr. De Luca—that's my father." Lorenzo smiled.

He'd grown up with servants, and he had befriended them all. Alan had been a part of his household since he could remember, and no matter how many times Lorenzo told him not to call him Mr. De Luca, he always did. Lorenzo's father had always been miffed at how friendly Lorenzo was to the people who worked for them.

"Come into the study, please."

Lorenzo's mother walked into the dark room with walls of floor-to-ceiling bookshelves. She turned on the golden lamps. The dark leather furniture, huge antique desk and the hundreds of books had been some of his favorite things growing up. Now the study looked out of place—or maybe it was him that was out of place.

"I can't stay long." Lorenzo stood in the doorway not sure what to do.

"Sit down, son." His mother offered him a glass of whiskey from the crystal decanter.

He shook his head and sat in one of the oversize chairs. The room smelled like his father: smoke, maple and sandalwood. Those smells used to strike so much fear in Lorenzo. It stunned him how much the scents smelled like home now.

His mother sat in the chair next to him and took his hand in hers. "I've missed you so much. Our phone calls are the highlight of my day, but there is nothing like seeing your face." She touched his cheek and smiled brightly. "I've missed those beautiful eyes of yours, my son."

"I'm sorry I've not been around, but you know how Father feels toward me. Coming here would've served no purpose."

"Your father loves you, Lorenzo."

Lorenzo didn't respond. His mother stood and picked up her drink from the bar cart. She paced back and forth.

"What is it, Mother?"

Lorenzo hated to see his mother wound up. He'd come immediately when he'd heard the panic in her voice. He'd been in the middle of discussing hiring a new singer with Jeb, his second-in-charge, but he'd run out of the club after receiving the phone call from his mother. She'd refused to tell him what was going on over the phone.

His mother looked over Lorenzo's head toward the doorway. Lorenzo followed her gaze. His father stood there, brooding and breathing heavily like he'd just taken a run.

"What's going on?" Lorenzo stood and turned to his mother. "You said he wasn't going to be here."

"He has something important to tell you, son. You need to hear it from him. Please, sit."

Lorenzo stared at his father for a long moment. He couldn't interpret his father's expression, but it wasn't the anger he'd expected. He sat heavily in the chair and his mother sat next to him again, clenching her drink in her hands and avoiding his gaze.

His father walked in and sat behind his desk. "I have some bad news to share, which might change your mind about being a part of the family."

Lorenzo started to protest, but his father held up his hand to silence Lorenzo.

"Your cousin Vinny has been missing for the last week. His body was found this morning, along with that girl he's always with."

"You mean his fiancée, the mother of his child?"

"Yeah. We aren't sure yet if this is mob related or related to the insurgence of the KKK in the city. Getting involved with Negro women is trouble. They're only good for one thing."

Lorenzo's mother cleared her throat. "Lorenzo, are you going to be okay? I know that you and Vinny were close."

Lorenzo couldn't speak. There was so much wrong with what his father had just said that it took Lorenzo's breath away.

He wasn't sure there was any point in arguing with his father about the importance of treating all women with respect. His father had many Black mistresses for the better part of Lorenzo's childhood. One of his father's favorites had a daughter, Mildred. She was one of Lorenzo's closest friends… Dred was like family to him.

Unable to stomach his father any longer, Lorenzo stood. "I'm not sure what you thought I could do, but I hope you're able to find out who murdered Vinny and his fiancée. Who's going to take care of his son?"

"The boy will go to his colored grandmother. Vinny's mother and father don't want him."

Lorenzo couldn't imagine how the four-year-old boy was handling losing both of his parents. He would go see the boy as often as possible, so he wouldn't forget his father.

"I find it really disgusting that in a family that claims to be built on the idea that family comes first, you would let Vinny Jr. be raised without the resources of the De Luca family. He *is* a De Luca."

"For someone who turned his back on the family name, *I* find it odd that you would want us to be involved with Vinny Jr." His father's voice rippled with anger.

"Believe me, it isn't my first choice for Vinny Jr., but he's too young to fend for himself. He will be a target because he is a De Luca. He needs the protection of the family until he's old enough to protect himself. Don't compare me, a grown man, to a child. I don't want or need the protection of the family."

"Whether you think you need the protection or not, you still have it, son."

Lorenzo inhaled sharply. He had become increasingly

aware of all the ways in which he'd benefited either directly or indirectly from the De Luca name. "I know, and I have to figure out how to disconnect who I am from this *family*."

Lorenzo had been roiling over the fact that he had been a benefactor of his family's power and influence for his entire life, and he had been so naive about it. Even when he'd decided to leave the family, he'd still had their protection and their influence.

"Listen, Lorenzo, I just want you to know your onions and think long and hard about how abandoning your family now will put us in danger. If it was the KKK who murdered Vinny, then we need to teach them a lesson. We need you. I'm getting old, and the idea that my own *ragazzino* has abandoned everything he is shames me. I die a little every time I look at your empty chair around the table. You must come back to take your place as the new Don. You're abandoning your responsibilities like a coward. And I didn't raise a coward." His father's voice thundered.

"I haven't abandoned my family or my responsibilities. I just finally decided that getting money and influence by killing and destroying others is not how I want to live my life. I would rather be my own man and work for my power and respect, than crawl over the backs of others to get it." Lorenzo walked to the door. "Bye, Ma. I'll give you a call later to find out more about Vinny."

Lorenzo's heart broke at the thought that he'd never see his cousin again.

"Son, I will always love you and hope that you will see the error in your judgment before it's too late. Everything I've done, I've done for you." His father sighed tiredly.

Lorenzo laughed without humor and walked out of the house. He wasn't naive enough to think what his father had just said wasn't a thinly veiled threat.

His palms were sweaty, despite the chill in the air. He'd be lying to himself if he said he didn't want to avenge his cousin's murder. His blood boiled with the venom of revenge: the kind that only blood on his hands could satiate.

There was an emptiness in his gut. He should have done more to get Vinny to leave the family with him. They'd argued the last time they'd talked about Lorenzo's decision. Vinny had called Lorenzo a coward. Lorenzo had told Vinny that the way their family stood behind the De Luca name was the definition of cowardice.

They'd never talked again after that argument, and now they never would.

Lorenzo blinked back warm tears in the night air as he opened the door to his car.

Chapter Two

Evelyn

Sunlight streamed through the sheer blinds covering the only window in the tiny room. The heat should have been stifling on an August morning in the Midwest, but Evelyn Laroque shivered from some internal cold that grew out of her fear.

She wiped away a warm tear from her cheek as she took another box off the shelf in her grandmother's closet. She had to find the bills to see how much debt her grand had. She knew the medical bills continued to pile up as she recovered from her latest fall. Her grand had hidden them from Evelyn, but she had to know what she was dealing with if she were going to make a plan to help her grandmother keep her house.

The slip of paper threatening to repossess her grandmother's home served as a constant reminder that her family's financial situation had taken a turn for the worse, and Evelyn was the only one who could do anything about it.

Evelyn was desperate. She'd finally broken down and sold her parents' car—the only thing she'd had left of them and their life before. Having a car had been a luxury anyway, and Evelyn would have to do without.

Her brother, Carmichael, had used most of the money left by their parents to purchase land with a small house and a used car in Kansas City. Evelyn hadn't fussed over

Carmichael taking the majority of their parents' money because she wanted her brother to be able to make a life. As a man, he would need to find a way of making a steady income to provide for his family. Evelyn, on the other hand, would be expected to marry someone who could take care of her.

No matter how much Evelyn resented that fact, she wouldn't keep Carmichael from having a family if that was what he wanted to do.

Her mother and father had not been traditionalists. Her mother had been highly educated and had married for love. Her mother had used to say that Evelyn's father had come into her life like a whirlwind, and even though she'd fought against falling in love with anyone, she'd had no choice where Evelyn's father was concerned, so they'd got married.

The comforting scent of lavender and oranges drifted through the air. Evelyn took a deep breath to fight back the tears. Her grand would be okay. She had to be.

The dusty box held old pictures of her mother as a young girl. Evelyn reeled at how much she resembled her—from the high cheekbones to the rich brown skin and almond-shaped eyes. It was like looking at herself from another time. The pictures were grainy, but her mother's smile shone through, just like she remembered it.

Evelyn thumbed through the box, stopping when she came across an old newspaper clipping from the *Tulsa Chronicle*. The headline sent Evelyn hurtling back in time to that awful night. The picture of bodies piled on top of each other accompanying the article made bile churn in her stomach.

May 31, 1921
Hate-Filled Mob Sends 200 Blacks to Fiery Grave!
The death toll continues to rise as bodies are re-

*covered from the burned houses and buildings of
Tulsa's affluent Black town. Greenwood was home
to hundreds of successful businesses, including hospitals, banks and grocery stores.*

*It has been reported that a White mob descended
on Greenwood in the early hours of the morning and
by afternoon the entire town had been burned, many
residents included.*

*Some of the recovered bodies have been iden-
tified. Dr. Juliette Laroque and her husband, Mr.
Ernest Laroque, were among those identified. Dr.
Laroque had been a revered gynecologist in her
field.*

Evelyn threw down the paper, unable to read any more
about her mother and father. Her nightmares kept that night
alive in her mind, and she didn't need to read the details
to remember how that mob had massacred her parents and
stolen the future her family should have had.

She had put the box back on the shelf and grabbed a
different one when a knock on the door nearly made her
drop everything. She was expecting the new owner of her
parents' car, but the sudden noise in the otherwise silent
home startled her. She put the box down, wiped her cheeks
and walked to the door.

She sighed inwardly, even though she knew the person
who was coming over to get the car. Opening the door,
she plastered a smile on her face. "Ronald, let me get the
keys for you."

The middle-aged man stood at least a foot taller than
Evelyn. He was handsome, but she had determined a long
time ago that he was too eager and she didn't trust that.
As she turned to get the keys out of the dish on the table,
Ronald grabbed her arm. She turned to face him, strug-
gling to keep the irritation out of her expression. She didn't

trust him, but it wasn't his fault she was having to sell the last piece of her history with her parents.

He released her, seeming to notice her disapproval of being touched. "I heard your grandmother is back in the hospital. I wanted to see if you needed anything." His voice rumbled from his chest, laced with nefarious undertones.

The fact that he was almost twice her age didn't really bother her. What did bother her was that he completely ignored the signals she sent him, which said that she wasn't interested at this time in a serious relationship. The fact that he continued to pressure her made her dislike him.

"I really appreciate your concern, but I'm about to leave. I don't need anything except the money for the car, but you're welcome to stop by the hospital and see my grand if you have time."

"I'd love to go with you to the hospital." His smile sent a chill down Evelyn's spine.

She hadn't asked him to go with her. And she knew he had no real concern for her grandmother. He was only continuing his pursuit of her because she hadn't agreed to marry anyone yet.

Evelyn thought it ridiculous that she had to agree to marry someone. She was only twenty-two. She was her own person and had her own dreams to pursue. Marriage was not one of those dreams.

Her parents had done all the right things. They'd gone to college when no one had thought they should and gotten advanced degrees. They'd married and had two children, and then they'd been murdered.

Evelyn wouldn't allow the same world who'd killed her parents to dictate how she lived her life. Seeing Ronald solidified in her mind what she had to do.

Leaving him at the door, she quickly retrieved the keys then dropped them in his hand. He'd pulled the money from the pocket of his white dress shirt.

"Thank you for coming by on such short notice, but I have to go now." Evelyn closed the door in his face. Her grandmother would be very upset with her treatment of Ronald, but she had to start putting her plan into action. There was no more time to waste.

She would go to Kansas City. Get a job as a blues singer. Send money to her grandmother and pay for her to have the best in-home care money could buy. She'd also put her foot down with her grand about doing the physical therapy the doctor had prescribed.

Evelyn had been saving as much as she could from her job at the pharmacy. Now, with the money from the car, she would be able to buy her bus ticket to Kansas City and pay her grand's bills for the next month.

She went to her room and dug out the box where she kept her valuables. She'd saved close to five hundred dollars, in spite of giving her grandmother money every week. Her grandmother kept saying she didn't need the money, and Evelyn had started to believe her until she'd got the notice of foreclosure while her grandmother was in the hospital.

Evelyn would pay her grandmother's house bills through the month and then get what she needed to make the trip to Kansas City in another couple of weeks. She would pursue her dream and help her grand.

With that resolution, a wave of guilt flowed over her, causing her to close her eyes for a long moment. She had to remember the only reason she was going to Kansas City was so she could take care of the woman who'd taken her and her brother in when they'd lost everything. Her grand was all the family she and Carmichael had left, and Evelyn would do anything to keep her safe—something she hadn't been able to do for her parents.

Chapter Three

Sunny afternoon, September 1926
Lorenzo

Lorenzo blatantly ignored the sputtering red-faced man across the desk from him. The impulse to strangle the man was strong, but Lorenzo contained himself. He had to get information about his cousin's death first. He'd told his father that he wouldn't be a part of whatever revenge the family was planning, but he couldn't sit by and do nothing. The KKK had just fallen into his lap, and he planned to take full advantage of their stupidity.

Running his hand through his hair, Lorenzo said, "I'm afraid I'm going to have to ask you to leave."

Sighing loudly, Lorenzo moved from behind the oak Renaissance-era antique desk, positioning himself at the door to his office. The man, apparently one of the head cats in the KKK, stood statue-still, beady eyes focused on Lorenzo.

The man had no idea that Lorenzo planned to put his head on a spike in the middle of the city for all other KKK members to see. The only reason it hadn't already happened was because Lorenzo needed information about who else was involved in his cousin's murder.

Three years ago Lorenzo's nightclub, Blues Moon, had opened up at the beginning of one of the hottest summers in Kansas City. He hadn't used his father's money to start the club, like his father had wanted. That fact, however, hadn't removed the stain of Lorenzo's mob family from Lorenzo's elegant club.

Lorenzo had started off small. He'd worked for another club for four years as the money man, saving everything he could to start his own establishment. Lorenzo had fallen in love with the blues and the new sounds that were coming out. He knew exactly what kind of band and atmosphere he wanted to create, and he'd done it. He'd exceeded his own expectations, crediting his success to the fact that he was an inclusive club owner who served everyone equally.

It was more than making money for him, though. It was about being one of the only places people could come and commune together with great music, food, and booze. He and his cousin Vinny had snuck into speakeasies when they were young and fallen in love with the music and the dancers. With Vinny gone, it was even more important to Lorenzo to make his club something spectacular.

Now the KKK thought Lorenzo should be an active leader in the organization, to solidify the KKK's influence in the city with backing from the mob.

No one knew Lorenzo had declared his independence from his family. He'd been shocked that his father had directed all the bosses to keep that information hushed. Lorenzo's mother had told him it was because his father still wanted Lorenzo to be protected, and still held on to the belief that Lorenzo would change his mind. So Lorenzo continued to reap the benefits of the family name, and he wasn't sure how to change that. He didn't *want* to be a benefactor of his family's malevolent deeds, but what choice did he have aside from leaving the city or changing his name?

The KKK openly hated Italians, but the hold Lorenzo's family had on the city and its politics had caught the interest of the vile organization. The leaders of the KKK had no idea that the De Lucas suspected the organization's involvement with Vin's murder.

After Lorenzo had gotten home the day he'd visited his mother, she'd called to apologize and let him know that his father had information about the KKK and one of its leaders who had been connected to the disappearance of several young Black women in the city in the last few months, and now that man stood blubbering in Lorenzo's office. It was like Lorenzo was *supposed* to avenge Vinny's death and the deaths of those young women.

Lorenzo looked through the window of his office. He had a view of the dance floor, which could easily hold one hundred people. He still marveled at the chandeliers, strategically placed over tables with red velvet cloths and patrons of all races.

"As you can see, Mr. Simmens…" Lorenzo motioned to his patrons "… I don't care what race my customers are. They all have green money. And, while we are on that subject, your presence here is making some of them nervous. When they get nervous, they leave. And I lose money. I get angry about losing money. Do you see where I'm going with this?"

Lorenzo needed the information about Vinny's killers, but he had no intention of joining such a disgusting organization. He would figure out another way.

Mr. Simmens, to his credit, didn't respond to Lorenzo's thinly veiled threat. "Mr. De Luca, boy," he said, drawing out the "b" sound, "you better rethink your business ventures before something happens to this beautiful place."

Lorenzo didn't like being threatened, especially in his place of business. He grabbed Mr. Simmens by the collar and shoved him against the wall. "Don't come back in here, or the next time you might not walk out. Don't forget who I am. I can make you disappear, and no one would dare ask me about it."

Lorenzo tightened his grip around the man's throat, seriously considering choking him until he passed out. It had been a while since Lorenzo's temper had gotten the best of him, but Simmens had brought out a side of him he tried to hide even from himself.

This side—the anger and violence—took Lorenzo back to a time when he'd thought he would follow in his father's footsteps. That was before what had happened to Holly, his high school sweetheart, the only girl he'd ever cared for. They'd been planning a future together all those years ago. He'd thought he loved her, but as he'd grown up he'd realized he'd been infatuated with her. He'd wanted to possess her as his father had done his mother. After Holly's death, Lorenzo had learned that possession and infatuation were not love.

Holly had been outside of the mob. Her family had been moderately wealthy, but even they hadn't been able to escape the catastrophic consequences of one of them being involved with the mob. Holly had been just an innocent girl who fell for the wrong boy.

When Lorenzo released Mr. Simmens the Klansman clutched his throat, gasping for air.

Lorenzo rolled his eyes and took a threatening step toward the choking man. Mr. Simmens straightened himself up quickly and left the office.

Turning around once he was in front of other patrons, Simmens said, "You have one week to confirm your membership."

Sweat beaded on Mr. Simmens's forehead and slid down his cheeks. He pulled a handkerchief from his pocket, yellowed from age or use, and rubbed his brow.

He hurried toward the door and called over his shoulder, "One week."

Lorenzo's club brought glamour and opulence to the downtown Kansas City area. No matter the time of day, his customers wore three-piece suits, flapper dresses, boas and floor-length fur coats in the winter. They paid for its opulence with overpriced whiskey and the best moonshine for two hundred miles. The smells of hot ham and fresh pretzels wafted through the air.

Before Mr. Simmens could reach the entrance, the door swung open and the most beautiful woman stepped through the threshold. She paused a moment, probably letting her eyes adjust to the dimly lit club, before walking—or gliding like an angel, more accurately—to the bar.

Lorenzo's mood immediately lifted. The woman had skin the color of wet sand. Her wavy hair, thick and dark, had been pinned neatly away from her face, highlighting her rosy-colored high cheekbones and sensual full lips. Lorenzo wanted to know this woman. He wanted to touch that satiny skin, nuzzle his nose in the crevice of her slender neck just above the collarbone that showed so seductively.

Mr. Simmens picked up his pace. As the dame with the form-fitting dress and matching lavender hat and gloves passed, Simmens grabbed her slender arm and said, "I'd love to teach an uppity n—"

Mr. Simmens didn't have a chance to finish his sentence.

Lorenzo couldn't remember socking the Klansman, but seconds later Mr. Simmens was on the ground, and Lorenzo's hand was throbbing and red. Blood gushed from Mr. Simmens's nose. His body went limp. His eyes rolled and closed seconds later.

Silence filled the air, smothering the usual baritone sounds of Lorenzo's bass guitar player.

Lorenzo looked up to see the woman staring at him. Her eyes were a light brown, almost gold, framed by long curly lashes, and her gaze tore into him. He took a step toward her, hand outstretched. Realizing he was about to cup her face, he let his hand drop to his side. He didn't even know her.

"Are you all right?" he said.

She didn't respond right away. Lorenzo worried she was in shock from the near assault.

"I'm fine, and I don't need you acting like a Neanderthal for my benefit."

Her hands were balled into fists. Lorenzo wondered if she'd planned to hit Simmens herself.

"Is this how you behave regularly, or was this show of testosterone for my benefit only?"

Lorenzo couldn't understand why this woman would get sore when his gesture had been nothing less than chivalrous. It seemed like she'd been offended by his defending her.

"I… I was just… He was going to say…" No one had made Lorenzo stutter in his entire life.

"I know what he was going to say, Mr….?"

"De Luca. Lorenzo De Luca." Lorenzo tried to regain some semblance of composure. He forced his voice deeper, to sound more authoritative, which was actually his normal register.

"Mr. De Luca, it wouldn't be the first time, and it won't be the last. I don't need your help."

Lorenzo, aghast at her words, couldn't think of anything to say—partly because of her harsh tone and partly because of how beautiful she was. The demure dress couldn't hide her womanly figure. With her high cheekbones and sharp chin, brown skin and pink lips, she should have been a movie star; maybe she was.

"I'm looking for the owner of this club." She looked at him with her brows furrowed.

"I'm the owner," Lorenzo said, still confused by her reaction. He realized everyone in the club was looking at him, this woman and the unconscious man on the floor.

"I would like to audition to be your lead singer." She switched her handbag to her right forearm, seemingly unfazed by the blood pooling at her feet. She had a slight accent—Southern, maybe. Her hands were covered by gloves.

"Boss, you want us to take care of this?" Lorenzo's security guard asked, pointing to Simmens on the floor.

Lorenzo nodded, not looking away from the woman. He hadn't taken his eyes off her. Suddenly the air swirled warm around him. Lorenzo's last lead singer had gotten a record deal and had gone on tour. He was happy for her. His goal was always to uplift someone if he could. But it had left him tasked with finding a replacement for his most popular nights last-minute. His club had a combination of live music, instrumental nights and nights with singers. He had been on the search for a singer for three nights a week. The other nights were already taken care of by his current singers.

The gorgeous woman shifted her weight, looking around at the other patrons who'd started talking, dancing and drinking again, but still stared.

The light from outside shot into the club when Lorenzo's security guys opened the door to carry Simmens out. They would take him and dump him somewhere his own kind would find him. The Ku Klux Klan had set up shop just east of the city limits, in a large barn that sat on a couple of acres of land. Lorenzo's men would drop him near there, so he'd be found.

The woman smoothed her dress with her gloved hands repeatedly.

Lorenzo, remembering himself, said, "So you can sing?" It didn't seem fair to Lorenzo for one person to have beauty like hers *and* have a beautiful voice.

"That's what people tell me. I've been singing since I was a child. My aunt sings, and I heard your club was a good place for…everyone." The woman averted her eyes from Lorenzo.

Lorenzo smiled at that. He liked that his club was known for treating people right. Maybe him being a mobster's son wasn't all people said about him and his establishment.

"I'd love to hear your voice. You want to sing something now?"

Lorenzo had, in fact, already hired a lead singer, but for some reason he didn't care about that. He'd auditioned probably a dozen beautiful women. Most of them had pretty good voices, but Lorenzo wanted—no, he *needed* to hear this woman sing. He'd got that feeling in his gut that something spectacular was about to happen.

However, in spite of his gut feeling, he couldn't get the woman's anger out of his mind. He'd thought he'd done the right thing. It bothered him how consumed he already was by this gorgeous woman. She was a looker. He had to know what he'd done that had upset her. Simmens *deserved* to have his big beezer broken.

"Yes… I'd love to sing for you." The woman scanned the club again. "Um…in front of all your customers?"

"Yes. They're who you'll be singing for if you get the job, Miss… I'm sorry, what is your name?"

She smiled, rosy lips revealing bright white teeth. "Evelyn—Evelyn Laroque."

"Miss Laroque, it's a pleasure to make your acquaintance." Lorenzo held his hand out to shake hers, remembering when he'd almost embraced her. The idea of touching her stunning face made his heart beat faster.

When their hands touched, Evelyn sucked in a quick breath. That small gesture nearly did Lorenzo in.

He wasn't sure what he'd do about the woman he'd hired if Evelyn's voice was as outstanding as her looks. But Lorenzo was a shrewd businessman. He'd never second-guessed his decisions and that confidence in himself had always led to more success. So he wouldn't start questioning his gut now. Besides, hearing Miss Laroque sing was the right thing to do. After all, she'd almost been assaulted in his club. And if she was indeed an amazing singer, he would have to do what was best for his business—hiring Evelyn and firing the other woman.

The only problem was that Lorenzo prided himself on being a man of his word. The woman he'd promised the position to would need some sort of compensation.

Lorenzo couldn't believe he was already thinking of hiring Miss Laroque and firing Nelly, an amazing singer in her own right, before even hearing Evelyn sing.

Chapter Four

Evelyn

The club smelled of savory meats and breads. Evelyn hadn't indulged in food like that in forever. She'd been careful with her money, saving for the things she would surely need if she got the job as lead singer for Blues Moon——new dresses, reliable transportation from West Eden to Kansas City…

Her grandmother continued to be a seamstress, but the more often she fell, the harder it was for her to keep up her business. When Evelyn was growing up, before her parents were murdered, she'd never worried about money. Whatever she'd wanted, her parents would get for her——and her brother. Now Carmichael helped their grandmother as much as he could, but he'd purchased land just outside Kansas City, and his crops hadn't made a profit yet.

Evelyn walked with Mr. De Luca, still unsure what to think of this man. He was beyond handsome——dark hair against pearl skin, beard with just a dusting of silver, making him look distinguished.

The way his suit stretched across his shoulders made warmth rise to Evelyn's face. Her mother had always told her that she wore her feelings in her expression. Evelyn's heart raced, and she wasn't sure if it was because she was about to sing in a twenty-four-hour club in front of strangers for the first time, or because of the way Mr. De Luca looked at her, so intense, with those gray-green eyes. Evelyn had never seen eyes like his…

"Benny, this is Miss Laroque. She's going to sing something for us."

Evelyn had been so caught up in her own mind that she hadn't paid attention to where Mr. De Luca was taking her. Now she was on the side of the stage waiting while Mr. De Luca spoke to his bass guitar player. Evelyn didn't miss the look that passed between Benny and Lorenzo. Benny seemed taken off guard by Lorenzo's introduction.

"Sure thing, boss. Miss Laroque, it's a pleasure. What song would you like us to play for you?"

The gentleman with the guitar wore a red shirt with black pants. He had an elegant burgundy guitar that seemed to glow under the low lights of the stage. There was also a pianist—an older gentleman with a kind smile—a drummer and a saxophonist.

Evelyn hesitated at first. She couldn't seem to make her feet take a step toward the center of the stage. And Mr. De Luca must have noticed her hesitation because he motioned for her to come forward to join them in the spotlight. His reassuring gaze broke her trance.

"Do you know 'Crazy Blues' by Mamie Smith?"

"Do we know it?" Benny smiled at the others in the band and struck up the first chord of the song.

The gentleman eased Evelyn's anxiety a little. His smile was so welcoming and warm, she couldn't help but relax a little. She'd wanted to be a singer for so long, but she hadn't thought what being a part of an actual band would feel like; so far, so good…

Mr. De Luca held out a microphone before Evelyn had a chance to think about it. It was the first time she'd used one. She faced the crowd, closed her eyes and let the melody carry her remaining fears away.

The first words floated from her like they were part of

the atmosphere; she dug deep for strength and courage. Benny and his band kept up with her easily. She did the runs, and finally started to relax into the flow of the song. People were out of their seats dancing. When she finished, the patrons cheered, and Mr. De Luca clapped slowly, staring at her from the side of the stage. His expression didn't give away his thoughts.

She picked her purse up from atop the piano. "Well, what did you think?" she said as Mr. De Luca led her off the stage and to a back office.

He closed the door behind them. Her pulse quickened. She took a deep breath, trying not to panic.

"Have a seat, please." He motioned to a beautiful paisley-patterned chair across from a very grand desk. "Drink?" he said.

"Um…no, thank you." Clearing her throat, she said, "Are you going to tell me what you thought of the song?"

He poured himself a drink, seeming unfazed that she didn't wish to join him. "I thought it was sensational," he said with his back to her. "I'm trying to think of words to describe your singing, but nothing seems adequate."

His voice was like a smooth baritone note with perfect inflections. He turned to face her. Evelyn searched his expression to see if she could determine if he was filling her with lies or not. She couldn't tell.

"So, am I hired, then?" she said.

"Absolutely. I can't let you go to another club. That would be bad for my business now that my customers have heard your voice. I do have other singers for the less popular nights, but your voice is so…unique and beautiful. I can't pass up the opportunity to introduce you to the music scene in Kansas City. My last lead singer got offered a record deal, and now she's touring."

Mr. De Luca sat back, taking a long pull on the brown liquid in what Evelyn imagined was a crystal glass. Her parents had used to drink out of crystal glasses in the evenings when they came home from work.

"That's…that's wonderful. When can I start?"

"Honestly? I already hired a lead singer." Lorenzo sighed.

"I don't understand. You said you were hiring me."

"I am—and I want you to start right away. It's just I'm going to have to figure out what to tell the young woman who thinks she's starting as well."

"Oh, Mr. De Luca… I don't want you to go firing anyone because of me."

"Luckily, that's not up to you. Besides, there are many other clubs she can work at. Matter of fact, I'm going to call in a favor and I'll have her another job in an hour." Lorenzo stood. "I'm going to have you talk with Benny about a playlist. Songs you don't know, you'll have to learn quickly. Any songs you want to sing, just give Benny a heads-up. I've yet to find a song they don't know."

Evelyn stood. "Thank you, Mr. De Luca. This is something I've wanted for a long time."

"Well, I think it will be good for both of us—and, please, call me Lorenzo."

Evelyn nodded, unsure if she felt comfortable being so informal with this man.

Lorenzo extended his hand to her. "We're happy to have you here, Miss Laroque."

"Evelyn." She shook his hand, and a jolt of energy passed between them as they locked eyes.

She couldn't help but notice how his callused fingers warmed her skin, but that the back of his hand was smooth and soft. He had many discrepancies, Evelyn imagined. He was nothing like she'd been expecting the son of a mobster to be. She had a feeling she had only seen the beginnings of the dichotomy that was Lorenzo De Luca.

When she turned to leave, she saw a large man in a white chef's coat, holding a boy by the collar.

"Boss, look what I found, trying to steal food. He must have snuck in the backdoor when I was taking the trash out. Whatcha want me to do with him?"

"Give him some food."

"But, boss…"

"Give him some food. And let him go." Lorenzo walked up to the boy and knelt down in front of him.

"I ain't going to jail."

The little boy looked to be about seven. His pale skin was covered with dirt or soot. He stared at the floor.

"Look at me," Lorenzo said. "Please."

The little boy looked at Lorenzo with big blue eyes and the longest lashes Evelyn had ever seen. Matted blond curls hung down to his shoulders.

"You're not going to jail. We're going to get you something to eat and find your mom. Where do you live?"

"We live on the street."

Lorenzo looked over the little boy's head at the cook, indicating that he should leave. "What's your name?"

The little boy was silent.

"I want to help you. What's your name?"

"Malcolm."

"Is it just you and your mom?"

Malcolm shook his head.

Evelyn wondered what Lorenzo was going to do with the little boy. It broke her heart to see his ragged clothes and his hollow cheeks. He looked like he hadn't eaten in several days.

"I have a baby sister. Her name is Nina."

"That's a beautiful name." Lorenzo looked up to the tall man now standing in the doorway. "I want you to meet someone, Malcolm. This is my really good friend Jeb. He's going to get you something to eat. Then he's going to go with you to find your mom. We have a place for you all to stay. We're going to help your mom get on her feet, so you all can eat and stay safe. Does that sound like a good plan to you?"

Malcolm nodded. Tears formed in his big eyes.

"Great. Go with Jeb, and I will come check on you, your mom and Nina tomorrow. It was a pleasure to meet you, Malcolm."

Lorenzo held out his hand and Malcolm shook it. Then the little boy grabbed Lorenzo around the neck.

"Okay, son. I'd come with you now, but I have somewhere I have to be. I'll see you tomorrow. Take care of your mom and sister."

"Yes, sir." Malcolm left with Jeb.

Lorenzo turned to Evelyn. "I'm sorry about that."

"No, not at all. Is there anything that I can do?" Evelyn had been standing by Lorenzo's desk, but now she moved to stand directly in front of him.

Lorenzo looked at her. "Well, since you'll be working here now, would you be willing to help me plan a fundraiser to help families like Malcolm's? It's something I've been wanting to do for a while. I've been using my own money to help as many families as I can, but I want to do more. We're having a gambling night here in a few weeks, and I really could use the help."

"Yes, I would love to."

"That's fantastic. Thank you."

Lorenzo took Evelyn's gloved hand and kissed it. He hesitated, like he wanted to do more but had thought better of it.

He took a step back from her, his eyes going blank again. "I'll see you tonight."

"I'll see you tonight."

Evelyn turned to walk out of Lorenzo's office. Her body was alight with a tingling sensation. Like the budding of flowers in spring, all her senses came alive when Lorenzo touched her, but she couldn't help but wonder about his sudden change in demeanor.

She looked back only once, to see him putting books in a canvas bag with that same blank look on his face. She wondered where he was off to.

Chapter Five

Lorenzo

Enraptured—that was how Lorenzo had felt, listening to Evelyn sing. This dame came out of nowhere and had him spinning already. He'd had to hire her, and not only because she was talented. She was more than talented, but he had to make sure she didn't blow town before he could figure out what it was about her that had him wanting to clip any cat who looked at her too long.

When she'd left his office, she'd left him feeling empty. Her presence had filled him with something he'd thought long dead after what had happened to Holly. He hadn't thought anyone would be able to spark the kind of desire that made him question his bachelor ways.

But he needed to push those feelings down. He couldn't forget the danger anyone who got close to him would be in because of his family. Now that finding his cousin's murderers was his central focus, he couldn't allow anyone to get close to him—not even the most beautiful woman he'd ever seen, with the most amazing voice he'd ever heard. Lorenzo couldn't risk letting anyone in. He had a circle of stone-cold killers around him at all times, who could definitely take care of themselves—anyone else was too vulnerable.

He gulped down the rest of his whiskey before returning to his usual position at the end of the bar. Walking through the club, he noticed that his patrons seemed more energized than usual. Flapper dresses swished as riffs from the saxophone filled the air, He wondered if Evelyn was the cause of this change in them. She certainly had changed him.

"Tommy, would you bring me another whiskey and something to eat?" Lorenzo said to his bartender as he took his usual seat.

Tommy was Italian, like Lorenzo, and people often thought they were brothers. They had similar builds. They sparred with each other often to keep in shape and in fighting condition. They both had dark features with the exception of their eyes. Tommy's were blue, and Lorenzo's were gray. Tommy had been able to pass for White his entire life because of his lighter skin and the look of his features. Only Lorenzo and a few other people knew Tommy's mother was Black.

Lorenzo had a leather-bound book of numbers in front of him. A casual onlooker wouldn't be able to figure out what the book was, let alone what the numbers meant, but Lorenzo knew his code. The soft feel of the journal soothed Lorenzo. He was comfortable with numbers. He could understand numbers. Things were black and white when it came to keeping track of the flow of money through his club and through the winery and distillery. He went out of his way to make his life simple—as simple as the life of a mob boss's son and bootlegger could be.

The music seeped into his blood, matching the rhythm of his heartbeat. He relaxed into his task. His club had exceeded the previous three quarters in profits. He was ready to expand. He was ahead of his schedule by three years. He hadn't planned to open another club for another couple of summers, but now he had no reason to wait.

Not able to get Evelyn off of his mind, he decided to retreat to his office. Grabbing his notebook, he stood up off his bar stool. "I'm heading to the back, Tommy. I need to focus."

Lorenzo walked to his office. He didn't like working in his office. He felt cut off from the action. He hadn't become a club owner to sit out all the fun. He liked to interact with his patrons usually, but his interaction with his new lead singer had left him reeling. He needed to get his mind right. His relationship with Evelyn was to be purely professional. So why did he keep imagining his lips on her soft, gorgeous skin?

Lorenzo closed the door to his office, dulling the lively beat of the music. He could still see the club, but from behind the glass window. He felt like a voyeur, not the owner of the most popular twenty-four-hour spot in town.

He sat down at his desk. He did love the antiquated thing; it reminded him of his father's desk. Lorenzo believed strongly that he had no place within his family's business. Yes, there were killers around him, but he wasn't a killer himself. Killing wasn't a solution to anything, but a gateway to something much darker, and Lorenzo already had a one-way ticket to hell because of what happened to Holly.

He had vowed then, while holding her dead body in his arms, that he would never be responsible for the loss of another human's life.

Sighing, he pushed those thoughts from his mind. They made him remember, and he didn't want to remember.

It wasn't long before he lost himself in his calculations, and a knock at the door interrupted Lorenzo's work. He crossed the room in two long strides and opened the door.

Tommy stood there, holding a glass of whiskey and a pretzel. "I thought you could use some sustenance."

Lorenzo backed up to let Tommy enter, closing the door after Tommy set the drink and food on the desk. "Thanks... you know I wouldn't have eaten anything if you hadn't come."

"I know." Tommy lounged in the chair across from Lorenzo. "So, the new singer is incredible."

"Yeah, she is."

Lorenzo ran his hand through his hair and picked up the glass. He gulped the brown liquid, thinking of how gorgeous and talented Evelyn Laroque was and what that could mean for his club. He'd be lying if he said he wasn't intrigued by her on a personal level, but he'd never let it get to that point.

"I'll be honest, Lorenzo. I've never seen you so mesmerized by a dame."

Lorenzo looked up to find Tommy staring at him. "What are you talking about? I'm not…mesmerized. Don't be ridiculous."

Tommy arched a brow and stayed silent.

"Fine, she definitely is something. I mean, did you see how she carried herself? She's real class. I have no business with a woman like that. You of all people know that."

"So, you're going to keep it professional?" Tommy said with skepticism in his voice.

"Of course. I'm not a Neanderthal," Lorenzo said, using Evelyn's word.

"I'm just asking because we have to figure out what happened to Vin, and we can't afford any distractions. You asked me to help you stay on the straight and narrow, and that's all I'm trying to do, boss." Tommy leaned forward in his chair. "Distractions end up dead around here."

Lorenzo didn't want to admit it, but Tommy was right.

"Have you gotten any more information about if the KKK killed Vin and Edith?" he asked.

It was the first time that Lorenzo had said his cousin's fiancée's name since the murder. He'd grown close to Edith because of his relationship with Vinny. When Vinny Jr. was born, Vin and Edith had asked Lorenzo to be the godfather. He'd been elated, but had belatedly thought about the danger Vin Jr. would be in if anything happened to Vinny and Edith. Not long after they'd asked Lorenzo, he told them he couldn't accept. Since they hadn't had a chance to choose anyone else before they died, Vin Jr had gone to Edith's family, which was probably best anyway.

"Yeah, that cat that was in here… Simmens…he has a thing for young Black women. He's been involved in several assaults, but he never gets caught. We think this was an assault gone wrong because they weren't expecting Vin to be there."

"Did they know who Vin was?"

"I don't think so. From talking to my informant, seems to me the KKK leaders have no idea that the De Luca family is after them."

"Good. Let's keep it that way. A surprise hit is best. We don't know who all is involved with the KKK, but I know their hold on the city is growing."

"Are you going to take out the entire organization? Or just the head cats who were involved in what happened to Vin?"

"You know my father's philosophy is to leave no loose ends untied."

"But is that your philosophy?"

Lorenzo took a moment to think. He'd left his legacy behind because thoughts of the families his father had destroyed haunted him. Holly's death had tortured his sleep for years. Lorenzo's insomnia was one of the main reasons he'd started working at a speakeasy in the first place.

In the heat of anger, yes, his philosophy was exactly like his father's—which was why Lorenzo had spent so much time trying to master everything about himself. He didn't want to be ruled by emotion, as his father was. Lorenzo knew that Tommy wouldn't hesitate if Lorenzo told him to take Simmens out, but Lorenzo couldn't be that person. He *wouldn't* be that person.

"No, we'll do it the legal way. We'll put Simmens out of action and whoever else was involved. But we'll send a message to the entire organization that they need to leave the city if they know what's best."

"That sounds like the plan. I'll get Jeb and Dred and fill them in."

"Thanks, Tommy." Lorenzo stood and embraced his bartender and friend before sitting back down to finish his work.

Lorenzo finally looked up from his notebook to see that his club had gotten to capacity. All the tables were filled with glittery, shimmering women and suit-clad men. The servers didn't miss a step. Glasses were full and the dance floor vibrated with the excitement and the flood of dancers.

Ten o'clock had come around quicker than Lorenzo had expected. He'd been hopeful that Evelyn would come early, so he could talk to her again, learn more about her— preferably not with a man bleeding at her feet.

Opening his safe, Lorenzo slid his notebook inside, along with the cash he still needed to drop at the bank— the bank his family owned—and his piece. Closing the safe, he turned to find those gold eyes staring back at him.

"Evelyn, I… I didn't realize you were here." Lorenzo's heart pounded in his chest. This woman had some effect on him that he couldn't explain—which was all the more reason to stay away from her.

She stood at his door in a gold-sequined, black-fringed, knee-length dress with a matching headband. Her beautiful thick hair was neatly pinned in waves falling around her face and her shoulders.

Lorenzo's mouth went dry. He searched for words, but he couldn't get any sound to come out.

Her lips, rose-pink, matched her cheeks and the lids of

her eyes. Her beauty was unparalleled. The way her lashes fluttered each time she looked down, like she had no idea how beautiful she was, made Lorenzo want to fall to his knees in front of her and beg her to… He wasn't even sure what he wanted to beg her for…just something…anything to keep her near him.

He had to get a handle on himself. Lorenzo De Luca didn't fall like this for a dame.

"Did you want me to come back later?" Her brows knit together. Concern shadowed the features of her face.

"No…no, you're right on time. Benny's ready whenever you are."

Evelyn shifted her weight.

Lorenzo noticed her handbag. "Would you like to keep that in my safe while you're on stage?"

"No, I don't want to be a bother."

"No bother, really."

He walked up to her. And why had he done that? She smelled like summer, and freshly picked fruit, coconut and candy. His mouth, formerly dry, now watered with the desire to taste her soft skin. She smiled, sending a shock straight through his chest. He took a deep breath and hoped his smile didn't give away the turmoil of emotions roiling inside of him.

"Let me take that for you."

She handed him her bag. Her gloved hands brushed his and their eyes met.

"Thank you," she said, somewhat shakily.

Lorenzo attributed it to nerves. "I'll take you around and show you the club. I want you to be comfortable. We have an area for the band. Or I can get you your own room if you'd like."

"No, that won't be necessary."

"Well, you'll be spending a lot of time here. I'm sure

you'll want somewhere to go to relax between sets. I want you to be happy here."

He meant that. His own sincerity rattled him, and he knew it was more than just about his business. But he would stay away from her. He had to for her own safety.

Lorenzo led her to the back of the club first. "This is the kitchen. They can make you whatever you want—on the house. We serve the best homemade pretzels and hot ham this side of the Missouri River, but we usually eat breakfast together as a staff, while we have the fewest customers."

Showing Evelyn around made Lorenzo look at his club through fresh eyes. He'd renovated the old building to include a state-of-the-art kitchen. Most nightclubs served only a few items, but Lorenzo wanted his speakeasy to be different. He served what the other clubs served—pretzels and ham—but they were the best pretzels and ham you could get in the city, and that wasn't an exaggeration. Lorenzo had to put in a lot of effort.

"This is lovely. I've never been in a kitchen like this. You have three iceboxes. Why do you have so many?"

"The largest one is for the bar. The other two are for the kitchen. If you have a special request, I can have it ordered and keep it in stock for you. What's your poison of choice?"

Evelyn looked down and said in a small voice, "I… I don't drink."

"You've never had a drink?" Lorenzo suddenly noticed how young she looked. Her body was all woman, but her face was innocent.

"Yes, I have. I just don't like to."

Lorenzo stared at her for a moment. "May I ask how old you are?"

"I'm twenty-two." Evelyn's gaze dropped to the floor and she wrung her hands together.

"Baloney," Lorenzo said, immediately regretting it.

"Excuse me?" Evelyn's eyes narrowed as she looked at him once again.

"No, I mean…you look young, but you're so sophisticated. How could you only be twenty-two?"

"I guess you could say I've been through a lot. Seeing death ages you."

"What do you mean?" Lorenzo knew the expression— he'd seen his share of death, and knew exactly what she meant—but he wanted to know *her*, know her past.

"It's not important," Evelyn said.

"Watch out," the cook said, grabbing a fire extinguisher.

Evelyn looked at Lorenzo with concern etched in her features.

"He's an excellent cook—just a bit accident-prone." Lorenzo laughed.

Evelyn smiled. "I better get to the stage. I hear the band playing the song I requested to sing first."

With that, she turned and walked away from Lorenzo. Her dress swished as she headed toward the stage.

Chapter Six

Evelyn

The club throbbed with all the writhing bodies on the dance floor. Evelyn didn't have time to be nervous. The band was playing her song and she appreciated the excuse to put some distance between her and Lorenzo.

She'd had to get away from him. Something about him had her wanting to be on the level with him, and she couldn't afford that. How could she tell him that people who looked just like him had burned her home and killed her friends and family? She couldn't trust him or anyone else.

As she'd grown up, she hadn't wanted to believe that race mattered, but since the massacre she had thought differently. Hatred was real, and it lived inside of people until it couldn't be contained anymore.

She hadn't even heard anyone talking about what happened in Greenwood; it was like it hadn't happened. He probably wouldn't believe her anyway…

That night still played in her mind whenever she closed her eyes. The smell of scorched flesh still haunted her. She woke in the middle of the night panting because the smell smothered her in her dreams. Her heart broke every time she thought of her mother and father, of how her refusal to pack and leave had led to their deaths. If they'd just gotten out sooner…

A tear fell and Evelyn swiped it away. She wouldn't

allow anyone to get close to her. The pain of losing the people she loved most was still ripe, like it had happened only hours before. Lorenzo was an unknown danger that she had to be wary of or she would regret it.

With more resolve than she'd thought possible, she vowed never to let Lorenzo or anyone else get too close.

"We have a special singer coming to the stage tonight. She's one of us now, so y'all give her a Blues Moon welcome."

Benny's deep voice matched his bass guitar. It was deep and throaty, not completely unlike Lorenzo's voice. But Lorenzo's voice held that tone of authority, like he knew he was a big shot.

The crowd cheered loudly and started chanting, "Blues Moon!"

Evelyn took a deep breath, smoothed down her fringed dress and straightened her gloves before walking out into the spotlight. Once she had the microphone in her hand, her nerves eased. As the band picked up the tempo of the blues melody Evelyn opened her mind to memories—the way her home had smelled when the fires started, the way her dad had fallen silent after the first gunshots rang through the air.

But the image that played on a loop in her head was of her mother's shaking hands. Each image was like a knife in her stomach, and she let the pain come out in every note she sang.

Time passed like she was watching a film. She saw people come to the dance floor in droves. Most of them stayed on the floor for the entire fifteen-song set. Evelyn hadn't sung so many songs without a break before. She was exhausted.

"We'll be right back after a short break."

Music was piped through the speakers.

When Evelyn turned to leave the stage Lorenzo was

there, waiting. He held out his hand to her, and she allowed him to help her step over the leads of the instruments.

"You've got the goods, Miss Laroque."

Lorenzo didn't drop Evelyn's hand, even though she didn't need his help stepping over anything else. His large warm palm comforted her, made her feel at ease. Adrenaline from performing thrummed through her, but her hand in Lorenzo's made her heart beat steadily. A calm came over her as he guided her through the back halls of the club.

He led her to a small room across from the kitchen.

"I'm making this your dressing room. You can come here when you want to get away from it all."

Stepping into the room, Evelyn smelled the flowers first, then she saw them. Bouquet after bouquet lined the wall and covered the table and small vanity.

"Where did all of these come from?" She took a step into the room. Someone had placed plates of food and water on the table as well.

"I had one of the cats who works for me pick some things up. We have to celebrate your first night."

"This is too much. I… I can't accept all of this."

Evelyn stared at Lorenzo in shock. She couldn't be swayed in her mission to keep everyone at a distance. She wouldn't be swayed.

Lorenzo's expression was unreadable. Evelyn hoped she hadn't offended him, but she didn't know what to say. She'd never been given flowers—not even when she'd gone out on that date with the future dentist…the only date she'd ever been on.

She didn't know how to process Lorenzo's generosity. It was counter to what she had been expecting—so much so, she didn't think she could trust it, trust *him*.

"Please, don't think of it as a gift from me. This is how we welcome new members to our family. You've already won over the crowd out there. Now I will let you get some rest. You won't sing again for about an hour. These are really late nights, so we try to make sure the band has plenty to eat and somewhere to put their head down to rest. That sofa is comfortable." Lorenzo said as he backed out of the room. "And before I forget, your purse is in that safe in the corner."

Lorenzo dropped a small key in her palm. He turned and started to close the door behind himself.

"Wait—don't leave," Evelyn said before she could stop herself.

She regretted the words as soon as they were out of her mouth. It was like someone had taken over her body for a split second, allowing her desires to rise to the surface.

"Are you okay? Do you need anything?" Lorenzo's soothing voice filled the room again as he stepped back into it.

"No, I'm fine. I just wanted some company. I'm a little too excited to rest just yet. Would you stay for a moment?"

Evelyn told herself that just because she was going to keep her distance from Lorenzo, that didn't mean she couldn't get to know him better. It was in her best interests to understand who she was dealing with. That was the best way to protect herself.

"Yes, of course." Lorenzo came all the way into the room, shutting the door behind him. He pulled a chair out from under the table and sat down.

Being alone in the room with Lorenzo made Evelyn's heart race. She decided sitting down was a great idea. She sat at the vanity, with her back straight and her eyes locked on the floor. She'd wanted his company—which was completely unsettling to her and counter to all the resolve she had to keep away from him. And now that she had him, she didn't know what to do.

"When did you decide you wanted to be a singer?" Lorenzo asked, moving his hair off his forehead.

If Evelyn had been more familiar with men, she might have been able to tell what he was feeling. She thought he might be nervous, but that couldn't be right. He was the one with so much experience.

"I've wanted to be a singer for as long as I can remember. My first memories are of my aunt, singing at church. As soon as I could stand up on my own I was in the choir."

"It must feel amazing to realize a dream you've had for that long."

Evelyn thought about it. She hadn't allowed herself to revel in the victory of the moment. Her mind had been consumed with doing what was best for her grandmother. She hadn't really thought about how long she'd wanted this very thing, but Lorenzo had helped make her dream come true. She owed him for that—another unsettling revelation.

"It is overwhelming, I guess. But I'm not here just because I love to sing. I *have* to be here."

Lorenzo sat forward in his chair, resting his elbows on his knees, and stared into her with those gray-green eyes. "What do you mean, you have to be here?"

The intensity in his eyes gave Evelyn pause. She'd said too much. His expression was hard to read, but concern flickered across his features like a storm cloud. It was brief, but Evelyn was sure of what she'd seen.

She wanted to take back what she'd said, but there was something about the way Lorenzo looked at her that made her continue, even though she knew better than to be so open with this man.

"I help take care of my grandmother. She's behind on some bills, so my singing is going to help her retire. She's a seamstress, but she's been having balance issues and keeps having falls. I don't know what else to do."

Lorenzo sat silently for a moment. Another fleeting sign of emotion shadowed his features and was gone just as quickly. Evelyn was amazed at this man's ability to keep himself in check. She'd become extremely observant since her parents' deaths—more out of a need to keep herself safe than any interest in people. If she hadn't been so perceptive, she might have thought that Lorenzo was an emotionless robot.

"I have a feeling that you've already determined what you need to do to ensure your grandmother is taken care of, but I will extend an offer of assistance if you ever deem it necessary. Just from the few interactions we've had I've learned that you can handle whatever is thrown your way. I admire that."

His lips quirked into a smile. Something about the expression made his handsome face even more irresistible. The way he looked at her, so intense and with absolute focus on her every move, overwhelmed her.

The room grew hot all of a sudden, and Evelyn stood. "I think I will take your advice and rest now."

Evelyn walked toward the door and opened it. She hated to be so rude, but when he touched her, her body tingled, and heat thrummed just under her skin. She'd never experienced anything like it before.

Lorenzo stood too, never taking his eyes off her. He walked to the door and paused in front of her. His lips parted, like he was going to say something, but he left without another word…so controlled. It made Evelyn envious of his ability to withhold so much of what he was thinking.

She closed the door and fell against it, sighing. When she finally opened her eyes again, she took in the room properly for the first time. The many-hued floral spread, the beautiful pink tufted sofa and the three-mirror gold vanity with a floral chair in front of it all vied for her attention. The table was black, with gold embellishments. It looked older than everything else in the room, and Evelyn loved that. She ran her fingers along the designs. The detail was remarkable. Evelyn had never seen anything like it.

She settled into the excitement that was thrumming through her body from being on stage for the first time as a lead singer. The band had played with her like they'd been together for years. The crowd had showed such enthusiasm. Her heart warmed at the memory of their reception of her. She knew that each time she performed—though previously it had only been in church—she poured her anger, pain and resentment into each song. Tonight had been no different.

Deciding to relax, she grabbed a pretzel from the elaborate spread of food. She chose from the variety of sauces, mustards, cheese and sweet butter, and sat on the sofa. She kicked off her black heels to give her feet a break. She was used to wearing heels, but she'd been standing for nearly two hours straight.

How had Lorenzo gotten all of this together in a matter of hours? Why had he gone out of his way for her—again?

Her mother would be turning over in her grave if she knew how Evelyn was treating Lorenzo. Evelyn hadn't shown it at the time, but she did appreciate what he'd done with the man from the Ku Klux Klan—even though he'd been a Neanderthal and all. She even enjoyed Lorenzo's gentle touch, now that she'd had a moment to consider what it might mean, but she just didn't want anything to get in the way of taking care of her grand.

Evelyn searched the room. It was larger than her bedroom at home—not the room she'd had in Greenwood, that room had been more than twice this size—but her room in West Eden was pretty small. Her mind drifted back to that night, the burning, but she pushed it away. She would save that for the stage.

Would she ever be able to put what happened behind her? That night trapped her in the past, and she didn't know how to move past it to live the moments she had now fully. The pain lingered in her heart, not allowing room for anything else.

A sharp knock at the door made her pause. She put the plate down and wiped her mouth. She'd taken off her gloves, and hurried to put them back on before opening the door. She checked her reflection in the mirror—her mother had taught her always to show her best self, every hair in place.

She walked to the door hoping, to her surprise, to see Lorenzo's strange-colored eyes that reminded her of ice-covered leaves.

"Miss Laroque? I'm sorry to be a bother to you, but Mr. De Luca wanted to make sure you have everything you need. I'm Yalaina—another singer here. I sing on week-nights mostly. I've filled in here and there, when we were without someone for Fridays, Saturdays and Sundays, but I'm in school, and Lorenzo wants me to focus on my studies. Anyway, sorry to ramble. Is there anything I can get you?"

Yalaina was young and quite gorgeous. Her long black curls hung down her back. Her eyes were brown with a hint of green and very large, framed by thick curled lashes. She and Evelyn were about the same height and build, but Yalaina's complexion was just a shade darker than Evelyn's. The bronzed brown tone seemed to glow gold in the dim light of the club.

Evelyn was young herself, so she figured Yalaina couldn't be much older than eighteen or nineteen. Evelyn wondered, much to her dismay, if Lorenzo was somehow romantically involved with this young woman. But Yalaina's smile made Evelyn feel like she was talking to a good friend.

"I have everything I need, thank you. Please tell Mr. De Luca that I really appreciate all he has done to welcome me to the club. We should talk some time. I would love to get the ins and outs of the club from a fellow singer."

Evelyn tried to discern whether Yalaina was mad about

being passed over for the lead singer role, but she couldn't find any malice in Yalaina's tone or body language.

Yalaina nodded. "That would be nice. I won't bother you now, but we'll chat soon. I heard you sing. You're amazing. I'm not surprised Lorenzo chose you."

Without another word, she left Evelyn standing in the doorway.

The music still boomed through the speakers. Evelyn allowed the rhythm to help her relax as she closed the door and returned to the couch. She hummed absently, tasting the assortment of sweet pastries and fresh fruit. She'd just popped a grape in her mouth when she heard a commotion coming from the front of the club. It sounded like a stampede, and several people were yelling.

Frozen, she wasn't sure what to do. Should she wait until things calmed down before leaving her dressing room, or should she go see what was going on?

There was only one answer.

She would never cower again if she could help. She'd run once when faced with danger. She wouldn't do that again.

She picked her heels up, but didn't put them on, and ran from the room.

When she rounded the corner, several White men she hadn't seen before were crowded at the front of the club by the door. One had a shotgun pointed at the crowd of scared patrons. Lorenzo stood in the center, between the crowd and the group of men who couldn't have looked more out of place. Their overalls, mud-caked boots and unkempt hair were a stark contrast to the glamorous customers of Blues Moon.

Lorenzo tilted his head from side to side, as if he was inspecting the men and truly puzzled by their actions. "Look, I don't think you guys want to go down this road. It won't end well for you."

His hands were at his sides. He stood in his tailored suit, voice calm, body relaxed, like he was talking to any other customer. But although his body language was casual, his voice was laced with danger.

"We're just here for payback for what you did to Simmens. You had no business putting your hands on him... call yourself defending some jig."

At the corner of the large room Evelyn saw several big men, moving toward the intruders. Lorenzo put his hand up, palm out, and the large men stopped.

"I'm giving you one more chance to leave my club. I'll even let you leave unharmed. But I can't promise that offer will last very long. I have some really eager friends who want to handle you the way we usually handle people who disturb my business and upset my patrons."

Lorenzo placed his hands in his pockets. Some of the outsiders looked nervously around the club, probably searching for the men Lorenzo had mentioned. The crowd of club-goers huddled closer together.

If Evelyn hadn't been at the back of the club she might not have noticed the woman in a sleek black bodysuit, her hair pulled back in a low ponytail, her skin the color of midnight, with the most beautiful eyes, as she slipped in the door. The woman was tall and thin, her figure accentuated in the tight, almost shiny material. She was stunning. If Lorenzo saw her, he didn't let on. His body language didn't change, and he didn't look in her direction.

Lorenzo's security team moved closer to the group of disheveled men slowly and the woman got closer. The intruders had no idea that they were surrounded.

"If you have beef with me, then let's take it outside. My customers have nothing to do with this. This is your last chance to leave unharmed." The edge in his voice had taken on a lethal tone.

The guy who talked for the group of angry men said,

"We're not going nowhere. Maybe we'll stay here and have some fun."

The other men nodded their heads, but their eyes betrayed their false bravado.

Then Lorenzo must have lost his patience because with one look at the guard who'd carried the Klansman out earlier and all the other guards and the woman converged on the unwelcome guests.

Evelyn didn't know what the woman was doing, but she moved so swiftly from the man holding the gun to the man next to him, and the man next to him, they didn't have time to react. The gun clattered against the tile of the club and the man dropped to the ground lifeless.

The security guards really didn't have to do much. The woman had shot something into the outsiders' necks, and the guards started throwing unconscious men over their shoulders and carrying them out. It happened so fast—the woman seemed to blur as she moved from one man to the next, and the guards got the men out without any fight.

That was not at all what Evelyn had expected. She'd prepared herself for something much more violent. She had a knife in her garter, which she kept on her in case someone tried to bother her. She wouldn't lie down without a fight. They'd have to kill her before she let them hurt her.

Her father had given her the knife on her seveneenth birthday. He'd been practical and had wanted Evelyn to be able to protect herself at all costs. He had known Evelyn would be on her own one day, and it had put his mind at ease to know she had some form of protection. She'd never thought she'd actually have to use it…

Now, seeing Lorenzo standing protectively in front of his patrons, shielding them from harm, made her reach for it. She was going to help him protect his patrons. She didn't want to stand by and watch people get hurt. She wouldn't live through that again.

Chapter Seven

⟨⟨⟨∾⟩⟩⟩

Lorenzo

Lorenzo looked around his club at the faces, some frightened and some furious. He would need to smooth things over and reassure his customers that something like this would never happen again.

He blamed his own arrogance. Everyone knew who he was—who his family was. No one in Kansas City in their right mind would ever dare to threaten him after the "civil war," as they'd called it, between the two mob families the De Lucas and the Riccis.

Despite all his efforts to leave a life of violence in his past, he carried with him the benefits of being the son of a mob boss. It sickened him that his father's legacy of intimidation and murder continued to influence Lorenzo's life, his business. Neearly everything he had was in some way or another tainted by the very things he'd vowed not to continue.

Lorenzo's family had come out on top after the "war," and thus now controlled the politicians, the police department and the city's transportation—but the KKK was a group of ignorant idiots who obviously had a death wish.

In a strange way, the KKK challenging him and his club might be a sign that Lorenzo was being seen as separate from his family—or maybe the Klan was just that stupid.

Lorenzo had allowed some of his security team to go

home early, and that had been a mistake. The KKK seemed emboldened, and Lorenzo would have to take care of that. He wanted to make sure he got the right cats for Vin's murder, but he was running out of time. The Klan had made a move against him now, and he wasn't going to be able to play nice with them for much longer. He'd have to get information about Vin's murder and handle the Klan all at the same time. He wouldn't let his patrons or his staff come to harm.

"Everyone, please stay and have fun. Drinks are on the house."

The crowd cheered, Benny thrummed the first notes of an up-tempo jazz song and the crowd started to move, talk and dance.

What happened tonight could not stand, but Lorenzo wouldn't call his father.

When he looked up he saw Evelyn, with her gold-brown eyes, staring at him. She didn't look scared; she looked indignant. He walked right up to her, stopping on the edge of what she probably considered her personal space. He wouldn't have to do much to kiss her…just bend down a little and press his lips to hers, finally taste her and pull her full bottom lip into his mouth…

"Are you okay?" she said.

"Yeah, I'm hitting on all eight. Are you all right?"

Lorenzo couldn't help himself. One of her curls had come undone and fallen in her face. He reached up and moved it so he could see her eyes. He wasn't sure what he'd thought her reaction would be, but he hadn't expected concern…for *him*.

"I'm fine. Are you sure you're all right?"

She looked deeply at him. Lorenzo wasn't sure he'd ever been looked at in that way.

"I'm fine. I'll handle the situation."

"I thought you just did."

Her eyes burned right through him, down to the smoldering fire of his soul.

"No, it's not handled yet, but it will be."

Lorenzo hadn't needed Dred for a long time. She was the daughter of one of his father's mistresses and one of Lorenzo's dearest friends. She closed potentially volatile situations with the least amount of commotion for Lorenzo. She was stealthy and lethal. She would have killed those men if Lorenzo hadn't told her years ago that wasn't his style. It might be his father's, but it wasn't his. Dred came at an extremely high cost, but she was worth it.

He didn't ever want his customers to witness a fight. When he gave Jeb "the look," he called Dred immediately. And she always seemed to be nearby whenever Lorenzo needed her. They'd grown up together...she was only three years older than Lorenzo. Her mother had been his father's confidante and his lover, and Dred and Lorenzo had been perfect playmates—more like siblings.

"The woman...what did she do to those men?"

Lorenzo knew Evelyn's question was steeped in curiosity—not empathy for the pathetic Klansmen.

"She drugged them. They'll be out for hours...maybe even an entire day. They'll remember what happened, but the details will be foggy."

Evelyn seemed to contemplate this for a moment before she responded. "Well, I don't want to keep your customers waiting. I should probably start the next set."

Lorenzo hated to let her go. He wanted to be near her as much as possible. She had an energy similar to his own, calm but dangerous, and that captivated him. But, without a logical reason to keep her from returning to the stage, he watched her walk away. He had to admit he enjoyed watching her round bottom in that dress...

He needed to get focused. If tonight was nothing else, it was a reminder that anyone close to him was in danger.

He *would* keep his distance from Evelyn, no matter how much he wanted her.

Even before he turned around, he could feel Dred's eyes on him. She stood by the door. He walked toward her and she turned and walked outside, not waiting for him.

Once under the canopy of stars Lorenzo breathed in deeply, taking in the crisp air. The coolness felt good. His insides were on fire, from both the excitement of the evening and Evelyn. Deep breaths helped him focus on what he had to do next.

He walked around to the side of his building where he saw Dred turn.

He didn't see his father's ink-black Ford Model K until he was deeper in the alley.

Lorenzo cursed under his breath. He had known his father would find out what had happened, but he'd assumed his father would send one of his minions to come in his stead since, technically, Lorenzo had been disowned.

Dred opened the car door and Lorenzo got in. "What are you doing here?" Lorenzo asked his father.

"Remember who I am and watch your tone, son. I come whenever it is in the best interest of *la famiglia* to come. I am the Don."

This was exactly what Lorenzo had been afraid would happen. "You have to let me handle it. They need to respect me and my establishment."

"Without the family's backing, how are you going to handle it?"

Lorenzo should have been expecting that question, but he wasn't, and the fact was he wasn't sure, but he wanted to do it his way. "I'm working on that with my squad. We'll take care of it. We already know of one definite player who needs to go. We just have to find out who else."

"Our family name is on the line. Just because you have shirked your duty, it doesn't mean you don't still carry the name, and your actions still reflect on us. It's not too late for you to come home, where you belong. You deserve to lead this family. It is your birthright. You know I love you, son."

Just then Lorenzo pictured his five-year-old self, sitting on his father's lap, laughing as his father played the tickle monster. That had been their routine. When his father came home from work, Lorenzo would jump into his lap and his father would say, "Uh-oh, here comes the tickle monster." Lorenzo would laugh until he cried, and his father would laugh too.

Lorenzo had a hard time reconciling that father with the man who sat in front of him now as a mob boss and killer.

"Think about what I said. You're my boy, and I will always be here, whenever you need me."

His father lit a cigar.

When his father lit a cigar, the conversation was over.

Lorenzo ran his hand over the luxurious leather interior, contemplating what his father had said. Then he took a deep breath, fighting his urge to accept his father's help, and got out of the car without saying goodbye. He had been dismissed.

Chapter Eight

Evelyn

The club didn't clear out even after the confrontation with the Klan. Lorenzo must have built up a lot of trust with these people. They all chose to stay and continue to spend their money in his establishment.

The way Lorenzo had commanded the attention of everyone in the room sent sparks dancing down Evelyn's arms, leaving her fingers tingling. She'd watched him, so cool and authoritative, wordlessly taking care of the situation in seconds. He'd even offered the Klan a way out, but they were too dumb to take him at his word.

Evelyn was learning that Lorenzo De Luca was the kind of man who backed up what he said, and he could do it with one look. The people who worked for him respected him, and they knew him so well that they could carry out his orders without even exchanging words. That was a kind of power Evelyn had never witnessed in real life. It had been amazing to see with her own eyes.

Evelyn replayed each moment with Lorenzo over in her mind—the way his eyes had bored into her, the way her skin prickled with fireworks whenever he was near…

"You ready?" Benny asked.

His gruff voice was a welcome distraction.

Evelyn had walked on stage, but she had paused when she'd seen Lorenzo follow the beautiful woman out into the night. She didn't want to care. She wasn't sure why she cared. But she did.

She nodded, and the bass started to play. Servers gave everyone glasses of what Evelyn assumed was bootleg liquor, which made the crowd cheer. Now Evelyn was singing, all seemed right again. Everyone smiled and danced and drank. The servers kept the drinks coming.

Benny must have seen the way Evelyn looked at the glasses because he asked her if she wanted anything when they finished the song. She shook her head. She might have experience with drinking, but she had a long journey home, and the only other time she had indulged she'd almost passed out. Her grand had been extremely upset with her when she'd had to be carried into the house. She'd never drunk again after that night. She wasn't going to start now and risk everything she'd worked so hard to get.

The next song started and Evelyn's thoughts unraveled into a stream of black billowing smoke rising out of Greenwood, the menacing faces of the KKK, and Lorenzo walking out of the club with the beautiful woman. Evelyn channeled her fear and her anger, and her—was that jealousy?—into the words and the melody like the only thing she could do was to sing.

She tried to focus on the faces in the crowd…some White, some Black, some she wasn't exactly sure about. She enjoyed singing and looking out at so many different kinds of people. The area around the bar had emptied some, due to most of the people now being on the dance floor. Evelyn tapped her foot and held on to the microphone as she sang. The words and the rhythm made her feel at home. Her confidence manifested itself while she was on stage.

The night went by fast and soon Evelyn was starting to feel the strain in her muscles as she used her diaphragm to give power to the notes. She'd been training for this opportunity, but it had come along quicker than she'd expected.

She would need to build up her lung capacity and her stamina for singing for long periods of time. She smiled at that.

"Thank you all for staying to hear us play. The Daytime Blues Brothers will start in thirty minutes. Please stay and enjoy your drinks," Benny said into the microphone attached to the stand in front of where he sat with his guitar.

Evelyn wanted to say something to the crowd too, but she wasn't sure what. Lorenzo hadn't returned, and Evelyn had an overwhelming desire to get home.

The crowd erupted in applause when she turned to leave the stage. She looked out at them, and then at Benny, who motioned for her to come back. "Say something to them."

Benny's smile warmed Evelyn's heart. She walked back to the microphone. Her eyes found Yalaina, smiling in the crowd with her hands clasped in front of her chest.

Evelyn took the microphone out of the stand and said, "I'm so honored to be here with all of you. This night has been something for the history books, and it's only going to get better from here. Have a good night—or morning."

Evelyn laughed as the crowd applauded again. She left the stage with her heart the size of a melon. She couldn't believe her good fortune to have been hired on the spot at such an amazing club. Aside from the two encounters with the KKK, this had been the best day of her life.

Her dressing room had been cleaned while she was on stage. There was a container of something sitting on the table. Evelyn opened it up. It was pretzels and ham. She smiled to herself. She was learning that Lorenzo thought of everything.

She shook her head at that thought. She hadn't seen him come back into the club, but maybe there was a back entrance. When she'd walked past his office on the way to her dressing room, the lights had been off.

Gathering her coat, she took off her headband and replaced it with her fur hat. After ensuring her hair was perfect and her gloves were pulled up, she left her dressing room. Then she turned back, remembering the flowers. There was no way she could take them all home, so she took just a few stems to give to her grandmother to celebrate. Her grand was back at home, resting with the healthcare nurse. Evelyn couldn't wait to see her.

"You were going to leave without saying goodbye?" Lorenzo's deep rasping voice filled the room.

Evelyn turned to see that he'd taken off his suit jacket and stood there with his top shirt buttons undone. He looked tired.

"Is everything all right?" Evelyn couldn't help herself. She genuinely wanted to know.

He smiled. "It'll be fine. I just wanted to say thank you. The way you sing... It's... The customers have let me know I better hold on to you. I'll see you tomorrow night, right?"

Evelyn tried not to get excited at the idea of seeing him again. Looking forward to seeing him was dangerous. "Do you always hide behind your tough exterior?" she asked suddenly.

Lorenzo chuckled. "I wouldn't say that."

"Then why won't you be honest with me?"

"I... I'm sorry. I just don't want to worry you. You've only just started and, believe me, this is not how things usually go here."

"I do believe you. But you can trust me. If you need to talk, I'm here."

"So you will be back?"

Evelyn smiled. "Yes, I'll be here. I better get going."

"Have a good night...morning."

He stepped out of her path, and when she passed him a wave of energy pulsed from him. He was upset, and though most people might not have noticed the slight clench of his jaw, or the hard set of his eyes, Evelyn did notice, and it worried her.

Chapter Nine

Lorenzo

Lorenzo hated to see Evelyn leave. He watched as she walked to the front of the club. Several men followed her every move with their eyes, and it didn't seem to matter if they had a dame on their arm already. She said goodbye to the band and Tommy, before going out into the early morning light.

When she opened the door, the gold light from outside formed an aura around her like she was a goddess. Her round, full bottom and toned calves nearly had Lorenzo on his knees. He wanted to show her what it meant to be cherished. Her voice, her presence, awoke something inside of him that he didn't really understand. He wanted to know more about her…the pain in her eyes pierced him each time she looked at him.

What had happened to her?

She was so beautiful and talented. And Lorenzo was learning that she was also fearless. He'd seen how she'd come from the back when the commotion started. She could and should have stayed in her dressing room, where she was safe, but she hadn't. She'd come to see what was going on, and she hadn't cowered. She'd stood defiant in the face of all those angry, racist, ignorant men who looked like they'd just crawled out of a flophouse.

But what touched Lorenzo the most was her concern

for him. She'd only asked if he was okay, but her face had said so much more. He wanted to tell her what was going on, but he didn't want to risk her deciding to dust out.

The sun was up, which meant it was time for Lorenzo to get a few hours of sleep. His entire life was his club. He rarely left. But, since it was a twenty-four-hour club, he had to get some rest in order to be the formidable force that he was in all his business interactions.

"You drifting, boss?" Jeb said.

Lorenzo hadn't even noticed his second-in-charge walking up to him. "Yeah, I'm going. Need a few hours of sleep before we do this all again."

"Whatcha gon' do 'bout the boys?"

Jeb always looked like he was ready for a fight. His brows were permanently creased and his expression was always a scowl.

"They're not even our biggest problem. My father paid me a visit tonight."

Jeb nodded and let out a breath that sounded like *woo*. Lorenzo figured Jeb had already known about his father's visit. Jeb seemed to know everything that happened at the club.

"He wants to take care of the Klan, and I don't think I convinced him that I can handle it myself." Lorenzo ran his hand through his hair. The stress of the day was settling on his shoulders. He closed his eyes and popped his neck.

"If Don De Luca gets involved, he's going to bop the whole lot of 'em."

Lorenzo laughed humorlessly.

"Man… Okay, well, let me know the plan. Those boys had to be gowed up to come in here like that."

Whenever Jeb said *that*, it sounded more like *gat*. It was his Tennessee twang.

Lorenzo agreed. The Klan had no idea what Lorenzo's father was capable of; death would be a gift.

Lorenzo nodded to Jeb and turned to leave out through the back door that led to the stairs. He took one stair at a time, dragged down by exhaustion.

His apartment spanned the entire top floor of the area above his club. There was another floor with three apartments right below. He hadn't decided what to do with the other floors. He'd considered opening a clothing store or maybe a hotel.

The seven-story building sat in the middle of Downtown, surrounded by hotels, other speakeasies, the courthouse, the bridge and the construction on the new theatre that was almost complete. Lorenzo had a view of all of it. He had floor-to-ceiling windows on every wall. It was a three-hundred-and-sixty-degree view.

Lorenzo opened the door to his apartment and closed it behind him. He placed his keys on the table in the entryway and hung his suit jacket. He took off his shoes and put on the house shoes that were by his front door. He didn't like outside dirt in his home. He thought of his home as a sanctuary of sorts, where he didn't have to be Lorenzo the mobster's son, or Lorenzo the club owner. He could just be.

He'd actually never invited a woman back to his apartment. He always insisted on going to her place. There was just something too intimate about having someone in his home. The only people who had been there were Jeb, Dred, Tommy and Vinny.

Lorenzo let out a breath at the thought of his cousin. He hadn't attended the funeral, even though his mother had insisted it would be okay. He hadn't wanted to take the focus away from Vinny. His presence at the funeral would have given his family false hope of his return to take his place as Don. He had arranged to view Vinny's body the night before the funeral, alone.

He'd kissed Vin's cheeks and left a single rose in the

casket. Then he'd sent ten dozen roses to Vin's mother, along with some meals that his cook had prepared. He'd also sent money to Vinny Jr.'s grandparents, to help with raising the little boy. Vinny's fiancée Edith had come from a wealthy family, but Lorenzo still wanted to help. With the extra money, Vinny Jr. would receive the best education from a private tutor. Then he would be sent to one of the Black colleges of his choosing.

Lorenzo remembered how important it had been to Vinny for his son to grow up knowing the importance of family and sacrifice, but Lorenzo hoped that Vinny Jr. would also be able to see that there were many options for him. He could have the life he chose.

Lorenzo sat down on his green couch, thinking about how he'd got it. He'd asked a department store to design and furnish his apartment. They'd filled his home with the flashiest things. He had no doubt that they'd thought that was what all mobsters' houses looked like. He hadn't returned the items because he didn't really care—and he actually liked most of what they'd chosen.

When he closed his eyes he saw Evelyn's striking face. That doll had invaded every thought he'd had since he met her.

A voice in his head said, *She's too good for the likes of you.* Lorenzo sighed.

His stomach rumbled and he got up to make something light. The sun had risen, and his apartment was lit with the warm glow. It made him think of that halo around Evelyn. He wondered if she'd gotten home safely. He shouldn't have let her leave alone… He decided right then that wouldn't happen again. She would have someone chauffer her to and from the club. Lorenzo would ensure her safety no matter what. She worked for him, so it was only right— even though he'd never offered such service to any of his other band members.

Lorenzo's phone rang. He walked over to the small table and picked up the receiver.

"Boss, there's something you should know about our new singer..."

Chapter Ten

Evelyn

Evelyn squinted into the sunlight. She'd never stayed up all night before. Her eyes burned with fatigue.

She was nervous about riding the train back to West Eden, especially being so tired, but she had no other choice. She couldn't afford another bus ticket.

She took a deep breath. She had packed an extra set of clothes that she'd brought with her in case a drink or something had been spilled on her while she was at the club. She didn't want to perform with a stain, so she'd come prepared. She also hadn't known how much touching up she would want to do between sets, so she'd brought her toiletry bag.

She lugged her bags to the train on Fourth Street. While she waited, she noticed the man from earlier—the one that Lorenzo had punched—staring at her from across the crowded platform. His beady eyes were focused on her. Surely that was a coincidence?

She averted her gaze to study her surroundings. There were families with little ones, men traveling alone, and women carrying groceries, all standing huddled together in the brisk early-morning air.

The railcars were segregated and Evelyn, for the first time, took comfort in that. The KKK member from the club wouldn't come to the Black section of the train, so he couldn't harm her. She would go about her day as planned, getting off on the stop that the people of West Eden had agreed upon because it was far enough away from the road to West Eden that no one would realize where they were headed.

Boarding the train with the other Black patrons, Evelyn knew that although in no way was segregation a good thing, but she had grown weary of White people like the man from the club after her parents' deaths. The men who had murdered her mother and father had had that same anger radiating in their glares. An anger that stemmed from something as arbitrary as the color of her skin. It made no sense to Evelyn. She had been raised to believe in science, and knew that skin color wasn't something that should have so much influence on how a person was treated.

Evelyn pushed the fear from her mind and settled into her seat across from a young woman and a little girl. She smiled at the little girl, who had the brightest brown eyes she'd seen. Her pigtails hung down low and the little girl played with one of them as she stared back at Evelyn.

Turning to the window, Evelyn stared out at the bustling city before closing her eyes...just for a moment...

Evelyn woke with a start. A gloved hand—a big gloved hand—was shaking her awake.

She sat up immediately, thinking of decorum, and rubbed her eyes. She couldn't make out who the person was at first, and her heart threatened to throb right into her throat. She didn't want to die—not when she'd just started living.

Her life for the past five years since the massacre in Greenwood had been a shell of the life she'd lived before. Before she'd been full of excitement and energy. Her future had been bright and nothing would have stopped her from pursuing her dreams of being a singer. Then that night of

May thirty-first 1921 had happened, and she'd become a different person. The fire had burned Greenwood, and now the fire burned out of her.

Her life flashed before her eyes as she contemplated the stranger at her side.

Finally, the man leaned down. "Miss, I didn't want you to miss your stop. I'm not sure where you're headed, but we're getting to the end of the railway line."

Evelyn shook her head at her hasty assumption that he was someone wanting to harm her. She really had allowed fear to take over her thinking. She looked out of the window to see if she had indeed missed her stop, but she hadn't.

"Thank you so much," she said as she stood, grabbing her bags.

He'd woken her just in time. Her stop was next.

When the guard opened the door, she exited. The cold wind of midday hit her hard. The tall Black man backed up and held the door open for her. He held his hand out to help her step down out of the car.

Evelyn put her gloved hand into his, savoring the small amount of warmth coming from the bright sun's rays. She decided that this gentleman was handsome—dashingly handsome, actually. He had a strong jawline, pleasing big, light brown eyes, brown hair cut really low, with a part on the side, and a muscular build. He was similar to Lorenzo in that they both had very symmetrical faces, but this man's features were more rugged and Lorenzo's were more a gentleman's features.

The comparison shocked Evelyn. Why had she instantly thought of Lorenzo while admiring another handsome stranger?

The man nodded knowingly at Evelyn, like he was well aware of where she was headed. She smiled as they walked in separate directions.

There were several people who exited the train car at

the same time as Evelyn. She started on her five-mile journey, carrying her bags down the dirt road. The crowd soon
thinned out, most heading in the opposite direction from
Evelyn. She found herself alone on the long stretch of road.

Suddenly, something hit her in the head. She gasped.
The wind had been knocked out of her. Her bags dropped,
stirring up a cloud of dirt from the road. Black crept in-
ward from her peripheral vision.

No, she couldn't pass out.

She shook her head. Her eyes rolled at the pain. She
looked around and saw two men progress toward her.
Blood ran down the side of her face, stinging her eyes.
Her vision blurred and her eyes watered.

"So we meet again."

She recognized the voice. It was Mr. Simmens. He had
a bandage around his head—probably from where Lorenzo
hit him, or maybe from where his head had hit the floor.

Evelyn was on her knees, frozen in the dirt.

"Get up!" Simmens yelled.

Evelyn wouldn't move willingly. They'd have to drag
her away from the main road.

She grabbed at the knife strapped to her thigh. They
would surely rape her if they could get to her. She'd heard
all the horror stories about Black women being brutalized;
she wouldn't be the next one—at least not without a fight.

Her head throbbed.

"Get the ax. I'm a put some White purity in this jigaboo."

Evelyn's eyes grew wide. The thought of his vile hands
racked her body with chills.

She wasn't ready to die.

That was the second time she thought that in a matter of hours.

She would fight, and they'd be forced to kill her. That
would be an admirable death.

Chapter Eleven

Lorenzo

Lorenzo pressed on the gas. He had a bad feeling about this. When Jeb had called to tell Lorenzo he'd seen Evelyn board the train, and that Simmens had been there on the platform as well, Lorenzo had flown from his apartment.

Jeb had been waiting by Lorenzo's roadster. They'd both jumped in without saying a word. They knew each other so well. Lorenzo's father had business with Jeb's father, so their friendship had been inevitable. And Jeb had a certain skill set that Lorenzo found valuable in many different circumstances.

Luckily, Jeb had seen which train Evelyn had taken, and Lorenzo's car was one of the fastest cars made. He had no doubt they'd catch up to Evelyn. She and Simmens had only a few minutes' lead. And it was Sunday, so most people were in church and off the roads.

"What's that?"

Lorenzo followed Jeb's gaze. There was a lot of dust being kicked up on the road. It was hard to see from a distance. Lorenzo pressed down on the gas pedal and the roadster revved ahead.

Lorenzo came to a stop. Gravel spewed everywhere, little pings hitting the car.

"That's Evelyn's coat," Jeb said as he and Lorenzo jumped out.

The road was empty. They looked toward the field.

In the distance, they heard a woman screaming.

They looked at each other and then sprinted into the tall grass. With the sun beaming down, the men who had Evelyn were hard to make out at first. But when Lorenzo got close enough, what he saw sent a seething fire of rage burning through him.

He ran toward the two men slapping Evelyn around. One held her while the other hit her repeatedly. The man Lorenzo knew was Simmens had his pants down around his ankles, and only stopped slapping Evelyn when he heard Lorenzo and Jeb approaching.

Lorenzo tackled Simmens to the ground. They rolled, but Lorenzo ended up on top. He beat Simmens over and over, until Simmens's face was nothing more than a blood-splattered mess.

"Lorenzo, stop. Lorenzo, please—stop!"

Evelyn's voice sounded far away at first. Lorenzo was so enraged he couldn't even see clearly. The sounds of rushing wind filled his ears.

A small glove-covered hand touched Lorenzo's shoulder and he stopped hitting the unconscious man. He looked up into Evelyn's medallion-colored eyes. She had bruises, and blood trickled down from a wound covered by her beautiful hair. Lorenzo stood up and cradled her face. She winced at his touch.

He looked at his hands, covered in blood. Simmens's blood. Immediately he dropped his hands to his sides.

"I'm sorry. Are you okay?"

Forcing himself not to touch her, even though his hands literally ached to feel the delicate softness of her skin, to make sure she was okay. His voice came out deeper than usual, thick with guilt for not preventing this from happening. He was both pleased and disgusted with how it had felt to beat Simmens. Rage still coursed through him.

He took in some deep breaths to calm himself. He'd never experienced anger like he'd felt when he'd saw what Simmens was doing to Evelyn.

"I'm okay. It could've been worse."

"Did they…?"

"No," Evelyn said, and she shook her head. "They were trying to, but I stabbed Simmens with my knife and that's when they started beating me."

A smile played at Lorenzo's lips at the thought of Evelyn stabbing Simmens. She was a fighter—but Lorenzo already knew that.

"Let's get you home."

He was leading her back toward the car when he finally remembered Jeb and the other man. He turned around to see Jeb standing over the second man, who was also unconscious.

"Did you kill him?"

"Nah, figured he wasn't worth it. Besides, they've got theirs coming soon enough. I slugged him, though."

Jeb smiled and walked toward Lorenzo and Evelyn, spitting on Simmens as he passed.

Lorenzo could hear the birds chirping again. The noise in his ears had subsided. He looked down at Evelyn and guided her toward his car. The roadster was a two-seater, but Evelyn's small frame would fit between Lorenzo and Jeb easily.

Lorenzo had a canister of water in his car and he used it to clean his hands of Simmens's blood. He wasn't a killer, like his father, but for the first time in his life he'd felt the kind of rage that might cause someone to commit murder. He was still trying to figure out where that rage had come from.

He was glad he hadn't done any permanent damage to Simmens. No matter how Lorenzo felt about the lowlife, he wasn't worth Lorenzo losing his integrity over. But when he'd seen Evelyn hurt, everything had gone black and he'd had tunnel vision.

If Evelyn hadn't stopped him, he wasn't sure what he might have done. Evelyn had saved Simmens's life. She saved the life of a man who had wanted to hurt her in the worst way. And she'd saved Lorenzo too.

To say Lorenzo was in awe of Evelyn was not sufficient to describe what he thought of her. His cousin's murder would be avenged, but this wasn't the moment to get it done. Lorenzo had wanted to send a very clear message to the Klan. Now he wanted to send a message about Vin, and also about Evelyn. He wouldn't allow anyone to hurt her. His wrath would be felt.

Jeb had helped Evelyn into the car. Once Lorenzo had cleaned up, he got back behind the wheel of the roadster. With Evelyn so close to him, he could see that she was shaking. He took the jacket that he had left in his car and wrapped it around her shoulders. The two men had taken her coat off, and all she wore was the beautiful shimmering gold dress she'd worn at the club.

"We will take you home," Lorenzo said, starting the roadster.

Evelyn put her hand on Lorenzo's arm. "I can't go home like this. Can you take me back to the club?"

Her eyes, still watery, punctured him. He would do whatever she asked. He nodded and turned the car around.

They were all was quiet on the ride back to the city, but Lorenzo and Jeb kept glancing at Evelyn. Experiencing something like she'd gone through could cause unseen damage. He would take care of Evelyn. Whatever she needed, he would get it for her.

When they pulled up at Blues Moon they took the back way inside. Lorenzo led Evelyn up the stairs, and Jeb went to check on the club.

She was walking fine, so Lorenzo didn't offer to carry her even though he really wanted to. He opened the door to his loft and let her walk in first.

She gasped. "This is where you live?" She looked around.

Lorenzo smiled. He liked that she liked his home.

Chapter Twelve

Evelyn

The wide-open space took Evelyn's breath away. The windows—there were so many windows—gave a view of the entire Downtown. She could see the river in the distance. She walked to a window to look out. They were very high up.

Lorenzo's apartment smelled of spices and lemon. She looked toward his kitchen as her stomach growled. "I'm sorry. I haven't eaten anything since last night." Embarrassed, she looked away from him.

"Let me get you cleaned up and then I can give you something to eat. I was just about to eat when Jeb called and told me what had happened."

Lorenzo disappeared down the hall and returned with washcloths, a bowl of water, and some alcohol.

"Have a seat on the sofa."

Evelyn obeyed. Lorenzo sat so close to her the warmth of his body warmed hers. She was still chilled from everything that had happened.

Lorenzo dipped the towel in the water and then moved toward her forehead. Evelyn winced.

"I won't hurt you."

Lorenzo's eyes poured into Evelyn's. She closed them and let him wipe away the dried blood. She focused on how the small vein in her neck beat more rapidly the closer he got to her. She wondered briefly if she should tell him she could do it herself. That would have been the smart thing to do. But her mouth wouldn't form the words. With her eyes closed, her sense of smell was intensified, and she felt a little intoxicated by the smoky mint scent that filled her nose.

"It doesn't look bad. Your hair will cover most of it. Are you okay?"

Each time Lorenzo touched her a new wave of warmth spread through her body, each one more intense than the last.

"I'm okay."

Evelyn's eyes were still closed when she felt the absence of Lorenzo. When she opened her eyes, she saw he stood in front of the refrigerator. He pulled out a pot of something. He put it on the stove and ignited the gas.

Evelyn stood and returned her focus to the windows. The sun shone brightly. She gingerly touched her face. She worried about going on stage. She didn't want anyone to know what had happened to her.

She decided to put it out of her mind and focus on where she was and the person taking care of her. The apartment was luminous, thanks to the floor-to-ceiling windows, and Evelyn saw Lorenzo had pictures of his family placed throughout the living space.

She picked up a frame from the small table where she stood. It was obviously a picture of Lorenzo, but he was a boy, and the beautiful woman she'd seen him leave with last night was the little girl in the picture. The two of them had their arms on each other's shoulders like they were the best of friends.

The picture both warmed her heart, to see Lorenzo so young and happy, and also sent a pang of jealousy through her chest. So Lorenzo hadn't just met this woman; she had been in his life for many years. Even if Evelyn had wanted to—which she didn't—she couldn't compete with that.

She felt his presence reverberating in the large room like a pulse. She could detect him no matter how close he was to her. She didn't want to think about what that could mean…

Lorenzo took the picture from Evelyn and gently placed it back on the table. "Ready to eat?"

The skin around his eyes had darkened some. He was tired; Evelyn could see that. She was tired too, but where would she rest? She couldn't stay here with him.

"I am. Thank you."

Evelyn followed him to a solid wood traditional table. There were eight seats. The table sat atop an intricately designed light blue rug. The color of the rug and the green couch made Evelyn think Lorenzo had extravagant taste. Her mother would have liked this decor.

Lorenzo pulled out a chair and Evelyn sat down. He placed a bowl of hot stew in front of her, a small plate with a soft buttery golden roll and, to Evelyn's amazement, a glass of red wine. Since Prohibition, wine had been hard to come by, but some people had wineries that would sell to anyone claiming they were using it for religious purposes.

"Where'd you get this?" Evelyn couldn't help herself. The question was out before she could think better of it.

"I own a winery and distillery just outside of the city— about thirty miles."

"But all the wineries and distilleries are owned or restricted by the government."

Lorenzo smirked. "Not all of them." He winked at her.

He sat in the seat at the head of the table, and she was right next to him on one side. She still had his suit jacket on, and he still had on an unbuttoned shirt. To a casual observer, they might have appeared to be lovers.

"Thank you for your hospitality and for coming to find me."

Evelyn couldn't meet his eyes. She hated that she'd

needed him, a White man, to save her from other White men. The irony of it all left her spinning.

She knew that in every race there were good and bad people, but she realized she was afraid to find out which Lorenzo was. All of his actions toward her so far had been kind and generous, but what exactly did he want from her? He had a beautiful woman who was lethal, and he had a thriving business. What could he possibly want with a country girl he had nothing in common with?

No matter how kind he was to her, Evelyn just wanted to know what he was really after.

"So, tell me about yourself," Lorenzo said. He looked at her over his glass of wine.

"What would you like to know?"

Evelyn took a small bite of the roll. It melted in her mouth. She had to stifle a moan. The savory sweetness was one of the best things she'd ever tasted. She hoped her face didn't give away how glorious she thought it was.

"Anything you wish to tell me."

"Well, I'm originally from Louisiana. We moved north so my mother could open her medical practice. We lived in Tulsa briefly, before my parents were…" She hesitated.

"Before your parents were what?"

"Killed." Again Evelyn couldn't meet Lorenzo's eyes.

"Oh, my God, I'm sorry. I didn't know. When you said you were taking care of your grandmother, I didn't put it together that… I'm sorry. Do you mind me asking how it happened?"

"Yes, I do mind." The curt reply was out before Evelyn could stop herself.

"I'm sorry. I didn't mean to be intrusive."

Evelyn shook her head. "I know. I'm sorry. You've been so kind to me, and I just keep…" She shook her head again. "It's not you. It's me. There are things in my past that I… I'm not sure I can get past."

"You don't owe me an explanation."

Evelyn looked up to see Lorenzo staring at her. "But I've been rude to you."

"No, listen… I want to get to know you better, but you don't have to share anything that you aren't comfortable sharing. I just wanted to extend the same offer to you that you gave me. I'm here to listen whenever you're ready."

Evelyn smiled. It seemed they both had things in their past that they didn't want to talk about. And a part of her wanted him to know what had happened to her, to her parents. But she was afraid to tell him.

"Thank you…really. You've been so kind."

Lorenzo reached across the table and took her hand. His eyes drilled into her. The grayish color threatened to slice her secrets open.

"I know all about running from the events of the past. Unfortunately, I'm a little too familiar with growing up amidst violence." He continued to hold her hand.

Evelyn sensed he was about to share something with her that he didn't like to talk about. She waited patiently for him to continue. She held tightly to the tingling sensation in her fingers from where his skin touched hers.

"I'm sure you are already aware of who my family is?"

Evelyn nodded, redirecting her gaze. She could see the burden on his shoulders from the weight of his very powerful, very dangerous family.

"I want you to know that I walked away from that life because I didn't want any part of the violence, the never-ending pursuit of revenge."

"That must have been really hard for you." She pulled her hand from his and used the napkin to wipe her mouth.

The regret that crossed his face was gone as quickly as it appeared and he was back to his usual expression, which was really hard for Evelyn to read. She hadn't wanted to stop touching him, but the desire thrumming in her body, deep down in her bones, frightened her.

Lorenzo took a drink of his wine. "I've realized that even though I've walked away, or 'neglected my responsibilities,' as my father says, every day that I'm Lorenzo De Luca I am protected by the very same violence I loathe. I scraped and sacrificed to earn enough money to start Blues Moon, but still my club is tainted by the protection of the mob."

He shook his head and chuckled without humor. He looked deep into her eyes.

"I will do anything I can to make you comfortable at Blues Moon. I want you to know that you don't have to worry about what happened on your way home happening again. Based on the direction you were headed, I assume you live in West Eden?"

Evelyn hadn't been expecting him to mention her town by name. Her mouth hung open for a moment, before she could recover.

"It's okay. I've heard rumblings about an all-Black town near the city, but I've never questioned anyone about it. I don't want my customers to be uncomfortable. I figure if they want it to be a secret, then it isn't my secret to tell."

Evelyn looked at him—really looked at him. He stared back at her just as intensely. Who *was* this man?

Chapter Thirteen

Lorenzo

Lorenzo's mother had used to make stew for him whenever he'd had a rough day at school. It was one of his favorite things to eat. She'd taught him how to make rolls that melted in your mouth—because stew had to have a roll to go with it, she would say.

Sitting at the table with Evelyn, Lorenzo thought a lot about his mother. His mother was the perfect balance for his father. She was kind and good where his father was harsh and morally ambivalent. His father had a sense of code and honor, but it was based on street rules: Omertá.

Lorenzo had grown up having both sides ingrained into him. He'd decided at a young age that he didn't want to go into the business with his father—he'd seen too many deaths—but that hadn't stopped his father from teaching him how to survive, how to be a boss and demand the respect of others.

Looking into Evelyn's gorgeous golden eyes, he thought of the kindness of his mother. He wanted to be something he didn't know if he was able to be for Evelyn. He was more like his father than he'd thought. He'd almost killed a man, and Evelyn was too good to be with someone like that.

Lorenzo could see weariness in Evelyn's gaze. "You should get some rest."

"Well, I don't think getting on the train to go home is a good idea at this point."

Evelyn focused on her bowl, avoiding Lorenzo's eyes. Was she nervous?

"I have space here, or there's an empty apartment downstairs that has some basic necessities, like a bed, if that would make you more comfortable. You definitely need to rest or you won't be able to perform tonight."

Lorenzo wanted her to stay with him, but mostly he wanted her to stay wherever she was comfortable.

He went over to the gramophone and turned on Bessie Smith. He loved her voice almost as much as he loved Evelyn's. He found that music helped him relax, which was something he struggled to do with everything that was leaning in on him.

"I should probably go to the apartment downstairs, if that's okay."

When Lorenzo turned back to Evelyn, he hoped the disappointment didn't show on his face. It wasn't proper for a single woman to stay in a man's apartment. He knew that. But he didn't care much about propriety. He just wanted to be near this woman.

He took a deep breath. The smell of the rolls still sat heavily in the room, making his home smell like a bakery.

The more he wanted to be near her, the stronger his resolve grew to keep her away from him. Just being seen with him, the son of a mob boss, could get her killed.

"Of course. I'll have Jeb handle getting it ready for you. Should take only a few minutes. Finish your wine, and please help yourself to more if you'd like."

Lorenzo walked over to the phone and called the club. He asked for Jeb, explained what he needed, and Jeb said he'd take care of it. Jeb had the same air of authority as Lorenzo, which was why Jeb was his second. He might even be better at some things than Lorenzo. They were a good team.

"I really shouldn't have any more wine. I had a bad experience with drinking."

Lorenzo was intrigued. "What happened?" He sat back down at the table with Evelyn.

She shifted in her seat and looked away from him. "I'll just say that I don't remember much, and that arriving home having to be carried to my room was not pleasing to my grand." She shook her head.

Before he could stop himself, Lorenzo used his index finger to lift her chin so she was looking at him. "We're all allowed a night of bad choices. Sometimes it's exactly what you need to wake up the next day and start making better ones. Don't be ashamed of your past. It has made you who you are, and so far I think you're pretty amazing."

She arched an eyebrow at him. "So far?"

Lorenzo smiled and sat back in his seat. He liked touching her, but he didn't want to get his hopes up when he knew he couldn't have her. He would keep his distance. She was young, gorgeous, talented and good. He would not ruin her. He would stay away from her.

"Let me show you the apartment downstairs. It's not as big as this one because there are two other apartments on that level, but it is very nice. Originally, I had the apartments renovated to rent out, but I haven't had time to find tenants."

He held out his hand to help her stand up. He kissed it before letting her go. Her eyes lit with what Lorenzo hoped was desire. Maybe he would let himself indulge in her... just a little bit. A kiss on her full lips wouldn't hurt—but what if he couldn't stop there?

He walked to the door and allowed her to exit into the hall first. Then he locked his door and showed her to the stairs. When they got to the sixth level, he opened the door of apartment 6A. When he held the door open for Evelyn her scent filled his nose as she walked past. She smelled of sunsets and rainstorms, warm days and cold nights.

"This is…lovely."

"It's yours if you want it."

She spun on her heels to glower at him. "Are you trying to buy me, Mr. De Luca? Because I am not for sale. I don't know what you think is going to happen here, but I will not be anyone's mistress."

The fire coming out of her golden glare made Lorenzo take a step back. He was taken aback by her response to what he'd considered an incredibly generous offer. The rent he planned to charge for this apartment was astronomical, and he'd be letting her stay for free because he didn't want to see her going back and forth on the train or a bus twenty miles every day by herself. This was the safest thing for her.

"Look, I don't know what you think I just offered you, but it was *not* a proposal to be my mistress."

"Then what was it? Why are you doing all of this for me? What do you want from me?"

Maybe it was his exhaustion, or maybe it was that he was so taken with this doll that he'd lost himself in her already, but he couldn't even respond. He had no words—which was unlike him. He'd been able to talk his way into or out of any situation he wanted to. But even he could acknowledge when he'd met his match.

"Are you going to say anything?" she asked.

He closed his eyes and shook his head. This entire scene was actually making Evelyn even more appealing. No one had challenged Lorenzo in this way. The sheer palpable anger radiating off her had Lorenzo's heart beating like a Duke Ellington song.

"I think I can make it just fine on my own, Mr. De

Luca, thank you. I will see myself out. And I'll return for my shift tonight."

With that, she stormed out of the apartment and down the stairs.

Lorenzo was left with a slight smile on his face, shaking his head. This woman was a spitfire, and he loved it.

Chapter Fourteen

Evelyn

Evelyn didn't know where she was going. She walked and did some shopping locally and then returned feeling calmer, eventually calling her brother from the phone in the club. She paced outside waiting. She fought back the tears that pressed against the back of her eyes. She would not cry over a man who would cheat on one of the most beautiful women Evelyn had ever seen.

She'd seen him walk out of the club with that woman who'd drugged the KKK members the night before. Then she'd seen that picture in his apartment, of that same woman as a child with a young Lorenzo. How could she entertain the affections of a man who had gorgeous women at his beck and call? No one would give a woman an apartment without expecting something in return.

Lorenzo De Luca must think Evelyn was just a skirt he could take out to play with whenever he was ready. Giving her gifts, playing soft music, offering her an apartment— he was out of his mind if he thought she was that type of woman.

The sun had retreated from the sky, resting on the horizon. It would be dark soon, and Evelyn would need to be back here by ten to start her set. She was so tired and, though she didn't want to admit it, heartbroken. She'd never been propositioned like that before. She looked up at the sky to keep the tears from falling down her cheeks.

Her brother had a Lafayette that he'd bought with his share of their parents' money when he'd come to the city. The car wasn't flashy, but it was drivable. When he pulled up in front of her she almost collapsed, right there on the sidewalk. She was so happy to see him. She hadn't seen him in a few weeks. He didn't come to West Eden often, and it had been Evelyn's first time to the city yesterday.

She'd been so excited to get home and tell her grand about her new job—she hadn't even thought to call her brother. Now he looked at her, with a knowing look.

He got out and hugged her. "Your first time to the big city not going well, little sister?"

Evelyn shook her head as a sob escaped.

"Miss Laroque—please wait."

Evelyn turned to see Jeb, Lorenzo's second-in-charge, walking briskly toward her with something in his hands. As he got closer, Evelyn wondered why he was chasing after her with what looked to be a stack of papers.

"Miss Laroque, please come back inside. Mr. De Luca wants to offer you a contract that includes room and board in one of the apartments above the club. He and I have discussed how best to keep you safe now that you are in our employ. I understand there was some sort of misunderstanding, and as this was partly my idea I wanted to make sure I explained it to you, since Mr. De Luca seems to have jumbled this up. Will you please come back inside so we can go over your contract?"

Evelyn looked from Jeb to her brother. Both men looked back at her, waiting for her response.

"I'm a foolish woman. I apologize for my abrupt retreat. It was my misunderstanding, not Mr. De Luca's. I've called my brother down here, and now I feel quite ridiculous."

"I'm sorry it took me so long to catch up to you. I was

in the middle of getting the contract drawn up when Mr. De Luca found me to tell me what had happened. I came as soon as he told me." Jeb smiled and turned to Carmichael. "It's a pleasure to meet the brother of this phenomenal singer." Jeb stuck out his hand and Carmichael shook it. "Why don't we all go inside to get a drink and discuss the details?"

Jeb put his hand on the small of Evelyn's back and guided her back toward the club.

Carmichael followed.

Evelyn squinted under the scrutiny of the setting sun. She was probably imagining it, but she thought everyone on the street was staring at her. They saw her for the fraud she was. She'd put herself on this pedestal, but she had no right to be so judgmental. That had always been her problem. She'd judged her own parents for wanting to keep her safe. She'd thought of them as cowards, and her last thought before they'd died protecting her had been how wrong she was.

Now here she was again—making foolish assumptions about someone who was attempting to help her. She needed to be cautious with Lorenzo, but she didn't have to be cruel.

Once back inside, she felt her cheeks warm immediately. She looked around frantically, to see if she could find Lorenzo. The feeling in the pit of her stomach when she realized he wasn't in the club was either relief or disappointment, and the terrible thing was that she really didn't know which one it was. It didn't matter because he would probably find ways to avoid her after her tantrum.

Jeb led them to one of the tables in the back corner, farthest away from the music. Evelyn decided she liked the atmosphere of the club during the day, even this early. The music wasn't as loud. No one was dancing. Everyone was sitting, chatting and eating. It was more like a restaurant than a speakeasy. It was a place she could see herself spending a lot of time, just getting to know people and writing songs.

A waitress set a glass of water in front of each of them. Jeb ordered eggs, ham and sausage for the table. He also ordered three cups of coffee.

"So, what is this contract you are offering my sister?" Carmichael's tone was the quiet, menacing tone of a protective brother.

If Jeb noticed, he didn't respond. He smiled and handed over the stack of papers he was holding. "I want to point out a few important things, and then you can take it back to the apartment and go over it in more detail with your brother, if you would like. The most important part is the wage you will be paid. I hope you find it to your liking. The apartment is what we're calling a perk of your employment, but if for some reason you were to quit, you would have free room and board for a month, to give you time to find new lodgings. Lastly, you will only sing three nights a week. There are other singers on the other nights, and if for some reason you need to take some time off you won't need to worry. There would be someone to cover for you. I'm sure the customers won't be happy, but there might be occasions when you need to have time off that fall on the days you usually sing. Do you have any questions?"

Evelyn shook her head and looked at her brother. He shook his head as well. Just then, the food arrived. It smelled amazing. Evelyn's stomach let out an embarrassing gurgle. She hadn't realized how hungry she was until the smoky savory scents created a cocoon of deliciousness around her.

They were all silent for a few minutes while they ate.

Carmichael was the first to finish. He always ate like someone was going to take his food at any minute if he didn't finish it. Evelyn noticed that Jeb was nearly done as well. She was famished, but she took her time savoring the way her mouth watered at the salty rich sausage. The eggs, fluffy and yellow, just like her grand made, felt like little clouds on her tongue.

"So, what exactly does my sister need to know about the mob boss who owns this club?"

Jeb looked up. He didn't appear to be taken off guard, but Evelyn knew the question was rude and he probably hadn't anticipated it.

He wiped his mouth and cleared his throat. "Lorenzo De Luca is not a part of the mob. Like anyone, he can't choose his family, but he has chosen not to have his business involved with any dealings that would put his clientele and those working for him at risk. Yes, he runs a speakeasy that sells illegal alcohol, but he is actually working to change the laws. He's put a lot of money toward fighting Prohibition the legal way. He's a good man, and I'm not sure what I'd be doing if I wasn't working with him."

Carmichael was quiet for a moment. Then he said, "I just want to make sure my sister is safe. She's been through enough and she doesn't need any trouble with law enforcement."

"I believe that Mr. De Luca will see to it that she is safe and doesn't have any trouble."

"I don't need you all talking about me as if I'm not sitting right here," Evelyn said, feeling her heartbeat speed up.

She was exhausted, and now that she'd eaten, she was ready to get some rest before she needed to sing again.

Picking up the papers, she kissed her brother's cheek. "Carmichael, I know you're busy, and I can't thank you enough for coming down here. I'm so sorry to have worried you. I will call you later. I need to get some rest now."

Carmichael nodded. "I have to get going, actually. I'm glad you're okay, little sis."

"Here you go, Miss Evelyn." Jeb slid a key across the table to her.

"Thank you again, Jeb. Please give Mr. De Luca my apologies."

With that, Evelyn stood and walked toward the back of the club, to get to the stairs that would lead her to the apartment. The only thing was to get there without running into Lorenzo…

Chapter Fifteen

Lorenzo

Lorenzo gulped down the moonshine, slammed the glass on the end table and fell back on the bed. His offer to Evelyn had not gone as planned, and to make things worse he hadn't responded the way he should have. Now he had no idea where she was or if she was okay. The waiting had his head throbbing and his eyes burning. Although he'd called in Jeb to smooth things over. Jeb was good at that.

The phone rang, and Lorenzo gasped at the sudden disruption of the silence. He stumbled from the bed to the phone. "Hello?" He was dead tired, but he didn't care. The only thing he wanted to know was that Evelyn was okay.

"She signed the contract and I gave her the key. She should be in the apartment now. Her brother was here with her. He doesn't like you." Jeb laughed.

"That's not funny, Jeb." Lorenzo sighed.

He laid his head back against the wall, letting out a long breath. He told himself that his concern for Evelyn was out of an obligation to protect a young woman who worked in his club, but he worried that there might be more to it than that. After all, there were other women who worked for him, and he hadn't offered any of *them* an apartment.

Yalaina still lived with her mother, not far away, and the others had stable living situations as well, so he didn't have to worry, but for some reason Evelyn traveling back and forth by herself unsettled Lorenzo. He felt the danger that surrounded his life like it was a second skin. He didn't want that danger to touch Evelyn.

No matter what, he would have to keep his dealings with her purely professional. If he reacted to her in this way and he'd only just met her, he couldn't imagine how he'd behave once he got to know her. He was protective of the people he cared about because he was so afraid of losing someone close to him again.

A barely audible knock at his door unsettled him. He wasn't expecting anyone. Running his fingers through his hair, he peeked at his reflection in the mirror by the door. His eyes were red and his skin had lost some color. He shook his head and opened the door.

"Hey, Malcolm. What are you doing here?"

"I'm sorry to bother you," said the little boy with sad blue eyes. "But Mr. Jeb said I would find you up here. I just wanted to say thank you, but my momma says we can't take no charity from the mob. I don't know what that means, but she says strings are attached to stuff like that and…well, anyway… Thanks for trying to help us."

He turned to walk away. The boy still had on the dirty clothes he'd been in when he'd got caught stealing food from the club. There was a bag outside of Lorenzo's door that held all the new clothes Lorenzo had had Jeb purchase for the boy and his family. It was just the essentials that they would need immediately. Lorenzo had more being delivered to the apartment that he'd set up for them a few blocks away.

He didn't think it was the best idea for children to live in lofts above a speakeasy, so he'd given them an apartment in one of the other buildings he'd renovated. He hadn't been intending to hold on to it, but with so many families in the city needing safe housing, now he planned to use money from the fundraiser to help create a charity to run his public housing venture.

"Wait—don't leave. Let me come with you to meet your mother. I want to help her understand that there are absolutely no strings attached to anything I will give you. I don't want anything from you or your family. I just want to help."

Lorenzo kneeled down in front of Malcolm.

"You see, I've been able to make a good life for myself. I've not always done the right thing, but I'm a different person now, and I feel like it's my...my job to help others because I'm in a position to do so. Do you understand?"

Malcolm's sad eyes were focused on the ground. He didn't say anything.

"Listen, I can talk with your mom. Will you let me walk with you? I want to meet your little sister anyway."

Malcolm nodded. He didn't look up, but he had agreed to let Lorenzo come with him, and that was good enough.

Chapter Sixteen

Evelyn

Evelyn nearly dropped the glass of water she was holding when someone knocked on her door. She wasn't used to living alone. She'd lived with her parents and then with her grand. Having her own apartment—and such a nice one—was a little unsettling.

"Who is it?" she said through the door, straightening the lounge shirt and pants she had on. She reached for the gloves she'd placed in the drawer of the table in her foyer for circumstances just like this. Sliding them on, she tried to look through the peephole.

"It's me—Jeb. I have a message from Lorenzo."

She closed her eyes for a long moment, trying to get her breathing to slow. The mention of Lorenzo's name made little pinpricks skitter across her forearms. She opened the door and tried to plaster a smile on her face.

"I apologize for stopping by unannounced. Lorenzo wants to know if he can speak with you briefly."

"I'll be at the club later. Can we talk then?" She was curious about what he wanted, but she hadn't yet mustered up enough courage to see him again.

"He said it was urgent. That's why I'm here. He didn't want to show up on your doorstep without permission. If you have a few moments, I can run up and let him know you're available."

Evelyn looked around the hall frantically, like the answers she was seeking were there somewhere. She didn't know what to say. She wanted to talk to him, apologize for her assumptions, but she hadn't decided what she should say.

Not able to think of a way out of it, she conceded to seeing him. "I'm not busy at the moment."

"Great, Miss Evelyn. I will go get him now."

Evelyn relaxed a little as Jeb turned and she closed the door. At least they wouldn't be alone. Jeb would be there, to offer a cushion between her and Lorenzo.

She went to the mirror to touch up her makeup and run a comb through her hair. She didn't have time to pin it up. It fell in waves down her back. There was something intimate about having her hair down that she couldn't describe. She always wore it pinned up in neat curls. Wearing her hair down around men she didn't know seemed scandalous.

She quickly whipped up a few curls and pinned them away from her face. The knock on the door was the only sound besides her pounding heart.

She walked slowly, giving herself as much time as possible to pull her emotions together.

When she opened the door, to her surprise Lorenzo was alone.

"Hi," he said, looking every bit as dashing as the first time she'd seen him.

His gray-green eyes glittered in the light of day. His perfectly sculpted face, beard and long lashes reminded her of the men on the covers of the latest fashion magazines. It was like he was unintentionally trying to give the impression of nonchalant dishevelment, but failing because he still looked perfect.

He ran his hands through his hair, and Evelyn realized she hadn't returned his greeting. "Hello, please come in."

Evelyn stepped aside to let him enter. When he walked

past her she inhaled the scent of honey, mint and rosemary. Evelyn loved to cook, so she could pinpoint the makeup of most fragrances just with one deep breath. Lorenzo's scent tempted her in a way she couldn't explain. Her mouth watered and she swallowed hard, trying to gain some semblance of restraint where this man was concerned.

She gestured for him to have a seat on the luxurious couch that had been delivered not long ago. She absolutely loved the furnishings in the apartment. She couldn't have picked better options herself.

Taking a seat in the chair opposite the couch, Evelyn said, "So, what is it that couldn't wait?"

She crossed her arms, not missing the way he looked so intently at her. She would be lying if she said she wasn't happy he'd come to see her. But she wouldn't allow herself to imagine what that could mean. He was probably just ensuring she was going to return to the club to sing because he wouldn't be able to find another singer on short notice.

"First, let me say that I would *never* try to proposition you in that way. I was only thinking of what would be safest for you, knowing you would be leaving the club at odd hours of the day and night and considering what happened with the Klan. I just wanted to make sure you didn't get hurt because of me and your association to me."

Lorenzo wore his confidence like a second tailored suit. He was all business now. And Evelyn regretted that she might never see him with his guard down again. He'd shared something painful from his past with her, and she had insulted him immediately after. Her behavior had been reprehensible. She blamed the men who had sown such a deep level of distrust within her after killing her parents...

"I know that now. Let me apologize for my abruptness and my unfair assumptions about your motives. It's not easy for me to accept help from someone like you."

"Someone like me?" Lorenzo's brow creased.

"Never mind," Evelyn said, looking away from his questioning expression. "I just want to say that I'm sorry. I have looked over the contract, and although it is way more generous than I'd been led to expect for this position, I am going to accept it. Because it is what's best for my grandmother at this time. I hope me staying here isn't an inconvenience to you?"

"Well, I own the entire building. I don't need to rent this apartment out. You've only just started, so I thought putting it in your contract as a part of your salary package would be the best idea." He leaned in closer to her. "And besides, having someone with a temper like yours, I won't have to hire any additional security for the club like I thought."

His lips quirked, and so did Evelyn's. She'd always had a temper.

"When I was a child, my parents nicknamed me Dr. Jekyll."

They laughed together.

"I can believe that. I was actually very mellow as a child. My parents valued a lack of emotion, so I learned not to show my feelings."

Evelyn smiled at him, but she couldn't help the sadness that invaded her thoughts. How awful to be just a kid and not able to express your feelings.

She nodded. "Here is the signed contract. Thank you again. Is it standard for nightclub singers to get contracts?"

"I'm a businessman, and I didn't get to where I am without thinking through every possible situation. A contract ensures there are no misunderstandings that would cause my club to lose money. And I don't want to lose you... for the club."

Lorenzo stared at her with that same intensity that Evelyn was beginning to enjoy very much. The tips of her fingers tingled as he reached over and squeezed her hand, grazing the top of her thigh where her hands were tightly clasped.

He was paying her a very generous salary, plus allowing her to stay in the apartment for free. How would she ever be able to repay him? She sighed loudly. She couldn't be indebted to him. He would have power over her. And the fact that he was a White man—well, she just didn't want to owe him anything.

"It puts me at ease," he said. "Knowing you won't need to travel back and forth to West Eden—especially when you're tired."

Her hair had fallen in her face. Lorenzo's callused hand moved it back behind her ear. She hadn't even noticed him get up and move closer to her. He kneeled in front of her. He had an effect on her that she had to figure out. She shivered at his touch.

"Now, how can I convince you that my intentions are only to make working at my club convenient and safe for you? Why were you so hesitant to take the deal?" His brow furrowed as he studied her face.

"I... I don't know." She wouldn't tell him all she'd gone through. She couldn't trust him.

Lorenzo stood, and Evelyn did the same.

"I won't take up any more of your time." Lorenzo clutched the papers in his hand. "Thank you for allowing me to see you on such short notice. I just couldn't focus on anything until I was sure you and I were okay."

He smiled genuinely down at her and squeezed her arm. Evelyn couldn't help but wonder why he cared so much. But, more importantly, she couldn't explain why she did as well.

Chapter Seventeen

Lorenzo

Unlike most women, Evelyn wasn't making things easy on him. She'd been resistant to him at every turn. She intrigued him. Yes, she was easily the most beautiful woman he'd ever seen in his life. She belonged in the movies. But her beauty was just an added bonus. Something about the pain in her eyes and the soul in her voice made him want to help make her dreams come true, and he would use every resource at his disposal to do so. While keeping their relationship strictly professional, of course.

He knew he was getting ahead of himself. He knew he should put some distance between them. But the idea of that made him uneasy. He didn't really care what all of this meant. All he wanted to do was run his business, get to know this incredible woman and take care of her if she'd let him—which she probably wouldn't.

Lorenzo laughed to himself as he climbed the stairs back to his own apartment, so caught up in thoughts of Evelyn he didn't notice the young man standing in front of his door until he was almost right on him. The man looked younger than Lorenzo, but he stood with confidence.

When their eyes met, the young man scowled. "What do you really want with my sister?"

His sister? Lorenzo let out a breath. The man had the same golden eyes as Evelyn. They had the same ginger-brown skin too, now that Lorenzo was really looking at him. He and the young man were almost the same height. Lorenzo stood six foot three, and this man was probably six two and a half.

"I don't understand."

Lorenzo took a few steps toward Evelyn's brother. He wanted to assure him that he would protect Evelyn. The defensive stance the young man had taken made Lorenzo want to put him at ease. He wasn't about to engage in a fight with one of Evelyn's family members under any circumstances.

"You do. My sister is innocent and she's been through a lot. She doesn't need someone like you trying to get whatever you want from her and then leaving her."

"Wait a minute. I wouldn't do that. I just want to help her," Lorenzo said, a little flabergasted at the venom in the man's voice. "I can help her with her singing career."

"I know men like you. I know what you want from a Black girl, and it ain't marriage."

Lorenzo, for the second time, had absolutely no words.

"Just stay away from my sister. She's not for you. She never will be."

Lorenzo stood in the front of his door alone after Evelyn's brother had stormed off without giving Lorenzo a chance to respond. What was *with* this family—and what was it they thought he wanted from Evelyn? He had been accused of a lot of things in his life—some warranted, most not—but this was new to him. He had no ill intentions toward Evelyn, but he wasn't sure he would ever be able to make her or her brother believe that. Especially if they both kept walking off before he could get his thoughts together and respond.

He continued to breathe deeply while he opened his door. Back in the comfort of his own home, he remembered he needed to refocus his energy on helping Malcolm and other families like his. The fundraiser would be a big deal, but he needed to continue to press the politicians to push for a repeal of Prohibition. He could make a lot more money and help a lot more people without Prohibition standing in the way of his progress.

The religious backers of Prohibition blamed immigrants like Lorenzo's family for the corruption surrounding alcohol consumption. Their logic was so flawed, Lorenzo couldn't believe that people were actually believing the lies these groups spewed. Alcohol and immigrants weren't the problem. Closed-minded self-righteous people were the problem.

He got on the horn to start planning the charity organization that he would give the fundraiser money to.

As soon as he hung up he wanted to talk with Evelyn and tell her the plans for the fundraiser evening.

He couldn't help but wonder if inviting her to his apartment was a good idea. Perhaps he should choose a more neutral location for their sessions. They couldn't go to the club. It would be too noisy and distracting. But if they went to a restaurant it might seem like a date.

Standing, Lorenzo sighed, and decided to think over his next move with Evelyn very carefully. Her brother had said she'd been through a lot, which wasn't a surprise to Lorenzo. He had seen the depth of her pain from the moment she'd walked into his club. What he wanted to know was how he could help her heal.

Lorenzo pulled off his tie and dress shirt. He stepped out of his shoes and lay across his bed. He fell asleep with Evelyn's gorgeous heart-shaped face in his head.

The patter of rain dragged Lorenzo from sleep. He'd been dreaming of Evelyn.

They were at Blues Moon. She'd just finished a set and received a standing ovation from the crowd. Her smile lit his heart as she ran to him, jumping up and down. She was so excited, and the only person she wanted to share her big moment with was him. He held her face and kissed her with all the passion of a man who hadn't been in love with anyone his entire adult life. She clung to him like he held the key to her last breath...

Sighing, and running his hands through his hair, he stood and lumbered to the window. He stared out at the street. People in raincoats and a sea of umbrellas swarmed below. Kansas City was *his* city. The music, the revitalization and all the new industries popping up excited him. He couldn't wait to leave his mark on this place he called home.

The rain, a consistent drumming matching the beat of his heart, lulled him into calm. He'd been so happy when he'd woken from his dream. The emotions had been so real. The smile on Evelyn's face had made him feel light and carefree—something he hadn't felt since he was a child.

The phone rang and he looked over his shoulder at it. He decided not to answer. He needed some time to think about the trajectory of his life and where he was going wrong.

He needed to handle the KKK, and he was determined to do just that, without any interference from his family. The Klan was a growing parasite on the city, and it was his duty to protect the place and the people he loved so much.

Even though he couldn't be with Evelyn, he owed it to her to make the city safe for young women like her. When he'd learned that Simmens had a thing against young Black women, and that he usually got away with hurting them because no one really looked into the crimes concerning the Black members of the community, Lorenzo's blood had boiled. He could do something, though. He could avenge Vinny and Edith and keep who knew how many other women safe from Simmens, and that was what he was going to do.

He got to the phone just in time. "Hello?" he breathed.

"*Bambino*, I'm glad you answered.'

It was his father.

"I want to talk to you. We have more information about your cousin that you really need to hear. I'm worried about you and this new singer that you have. Pictures have surfaced of you and her, talking inside Blues Moon. People are speculating about your relationship with her, and they're targeting her to get to you."

Lorenzo envisioned his father, helping him up when he was five years old when he'd fallen and skinned his knee. His father had called him *bambino* and brushed the dirt from Lorenzo's cheeks. The tears had kept falling, and Lorenzo had thought his father would yell at him for showing weakness, but instead his father had picked him up in his arms.

"*Bambino*, you're going to be okay," he'd said. "You're going to show that bike who's boss, and I'm going to help you. That bike won't know what hit it."

Lorenzo had laughed and squeezed his father's neck. And then he'd got back on the bike and shown it he was the boss.

"I've got the situation under control," he said now. "But I do want to call a meeting to discuss Vinny."

Lorenzo's father hesitated before grunting in agreement.

Lorenzo hung up and got dressed. He had to make sure his *famiglia* respected him and the way he chose to handle things.

His knock on Evelyn's door shattered the silence of the hall. He took a few long breaths before the door opened.

"Hey, thank you for seeing me," Lorenzo said.

"Of course—come in," Evelyn said.

She had on a long silk housecoat and gloves, which seemed odd with night clothes, but Lorenzo didn't question it.

"Have a seat. I'll be right out. I was getting dressed to go to the club."

When Evelyn re-emerged, she had on another gold dress and a beautiful headpiece that was thicker than a headband, with jewels that sparkled like diamonds. The floor-length gold-sequined dress showed her trim leg through the high slit. The sight of her skin had Lorenzo breathing hard and fast. Her hair was pinned away from her face, as Lorenzo was coming to realize was her usual hairstyle, and she had on fresh makeup. Her gorgeous eyes were lined in black and long curled lashes stared back at him. The air that came into the room with her was scented with vanilla and lavender.

He couldn't imagine how he must look, basically drooling over her—a woman he'd been told in no uncertain terms he could not have. But Lorenzo had never liked being told what he couldn't have. He understood her brother's hesitation, but every time he saw this doll he lost a little of his will to stay away from her.

"You look…beautiful."

"Thank you. What did you want to tell me?"

Lorenzo exhaled, walking up to her. He took her gloved hand and led her to the couch. They sat together, closer than necessary, but Lorenzo couldn't help but want to be near her.

"I have something important to tell you. I don't want to scare you, but it's important that you know, so you can stay on high alert."

"Lorenzo, what is it? You're scaring me."

"The Klan is trying to take a foothold in the city. The guy you saw at Blues Moon, and who attacked you on your way home…he has a thing for hurting young Black women. I've gotten word that he may target you again. I'm going to handle it, but that means I won't be at the club tonight. I need you to be careful. Don't leave the building. I will make sure Jeb and Tommy, my bartender, have eyes on you at all times when you're not in your apartment. As long as you stay alert, and where they can see you, you're safe. If you need to leave, one of them will go with you. Can you do that for me?"

Lorenzo stared into Evelyn's eyes, hoping her stubborn nature would not prevent her from heeding his warning.

She nodded after a long second. "Why me?" she finally said.

"Because of me. I'm sorry. I knew this would happen if anyone thought you and I were involved."

"Involved? But we're…"

"I know, but there's been someone in here, spying on us for the Klan. They have pictures of you and I talking. I'm going to meet with my family about what we're going to do. I will handle this."

"Okay…"

If Evelyn wondered about the mob's involvement, she didn't say anything.

"Thank you for everything," she said as Lorenzo stood.

"I won't let anything happen to you."

"I know." Evelyn smiled up at him.

"Do you mind mentioning that to your brother?" Lorenzo said, and laughed.

"What are you talking about?" Her expression changed instantly at the mention of her brother.

"He paid me a little visit."

"Oh, no—what did he say?"

Lorenzo sat again. "He told me in no uncertain terms to stay away from you and said that he knew what I wanted from you. What *does* he think I want from you?"

"To live out your fantasy of being with an exotic woman?"

"I… That's not… I'm not trying to…"

"It's fine. I told him that I can take care of myself."

Her golden eyes glittered in the dim light of the moon. She was a fantasy—but not for the reason her brother thought. She was so beautiful. Actually, that word wasn't sufficient to describe her because she was more than just external beauty. She was smart, and there was this fire inside of her that burned so bright.

And her voice sent chills through anyone who heard it. The pain in her voice when she sang made Lorenzo want to… His thoughts trailed off. He'd already fallen too hard for this woman he'd only just met. His father had taught him not to show his cards too soon in the game. He would have to shield his thoughts more carefully around her.

They stared at each other for a long moment. She searched his face as he searched hers. Maybe this could be something… Lorenzo let the thought take shape, not knowing what it meant.

Suddenly Evelyn stood and started pacing.

"Is everything okay?" Lorenzo said.

"Yes, I'm just tired of men who think they can dictate what I should and shouldn't do."

Her gaze burned into him. He knew that comment was for him as much as it was for her brother. He could be controlling—that was his nature—but Evelyn wasn't something to control or possess. He knew that. Yet he still couldn't help but want to protect her at all costs. He understood her brother's compulsion to keep men away from her.

"I think your brother was just trying to keep you safe and away from trouble. I get that desire. Now I better head out, or I'll be late." He walked to the door with Evelyn following close behind.

"When will I see you again?" she asked, with a strange look on her face.

Lorenzo couldn't decide if it was just general curiosity or something more.

"I'll come by when I return, if that's okay. It'll be after you're done singing. I can bring breakfast."

Evelyn nodded. "I would like that, Lorenzo."

He imagined how she might sound if she said his name out of desire and longing. He had to stay away from thoughts like that, though.

Lorenzo turned and walked toward the stairs.

He had one more thing to do before he went to meet with his family.

Chapter Eighteen

Evelyn

The club throbbed with excitement. The dance floor still overflowed with people, but the easygoing tone seemed to be missing.

Evelyn disappeared inside her dressing room. Her eyes had to adjust to the change from low lighting to the bright lights of her vanity. Just outside, dishes clanged loudly in the kitchen.

Evelyn couldn't stop thinking about seeing Lorenzo later. He was kind, but he would never understand what her life had been like—*was* like. Because of all she'd gone through, she couldn't open up. She was starting to think she simply wasn't capable of trusting anyone who wasn't family.

Tears burned the back of Evelyn's eyes. She'd been so sure she could give Lorenzo a fair shot, but maybe she wouldn't be able to after all.

She'd just closed the door to her dressing room when a knock came. She sighed before turning to answer it.

"Benny—so good to see you." She smiled at the older man. "Please, come in."

"Woo—this is a nice room. Mr. De Luca sure knows how to show his appreciation." Benny came in and set his hat on the table. He pulled out one of the chairs and sat.

That was when Evelyn noticed that there was fresh food on the table, with some pitchers of water and tea.

"Please, help yourself," Evelyn said, when she saw Benny eyeing the spread.

He didn't hesitate. He grabbed a piece of meat, some bread and cheese. Then he poured himself some tea and dug in. "So, how are you and Mr. De Luca getting along? I hope there isn't any trouble. We really like having you here."

Evelyn laughed, but there was no humor in it. "We are getting along fine. He is a very kind man."

"He is, Miss Evelyn. He really is. I know you're probably thinking what does this White man want with you, but I've never seen him so...so taken by a woman before. Now, I've seen them taken with *him*, many times, but never reciprocated. I like Mr. De Luca. He's a good friend of mine, and I don't want to see him hurt. Just be honest with him if he don't stand a chance. Okay?"

Benny looked at her with serious eyes.

She nodded.

"Well, I best be going and leave you to it. I'll see you on stage in about thirty minutes. We'll start with the list you gave us last night, then end with some of the songs we discussed." He finished his food and gulped his drink before he got up and walked to the door.

"That sounds wonderful, Benny. I'll be out in just a few minutes."

"You keep wearing dresses like that, Miss Laroque, you might cause some of our customers to have a heart attack." Benny smiled bright, then closed the door, leaving Evelyn alone with her thoughts.

She wanted to just focus on her singing and not deal with whatever was going on with Lorenzo. She wished it didn't have to be complicated, but she also wished there was a world where they could have feelings for each other and not be committing a crime.

Lorenzo didn't seem to worry much about the law. He had

a winery and a distillery where he made bootleg liquor… he owned a speakeasy. Evelyn needed to be a rule-follower. Most of the time her life depended on her doing the right thing and not being caught in situations where she might be accused of a crime.

West Eden and Greenwood were the only places she'd felt safe.

But that wasn't completely true. She felt safe with Lorenzo.

She ate some of the delicious food before touching up her makeup. When another knock came, right before she was about to go on stage, she opened it without thinking, assuming it was Benny again.

Lorenzo stood in front of her. He ran his hand through his hair and asked, "Can I come in?"

Chapter Nineteen

Lorenzo

Lorenzo had stopped by Evelyn's dressing room to remind her of the danger she was in, being associated with him. He had to make sure that she would be safe in his absence, so he'd met with Jeb again and now, on his way out to meet with his family about Vinny, he just wanted to make sure Evelyn was heeding his advice.

Evelyn's sweet lavender and vanilla scent hung in the air. The fresh flowers he'd had placed in her room the day before still bloomed, and added a sweet floral scent to the already full fragrances wafting through the air. He stepped into the room, not missing the perplexed look on Evelyn's face. He was just happy that she wasn't angry with him… yet. That could change very quickly, he was learning.

She stepped aside and Lorenzo walked past her, taking a seat on the sofa.

"Is something wrong?" she asked. "I thought you had something to do?"

"I'm leaving in a few minutes. I wanted to see you one more time before I left. I need to be honest with you about something."

She sat next to him on the sofa. He was truly in shock at the ease of talking to her, being near her. He'd gotten so used to being on guard all the time, that the freedom he felt with her took him a while to understand.

"Okay…color me interested…" Her delicate gloved hands fingered the delicate fabric of a pillow.

Looking into those dazzling eyes, he said, "With everything going on, I wanted you to know that by working here you will be associated with the mob. Whether you have anything to do with me or not, people are going to make assumptions."

He reached for her hand. Evelyn clearly wasn't expecting it, so she jerked. Her glove slid down, and Lorenzo saw the skin on her right hand was badly scarred. Evelyn pulled away quickly, but it was too late. He'd seen it.

"What happened to you?"

His jaw clenched. Seeing her burns, he wanted to kill someone for hurting her. Rage surged so quickly inside him he had to work hard to tamp down the emotion. All the years he'd practiced being calm and in charge of his emotions had gone with the wind the few times he'd thought Evelyn was being hurt, and this was no exception.

"It's nothing." Evelyn pulled her glove back up, covering her scars. "Why would anyone associate me with the mob? I have nothing to do with that."

Lorenzo didn't want to let what he'd seen go, but he could tell she wasn't comfortable talking about it. "Trust me, I know how unfair it is, but that's the way this city runs. You just need to make sure this is what you want. That's all."

Lorenzo anxiously awaited her response.

Evelyn took a deep breath and wrung her gloved hands together. "Thank you for your honesty. I guess I hadn't thought about that aspect of working here. I knew working in a club would come with some amount of danger, but I hadn't realized that your family would be involved."

"They aren't, but it doesn't matter. No one cares that I started this club with my own money, or that I'm a De Luca in name only. What they see is a mobster's son."

Lorenzo couldn't help the resentment that leaked into his voice. He resented how he'd benefitted even when he'd tried to cut ties.

"And there I thought you'd come to explain where this coat came from." Evelyn laughed.

Lorenzo looked at the long white coat that was draped over a chair. The coat looked familiar, but he couldn't place it. Then it hit him. "Yalaina must have put it in here. Jeb and I were talking about how the KKK tore your coat, and how we didn't want you to get cold if you had to leave the building for some reason."

"Yalaina?" Evelyn's gaze softened.

"Here, let me help you try it on, to make sure it fits."

Lorenzo stood, grabbing the coat. Evelyn stood too, with her back to him. His hands grazed her skin and their eyes met in the mirror. The chemistry between them was like an uninvited guest. The heat of her body against his pulsed between them. He remembered he'd been taken with her from the first moment he'd laid eyes on her.

She turned to face him, put on the coat. He slid his hand inside the coat and around her waist. He pulled her to him. His other hand cupped the back of her neck. He stared into her eyes.

"Can I kiss you?" he said.

He still feared for her, and he still didn't want to let her get close to him, but maybe one kiss would tamp down the fire building in his body, threatening to explode.

"Yes…" It came out as a whisper.

Lorenzo brushed his lips against hers, gently at first. Evelyn closed her eyes and her lips parted, just slightly. Lorenzo nudged them farther apart with his tongue. With her body pressed against his, his arousal peaked. A moan escaped her lips and he wanted to groan from the pain of his erection and the pleasure of her warm mouth.

Lorenzo backed her up to the couch, relishing in the

softness of her full lips and the sweet taste of her mouth. Together with her intoxicating scent, it made Lorenzo completely lose himself. When he laid her back on the couch her petite body melted into his. His hands explored her body through her dress, cupping her breasts. She moaned into his mouth and it ignited a desire inside of him he'd thought long burned out. He kissed his way down her slender throat. Her legs parted and Lorenzo positioned himself between them.

What were they doing? He knew it was wrong, but he couldn't stop.

"Oh, Lorenzo..."

His breath caught. He loved his name on her lips. His hands caressed her thighs as he slid her dress up farther. Her back arched, giving him greater access to her most delicate part...

The sound of crashing dishes broke them from their reverie.

They looked at each other, jerking apart. Lorenzo stood, noticing the door to her dressing room hung wide open.

"I'm sorry," he said.

"No, don't be. I... I wanted you to do—that."

Evelyn looked away. Suddenly, something was really interesting on the floor.

He wanted to ignore the way his heart beat faster just because he was near her, but he couldn't. A smile slid across his lips with such ease he couldn't hide it.

Not knowing what to say about what they'd just done, he decided to act as though nothing had happened. "I'm glad you like the coat. Now you'll be warm."

She stood and fixed her dress. Walking back to the mirror, she admired herself in the coat. "I actually hadn't given it a lot of thought, with everything that's going on. But now that I'm staying here, I do need to get back home tomorrow. I want to get some things and reassure my grand that I'll be okay."

"I can have Jerry drive you over." He walked toward the door.

"Um…sure. I think that would be fine, then I won't have to bother my brother for a ride."

The door was still wide open, but Benny knocked anyway. "Excuse me, Miss Laroque… Lorenzo, but we should get started. The crowd is waiting for our new star."

Happiness filled Evelyn's smile. Lorenzo loved that smile. He hadn't seen it before. She'd always been so reserved. This was a real Evelyn smile; he could tell.

"I was just going, Benny," he said. "Far be it from me to keep her from blessing everyone with her voice." He winked at her. "We can talk more after the show."

When she didn't argue, or refuse, he left with a small piece of hope in his chest. But hope for what, he didn't know.

Lorenzo made his way to his roadster. He hopped in and cruised toward the outskirts of the city. He was both anxious and elated about seeing his family. Getting to be a part of the family again, in the way he was meant to be, felt right—even if it was temporary. He knew they wouldn't like what he had to say, but they would respect him and his choice of how to handle the Klan.

When Lorenzo pulled up, he cut the engine. Owls hooted in the distance and the full moon was shining a spotlight on the ancient mansion. If Lorenzo were superstitious, he would worry that it was an omen for his continued involvement with his family, but he wasn't superstitious. He was pragmatic in his beliefs about the future. He was in charge, and nothing and no one would take his power to choose away.

Taking a deep breath, he got out of his car. He patted the hood as he walked around it, satisfied with who he had become in spite of the temptation to return to the family business. He wasn't naive any longer about the fact that he still benefitted from his family's power and influence. But he'd worked hard against the pull of the mob, and now he was here to find out as much as he could about what had happened to Vinny, so he could make his final break with the family.

"Hey, it's my *bambino*." Lorenzo's father stood proud at the center of the horde of De Lucas. He smiled brightly, walking to Lorenzo and pulling him into a big hug. He kissed Lorenzo on both cheeks. "My boy, it's so good to see you. Come, come…sit, drink."

His father put his arm around his shoulders and guided him toward the table. Drinks flowed and everyone smiled and laughed as they greeted him.

He was home, and he couldn't deny how right it felt, to be surrounded by the people who'd raised him, the people who had always protected him and had taught him everything he needed to know about being a successful businessman.

After everyone had settled down to eat and drink, Lorenzo said, "I'm happy to be back. I've missed all of you."

"We missed you too, son."

Lorenzo had never seen his father so happy, so proud—not even when Blues Moon had made the newspaper for being the top-grossing nightclub in the Kansas City area. And those numbers hadn't even included the liquor sales, since those were done strictly under the table.

"But I do want to be clear. I only came to get information about Vinny's murder."

What his family had shared confirmed what Lorenzo had already found out. Vinny had been murdered by the KKK because Simmens had targeted Edith, not knowing that Edith was involved with the mob. Simmens was a problem that needed to be handled. If the police wouldn't take the murders and assaults of women seriously, Lorenzo would.

Once his family had realized his presence at the meeting didn't mean he was taking up his role within the family, the meeting had gone very fast. He was thankful he would get to hear Evelyn sing for a little bit before meeting her for breakfast.

Lorenzo took up his spot at the bar with his book of numbers in his hand.

The spotlight cast an otherworldly glow on Evelyn. Her gold dress sparkled under the bright light. Her skin soaked up the luminescence like a sponge. The chatter in the club stopped as everyone listened, eyes glued to Evelyn. She closed her eyes and swayed as she released the first note. The saxophone came in right after her and the rest of the band a beat later. Her presence on stage consumed the entire club. Tommy had even stopped making drinks and was just watching her.

Lorenzo took in the effect she had on everyone, including him.

He wanted to ask her why she always closed her eyes when she sang. Sometimes she would open them and the glitter of unreleased tears sparkled, casting a watery shadow over her gold irises. He ached when she sang, ached and then froze in disbelief of the emotions crashing through him with each note. Her words hit him hard. She sang songs he'd heard, but she and Benny had also decided to sing some songs she had written. Those were the best ones Lorenzo decided.

He'd stopped by the club after meeting with his family to work, but he couldn't focus on the numbers. All he could think about was Evelyn. He'd meant to greet customers and make small talk as he usually did, but he couldn't. All he could do was watch her.

"She's sensational."

The familiar voice brought Lorenzo out of his trance. Evelyn was on her seventh song and Lorenzo had gotten absolutely no work done. Dred slid onto the bar stool next to Lorenzo with her back to the stage. Everyone else had turned to face the stage, only turning toward the bar to order another drink or food.

"Tommy, let me get a tequila with a lime, please."

Dred had on a long, sleek black dress. She always looked polished.

"So, where's Jeb?" she said.

"I haven't seen him since I got back. He's around here somewhere." Lorenzo eyed Dred suspiciously. "Why're you asking about Jeb?"

Lorenzo couldn't help the smile that played at his lips. He wanted Dred to find someone who could handle her, who might be as lethal as her. And Jeb was definitely a good candidate. But Lorenzo hedged seeing the venom in Dred's eyes.

"I'm just asking…making small talk. You know—what I've been trying to teach you to do," Lorenzo said.

Dred lacked some social skills. She preferred to be alone most of the time, only coming to the club when she wanted to spend a little time with Lorenzo. They'd grown up like siblings, and when they went too long without talking they genuinely missed each other.

"Well, I just came by to make sure you weren't dead and to see what all the hype was about. You know news of this girl is all over the city?" Dred squeezed the lime into her glass and took a long sip of her liquor.

Lorenzo didn't like the sound of that. If Dred had heard something, that might mean trouble for Evelyn—well, more trouble, that was.

"What did you hear?"

Lorenzo looked away from Evelyn to take in Dred's

body language. He could tell if she was uneasy about something, even if no one else could. She held tension in her shoulders when something wasn't right—just like she was doing now.

"The Klan boys are talking. You have really pissed them off. You know they don't like Italians anyway. They think all immigrants are ruining the country. Ignorant bastards."

Lorenzo took a deep breath and then let it out slowly.

"You thought they had beef with you before? Well, they want to bop you *and* the girl now. I heard the KKK has a hit on you."

"We have to protect Evelyn. This is what I want you to do: round up Jeb and meet me in my office as soon as possible."

Dred downed her drink. "Let me get another, Tommy."

"Sorry, Dred. That was the last of it," said Tommy.

Dred looked at Lorenzo. "Something going on with the supply?"

"Yeah, that's an entire problem of its own."

Dred's eyes grew hot with hate. Lorenzo assumed his looked similar. He knew that the KKK was behind what was happening with his liquor. And they would regret it. He had the fleeting thought that he should have killed Simmens when he'd had the chance. But then he thought again. One death would just lead to the birth of another bigot to take his place.

Lorenzo looked at Evelyn one last time before moving swiftly toward his office.

He would need to get the chopper squad together.

Chapter Twenty

Evelyn

During her second set, she noticed that Lorenzo had returned, but shortly after he was missing from the bar where he'd been watching her. It both thrilled her and scared her how intensely he stared at her. It was like she was a puzzle he just couldn't solve. She wondered what would happen if he ever did figure her out.

What had happened between them in her dressing room had played on repeat while she was on stage. She didn't know what to think of it. It didn't have to mean anything. She was grown, and she could have fun with a nice man without it having to mean something. She hated how women had this unrealistic expectation of being prudish. Marrying wasn't something she even wanted. She just wanted to be able to take care of her grandmother and sing.

She'd thought he might be in his office, but it was empty. Her heart sank.

She was headed toward her dressing room when a callused hand touched her arm—not roughly, but enough to stop her.

She turned to see a tall Black man with skin the color of red clay. He had eyes that were nearly the same color, and hair cut really low. With his muscular build and height, he towered over Evelyn.

"I'm sorry to bother you, but I couldn't leave without

telling you how beautiful you are. You took my breath away with your singing. I'd heard you were good, and gorgeous, but I had to come see for myself."

He let his hand drop from her arm after a long moment.

"I'm glad you enjoyed the show. I'll have one more set in about an hour."

"I know. I'm not going anywhere."

Evelyn smiled at him and turned to walk away. She probably should have stayed and talked with him, maybe even gone to the bar and had a drink with him. She was so inexperienced when it came to men. But something inside of her just wanted to find Lorenzo and ask him what he'd thought.

She went inside her dressing room, hoping he would stop by before she had to go back on. That hope proved futile because after an hour, when she'd eaten, closed her eyes to rest, she was awoken by a knock. She ran to the door, thinking it was Lorenzo, and sighed deeply when it was only Benny.

"Is everything okay, Miss Laroque?"

"Yes, Benny—and, please, call me Evelyn. I'm sorry. I must have fallen asleep. I'll be right out."

He shut the door, and Evelyn touched up her hair and makeup. Wondering where Lorenzo had gone was useless. However, she couldn't ignore the growing emptiness in the pit of her stomach. Something was wrong, and she was worried about him.

Walking out onto the stage, she channeled her angst about Lorenzo into each song in the same way she did the pain from her memories of Greenwood. Afterward, she didn't feel lighter, only heavier, noticing his seat at the bar remained empty.

She went to talk to Tommy and got stopped several times by customers telling her how lovely she was and how much they enjoyed her voice. Many told her that her voice was unlike anyone they'd ever heard. They commented on how young she looked.

By the time she got to the bar, Tommy's arched brow made her laugh.

"What?" she said.

"I'd venture to say you're more famous around here than the boss man." Tommy laughed, cleaning a glass for her.

She liked how the lights over the bar shone on him but left the patrons on the bar stools in shadow. She was weary of the spotlight and just wanted to relax. She wasn't really sure what to do since Lorenzo had offered for his driver to drive her back to West Eden to pick up her things so she could finish moving into the apartment upstairs.

"Where is the boss?" It was strange to call him that.

Tommy averted his gaze, and suddenly it seemed the glasses were that much more interesting.

"Tommy, where is he? Is everything okay?"

"I'll let him tell you. He should be back any minute. Have a drink. It's my specialty. I call it Blues E. I created it after hearing you sing for the first time."

He busied himself mixing the cocktail while Evelyn watched. He put a lot of different things in it.

When he handed the glass to Evelyn, the gold-colored liquid swirled in the glass. Evelyn lifted it to her nose and smelled it—citrus…maple, maybe…and something sour, like tea.

She took a small sip and looked at Tommy. "This is wonderful. What's in it?"

"Can't tell you. Enjoy, but don't have too many. It's sweet, but full of fire." He smiled at her warmly.

The smile touched her. She hadn't had many friends. There were a few people she had become somewhat close to in West Eden, but she hadn't been there all that long. And, to be honest, after losing her parents and so many of her friends in Greenwood, she just didn't want to get close to anyone like that again.

Blues Moon was making her efforts to stay secluded difficult. She hadn't given much thought to dating and romance until she'd met Lorenzo. Now she had Tommy and Benny who were being so kind to her. She hadn't planned to grow so many attachments so quickly. She'd thought all she wanted was to sing and take care of her grandmother. Maybe she'd been wrong.

The melodic, hypnotizing sound of Louis Armstrong filled the club. She drank and swayed gently back and forth to the beat. Her mind was still on Lorenzo, but all she could do was wait.

After she'd finished the Blues E, she felt like dancing. As she got up, she faltered a bit. Steely gray eyes were staring at her. Strong hands kept her from falling. She looked up into the silvery eyes of the most handsome man she'd ever met.

Lorenzo's concern shadowed his features. "Are you okay?" He helped her sit back down on the bar stool.

"I'm fine. I'm ready to dance. Will you dance with me?" She smiled up at him, chuckled at the concern on his face.

Lorenzo held out a protective arm to help her to her feet. "I think you've been drinking, Miss Laroque." He smiled.

Evelyn reached up to wrap her arms around his neck. "Well, aren't you perceptive, Lorenzo?" Then she started to sway to the music.

He took her hand from his face and kissed it. He wrapped his arm around her lower back and led her to the dance floor. She thought people were staring, but she couldn't have cared less. Lorenzo was with her, touching her, and that was all that mattered.

He pressed his body against hers and a flame travelled up from her toes, burning its way through her. She inhaled the scent of him and became more intoxicated by the mint savory-sweet smell than by the drink Tommy had given her. The press of his hand against her lower back steadied her. Nothing else mattered in that moment as they swayed, her head against his muscular chest, his lips against her ear.

"How was your night?" he whispered, his sweet breath warming her skin.

"I must say it was good, but it got instantly better when I looked up to see you staring at me." A smile played on her lips.

"Staring at you? No… I was looking at Benny."

They both laughed.

He pulled her body even tighter against his. The closeness left Evelyn wanting more. She wanted her skin against his skin. She wanted to taste his soft lips again. She remembered how safe she'd felt in her dressing room, when he'd laid her back on the couch. There had been a fleeting moment of thinking everything would be okay. She hadn't had a thought like that sense her parents had passed.

What was she doing with this man? She wasn't sure… and she feared she wasn't in a position to deny her feelings for him much longer.

Chapter Twenty-One

Lorenzo

Lorenzo danced with Evelyn, enjoying her in a way he hadn't with a woman, ever—not publicly. He didn't care what anyone thought as they moved together to the rhythm. His desire for her amplified with the beat of the music and her humming in his ear. He brushed his lips gently against her skin, wanting to do so much more. He held her to him like it was the last time he'd ever get to do it.

"I'm getting tired," she said, looking into his eyes.

Without hesitation he led Evelyn to the elevator. The operator nodded and took them to Lorenzo's floor. Lorenzo unlocked his apartment door. Leading her still, Lorenzo crossed the threshold and closed the door with his foot once they were inside.

He'd chosen to take her to his apartment instead of hers so he could keep an eye on her. Even though she'd only had one drink, he wanted to make sure she was okay. And the threat of the KKK also had him wanting to keep her close.

"Make yourself comfortable. I'll start breakfast."

Lorenzo started taking out eggs and other fixings for their meal. He looked back at Evelyn. She'd fallen asleep almost as soon as she'd sat down on his couch, and something about that simple sign of trust melted any remaining walls he had around his heart.

He picked her up, smiling to himself, and walked straight

to the bedroom and laid her down in his bed. He pulled a plush red throw over her. Going to West Eden would have to wait.

He went to the kitchen to get her a glass of water. When he returned to place it on the table beside the bed, her eyes opened. She stared at him, then grabbed a fistful of his shirt, pulling him down on top of her.

He resisted. He wanted his first time making love to her to be remembered. He allowed her to pull him down, but he moved his face to nestle her neck instead of kissing her. Taking in a deep, long breath of her scent, he grazed his lips against her skin. That was all he would allow himself until she sobered up.

"Go to sleep, gorgeous. I'll be waiting for you when you get up."

He kissed her forehead and wrapped the blanket tighter around her. He closed the door when he left the room. She needed to rest, and he would be there when she awoke for whatever she needed.

He busied himself while she slept. He actually looked at his books. The cash flowing into the distillery and the winery was accurate, but the product coming out was not. He would need to take a trip to visit it the next day. He'd ask Evelyn to join him. He told himself it was so that he could ensure she was safe, and that was a part of it—just a part. The other part was because he didn't want to be away from her.

When she'd stormed out of the building that first time and he hadn't known where she was, he'd lost it. He hadn't been able to focus. He hadn't been able to think.

Lorenzo settled in on his couch with his books all around him. He requested some clothes be brought up for Evelyn and some toiletry items. That was the nice part of being in the garment district. Everything was at his disposal. He soon had five outfits purchased for her and all the toiletries any woman might require.

He placed them in the bedroom, so she could get changed when she woke up. And he left her a note to make sure she knew the items were meant for her and that she should use all that she desired.

Evelyn slept for five hours. When she walked into the living room she was squinting her eyes like the sunlight hurt her. Lorenzo hopped up, setting aside the books he was working on, and closed the blinds over the windows casting light on the living room.

When she came out of the bathroom she was dressed in an off-white pleated skirt and matching sweater that hung low on her shoulders. Her face glowed in a way Lorenzo hadn't seen before. Her lips were pale pink and her long black lashes curled around her gold eyes. Her cheeks had the barest hint of rose to them and the skin around her eyes glittered in the sunlight.

Lorenzo had requested multiple styles and colors of gloves because she always wore them—he knew now it was to hide her scars—and she'd opted for off-white short ones.

Lorenzo had to make sure his mouth wasn't open before he stood up and walked over to her. "You look beautiful."

She smiled shyly, the corners of her lips turning up just slightly. He leaned down and kissed her cheek. He wanted to do more, but thought better of it.

She sucked in a breath when his lips grazed her skin. Her cheekbones, high and angular, needed to be kissed. He ran his thumb along the side of her face opposite where his lips had just been. Her eyes fluttered open when he pulled back.

"Come…have a seat." He guided her to the couch.

"What happened? Why am I here?" Confusion clouded her features.

"You had one of Tommy's special drinks. So I brought you up here to rest where I could keep an eye on you and make sure you were okay."

She looked at him with furrowed brows. "Thank you…" She said it as more of a question than a statement.

"It was my pleasure. I felt bad for making you wait when I'd offered to have Jerry take you home."

Understanding registered on her face. "Where were you?"

Normally Lorenzo would have told any woman who asked him that it was none of her business, but he wanted Evelyn to know. "Dred and I had to handle a situation with the KKK. We have some heat coming down on us—you included—that we need to deal with."

"Heat? Me included?"

She ran her fingers through her beautiful thick hair. This was the first time he'd seen it unpinned. He really liked it. It fell in waves around her face and cascaded over her shoulders. He reached up to move some behind her ear. She turned her face into his palm and took a deep breath. She looked at him with shock in her eyes, like that had been a natural reaction she hadn't even thought about. He pulled his hand back from her.

"Yes, everything started with Simmens, and it will end with him too."

"What do you mean? Are you going to kill him?" Her doe eyes captured him.

"If I did, would that make you think differently of me?"

Evelyn fell silent for a long moment and just stared at Lorenzo. Then she sat back on the couch and said, "My momma told me that life is about right and wrong. And even though some don't get punished for the wrong they do, that doesn't make it right. That has always stayed with me. But now I think perhaps that life is not just about right and wrong. That's too dichotomous. There are so many different levels of wrong. Killing is wrong—but what if you're saving a life by taking a life? I don't know... Some think singing in a speakeasy is wrong. Some think interracial marriage is wrong."

She looked at Lorenzo for a brief moment before focusing her attention on her hands.

"If you don't feel comfortable being here with me, I understand," Lorenzo said, reaching out to touch her hand but then thinking better of it.

"You know what's crazy? I feel more comfortable here with you, a mobster, than I've felt with anyone in a long time." She laughed without humor. "I'm tired of fighting past horrors."

It stung to hear her call him a mobster. Lorenzo cupped her chin and turned her to face him. He moved her hair from her face. "My *mamma* told me that if you want the nightmares to go away, then you should bring them out of the dark and make them face the light."

"What did she mean by that?" Evelyn blinked rapidly. Her long lashes brushed her skin.

"She wanted me to find someone that I could confide in to help me move past what happened."

"And did you?"

Lorenzo shook his head. "You're the first person I've wanted to tell, but I fear how you'll react."

She leaned in and kissed him hesitantly. She ran her hand through his hair. The sensation overtook him. There were so many reasons he shouldn't let things go further, but he couldn't think of one in that moment.

"I didn't bring you up here to... I wasn't going to..."

Evelyn pressed two fingers to his lips. "I know, but this is what I want. Do you want it too?"

"I do."

Lorenzo warred with himself. On one hand he wanted this dame more than he'd ever wanted anything in his life, but on the other hand he wasn't good for her. His life was dangerous, and she deserved better than him.

He leaned in and kissed her, taking a deep breath of her lavender sweet fragrance. He could fall in love with this woman, and that was a dangerous thought. Kissing her again, he laid her back on the couch, just like he had in her dressing room. He kissed her collarbone, and then her neck, enjoying her soft skin against his lips.

She let out soft moans of pleasure that sent him over the edge. "I'm new to all of this, Lorenzo. Will you go slowly?" Her sweet voice was barely a whisper in his ear.

Lorenzo looked up. He wasn't sure why her admission shook him. He'd figured as much. But hearing her say it ripped him from his lust-laden fog. He sat up.

"What? Did I do something wrong?" she said.

"No, it's just…your first time should be with someone you care about."

"Who says I don't care about you?"

Lorenzo stared at this beautiful woman. Sitting up, she pulled her sweater down and her gloves up.

"You don't know me. How can you care for me?"

"I know enough to know that you are a good man. You've given a lot of people opportunities that they wouldn't have gotten other places. You treat your customers with respect and kindness. How they feel for you is obvious. Everyone who works for you has gone out of their way to tell me you are good. You're the only one who doesn't believe that. Just because you've done things in your life that may have been wrong or against the law doesn't make you a bad man. Besides, all laws aren't necessarily right anyway."

They stared at each other for a long moment. He knew she was thinking of Jim Crow laws, as he had done many times. It amazed him, the ridiculous things people came up with when hate ruled their lives.

He didn't respond to her admission, opting instead to silently respect how hard her life was. "Are you ready to go?" he asked.

"Yes, I just need to grab my handbag and my coat from my dressing room."

"I had them both brought up. They're on the table."

"Do you always think of everything?"

"I try to." He took her gloved hand in his and they headed for the door. "Jerry needed to take the day off for some family emergency. Is it okay if I drive you instead? I can stay in the car if you would like, as Jerry would have done?"

Evelyn looked at him quizzically. He didn't know how he would feel if she rejected his offer.

Jerry had mentioned in passing that he needed to do something for his family after he'd returned from taking Evelyn to West Eden, and Lorenzo, being the generous boss he was, had offered to take Evelyn instead, so Jerry would have all the time he needed.

Knowing he might be the one driving her, Lorenzo had showered and changed into a different suit while she rested. He'd chosen a light gray pinstripe with black shoes. Seeming to notice, she reached up to touch it with a confused look on her face. He hoped she could remember what had happened right before she went to sleep. He kept replaying it in his mind for damn sure.

"I would love to have you accompany me. Thank you," she finally said, pulling up her gloves.

They rode the elevator down in silence. Walking through the club, Lorenzo greeted people as usual, introducing them to Evelyn and making excuses for their quick departure. People fawned over Evelyn, and rightly so.

Before Jerry had left, he'd had the roadster pulled around front. Lorenzo liked to drive the roadster more than his other cars. The picnic basket Lorenzo had had his cook make was sitting on the floor in front of the passenger seat. Lorenzo opened the door for Evelyn, and she slid in.

"What's that?" she asked.

He climbed into the driver's seat. "It's lunch for you. You haven't eaten. Go ahead and open it. I hope there are some items you like."

The way she looked at Lorenzo, with her eyes intense and her lips slightly parted, made his heart jump into his throat. He didn't want to acknowledge the other part of him she was having an effect on.

He shifted in his seat, hoping she didn't notice the bulge in his pants.

Chapter Twenty-Two

Evelyn

Evelyn opened the wicker basket at her feet. She pulled out a bowl of fruit. Her stomach growled and she devoured grapes, strawberries and pineapple chunks.

"Are you hungry?" she thought to ask when she had only one grape left in the bowl.

Lorenzo laughed. "No, I ate while you were sleeping."

She pulled out a small plate with a warm pie. She grabbed a fork from the side pocket. Lorenzo's cook was almost as good as her grand. It took her no time to finish off the pie. Next, she pulled out a small piece of chocolate cake. Her stomach was already full, but she couldn't turn down a piece of chocolate cake. That would be blasphemous.

Lorenzo reached over and removed some icing from the side of her lip with his thumb, then he licked it. The gesture, and his unexpected touch on the sensitive skin by her mouth, sent a shiver through her. Her eyes grew wide.

A pang of guilt hit her in that moment, as she happily enjoyed the afternoon with Lorenzo and fought back the memories of her family being murdered by the hands of people who would have spared Lorenzo's life because his skin was the right color. She and Lorenzo had had a couple of intimate close calls now, and she couldn't help but think it was better that things hadn't gone further.

"Is everything okay?" Lorenzo asked, seeming to notice her shift.

She nodded. "The cake is very good."

Lorenzo said, "Delicious. Cook sure knows how to make the icing creamy and sweet."

Evelyn had a feeling that he wasn't only talking about the icing being sweet, but she couldn't be sure. She wanted more of his touches. She remembered pulling him on top of her last night, and the way his soft lips had felt against the bare skin on her neck. He'd been warm, and his beard had tickled her.

Licking her lips at the memory, she said, "Yes, it is very sweet."

He looked at her, one corner of his mouth pulled up in a knowing grin.

"Did you want a bite of the cake?" she asked.

He nodded.

When she'd offered, she hadn't realized that meant she would have to feed him, but she didn't hesitate. She used the fork to scoop the last piece into his mouth. He licked his lips, sending desire cascading through her veins. The sensation was unfamiliar but pleasant—extremely pleasant.

She wondered what it would feel like to kiss him again. She'd been a little under the influence last night, but she'd known what she was doing when she'd pulled him to her. She'd known what she wanted and had been thoroughly disappointed when he'd denied her.

"Do you make a habit of denying the advances of women in your bed, Mr. De Luca?" Evelyn smirked.

"I've never had a woman in my bed, Miss Laroque. You were the first."

"You mean you've never—?"

Lorenzo interrupted. "Yes, I've been with women. I just don't have them in my home. It's my sanctuary, and

I never want a woman to get the wrong idea about our… encounter."

"So why did you take me to your apartment? You could have easily taken me to my own."

Lorenzo looked at her briefly, before returning his eyes to the road. His hands gripped the steering wheel tighter.

He took a deep breath. "You're different. I wanted you in my home…in my bed." He looked at her again.

That sideways smile he gave sent waves of longing straight to Evelyn's heart and it threatened to thrum right out of her chest.

She looked away, out of the window, to compose herself.

Focusing back on the road, he said, "You look like you're thinking about something. Anything you want to share?"

"No," she said hurriedly.

He laughed.

She'd been so consumed by him she hadn't had a chance to be nervous about him meeting her grand and seeing the secret town. How would she explain why she'd let someone like him not only know about the town but come to it?

The cement buildings of the city had been transformed into fields of grass and corn. They drove for a while longer before reaching the small, almost imperceptible dirt road that led to West Eden. Evelyn could always find the road because there was a small cross about a mile before they needed to turn right on the path.

"Turn here," Evelyn said suddenly.

Lorenzo jerked the car to the right and looked at her. "A little more notice next time?"

"Sorry, it's not supposed to be easy to find."

They rode in silence for miles before the buildings of West Eden emerged, set behind a canopy of trees.

Evelyn remembered the first time she'd seen this city beneath the trees. The buildings there were only permitted to have five or fewer stories, to ensure no one would see them from afar. Trees surrounded the entire town, making it look like there was nothing but forest in this direction from all angles.

There were cars as nice as Lorenzo's roadster buzzing down the busy streets. On the main street into town there was a bakery, owned by Evelyn's good friend's family, and the movie theater, the three banks, and the hospital were all Black-owned.

Greenwood had been very similar to West Eden. Evelyn's mother had been one of the head doctors there, in the field of gynecology. She'd had to prove her expertise to earn that position.

In West Eden, people bustled about dressed in suits, drop-waist dresses, hats and gloves. Evelyn was glad they'd come during the day. She wanted Lorenzo to get a full view of the beauty of this place.

At night, the buildings dimmed their lights, to make sure they weren't spotted from above. Around Thanksgiving, though, they put up Christmas lights, but they only kept them on for an hour in the evening. That time of year was magical, and the lights only made the surrealness of this place more evident.

The other thing that worked in West Eden's favor was that no one would believe a town like it could exist in total secret, run by Black business owners and politicians, yet here it was.

There were some members of the government who knew of the town and made sure it stayed off the map, but other than that, if you were not a resident, you didn't know if West Eden was real or a myth—which made Lorenzo an anomaly. Evelyn took a deep breath as people noticed the roadster and its driver.

"Are you okay?" Lorenzo peered at her.

"Yes, I'm just worried that people will be upset that I brought you here. You're not exactly... How do I say it?"

"I'm not Black."

"Yes, that's it!" Evelyn laughed.

This town had been created out of a need for Black people in the country to have a safe place to thrive and find the same American dream that others could find elsewhere.

"I'm not going to speak of this place," he said. "You know that, right?"

...

"I know, Lorenzo. It's just that there are two Americas, and you come from the one that kills people who look like me just because they can."

Lorenzo looked puzzled, like he wanted to ask a question, but wasn't sure what to ask. "There's only one America, Evey."

Taken aback by his term of endearment, Evelyn faltered and didn't say anything at first. She liked that he had a special name for her. His smile was so sincere, she couldn't help but smile herself.

Continuing, she said, "There are two. The one you come from offers prosperity and the pursuit of happiness. The one I come from—the one the residents of this town come from—says we were born less than human, that we're criminals who will never be as good as others because of the color of our skin. Our Americas are not the same."

Lorenzo fell silent. Evelyn didn't want to continue the conversation. She didn't like having to admit the reality of how Black people had to learn to survive by striving to be better and then were still not considered good enough.

"Take a left, and my house is on the right."

Lorenzo followed her instructions, and moments later they were at Evelyn's grand's home. The two-story gray and white house with the red door stood out on the street. The other doors were more muted colors such as beige, brown or white. Evelyn's grand had always had eclectic taste; Evelyn loved that about her.

"I like the red door," Lorenzo said.

"I figured you would, Mr. Green Couch."

They both laughed. Lorenzo got out of the car and walked around to open Evelyn's door.

"After you," he said, and he took her hand and helped her from the car.

Taking one more deep breath, she walked toward the front door. In some ways she felt like she was about to go to trial for a crime she didn't believe should be a crime.

Mustering as much courage as she could, she took out her key and opened the door. "Grand? Are you here?"

"Evelyn?"

Her grand's voice came from the back. She appeared in the front room wearing an apron and wiping her hands. She looked like an older, more distinguished version of Evelyn. She walked right up to her and cupped her face.

"Are you all right? Your brother called to tell me he had to come by that club."

Seeming to realize they weren't alone, Evelyn's grand let her gaze roam over Lorenzo appraisingly. Then she turned back to her with concern in her eyes.

"Who is this, Evelyn? Why would you bring him here?"

"This is Lorenzo. He's the owner of Blues Moon. He already knew of West Eden, and we can trust him. He's been so wonderful to me." Her grand didn't seem convinced, so Evelyn added, "He protected me, Grand, from the KKK—twice."

She didn't add that he was the son of a mobster and her association to him could get her killed. It still gave her pause, even though her attraction to him had severely impaired her judgment about him so far. She did believe that he would do whatever he could to keep her safe, but she couldn't risk her own life when it meant her grand wouldn't have anyone to take care of her.

Her grand's skin had lost its color. "I knew you shouldn't have gone to that city." But she backed up and allowed them to enter the room. "Have a seat, please. Lorenzo, is it?"

Evelyn's grandmother held her hand out. Her expression was still filled with concern.

"Yes, ma'am. Please don't worry. I have known of this place for many years. I would never share the location or its existence with anyone."

Evelyn's grand's eyebrow arched, and she pursed her lips.

Chapter Twenty-Three

Lorenzo

Lorenzo sat on a black couch. He rubbed his hand on the smooth fabric. He really liked how the couch had such modern lines but was incredibly comfortable. He'd have to have Jerry find him one just like it.

"You have a lovely home, Mrs....?"

"Dupre—but you can call me Delphine."

"My apologies, Delphine."

He took a quick glance at Evelyn. Her eyes were wide, and she looked nervous.

"Grand, have you been taking it easy like the doctor said?" Evelyn asked.

"No. These doctors think they know it all, but they don't know nothing about the healing power of food and herbs." Delphine took a seat in the large armchair next to the couch.

"Oh, no—what did you do?" Evelyn said.

"You worry too much, child. I'm fine. And I sent that nurse away. I don't want nobody hovering over me all day." Delphine said.

"You *what*?" Evelyn threw her hands up. "What am I going to do with you?"

"Nothing. You need to live your life and stop worrying so much about little ol' me. I've been surviving for sixty some years." Delphine stood and walked out of the room.

Evelyn shook her head. "She is so stubborn."

Lorenzo laughed.

"What's funny?" Evelyn asked indignantly.

"I see where you get it from." Lorenzo reached out and squeezed Evelyn's gloved hand playfully.

"Grand, I thought maybe you could come to the city and see where I'll be staying," Evelyn said, loud enough for her grandmother to hear her in the back.

Her grand reappeared with two glasses of tea on a silver tray with a plate of pastries. Her face softened at the idea.

"I'll have to ask someone to drive me up there, but it would put my heart at ease to know where you're spending your time—and with whom." Delphine gave Lorenzo a look of displeasure.

"That won't be necessary," Lorenzo said. "I will have a driver come pick you up."

"Oh, you will?" Delphine sat in the chair. She looked tired. "Evelyn, why don't you run up and get your things, so I can talk to Mr. Lorenzo?" She smiled a mischievous grin.

"Okay. I'll be right back down." Evelyn headed up the stairs, giving Lorenzo an *I'm sorry* look.

"So, what exactly do you do, Mr. Lorenzo, besides running a club?" Delphine asked.

"I have a few other business ventures, but my main focus is on the club. I would like to open another soon. I believe that music brings people together, and I love being a part of that."

Lips pursed and eyebrows arched in what Lorenzo was starting to think of as Delphine's "not amused" face. He honestly didn't know where he was going wrong with her, but he would continue to try because he wanted to have her validation.

He hadn't ever cared what anyone thought of him. Enter Evey into his life and all of a sudden his character was on trial—and he so wanted to be proven innocent. Even though he'd had some shady things in his past, he believed in certain ideals wholeheartedly and he would fight to protect the rights of others.

He wasn't just chinning. He meant what he said.

Delphine fired off a few more questions.

Lorenzo was very vague about his family, not wanting to give her any reason not to let Evey leave with him. He'd been thinking of her as Evey in his head for a while, and when he'd said it to her he'd thought she might be offended, but she hadn't even commented. That gave him a shred of hope.

Evelyn came back down the stairs and Lorenzo almost jumped for joy. He was in the hot seat with Delphine, and he wasn't sure how much more he could take.

"We're going to have to go now, but I'll see you this evening?" Evelyn walked to the front door.

Lorenzo was on her tail, anxious to leave.

"Oh, dear… I'd hoped to spend more time with you and your employer," said Delphine.

"Lorenzo's my…my friend as well."

She and Lorenzo exchanged a look.

They hadn't known each other long, but Lorenzo was glad she thought of him as more than just her boss. He didn't want her to think of him as a boss at all, actually. He wanted her to think of him as someone she could depend on and trust—her equal and her confidant and her lover…

Lorenzo mentally scolded himself for that last one.

Evey was looking at him as if she'd said something and he hadn't responded. "What did you say?" he asked.

"I said, are you ready?"

Lorenzo nodded a little too enthusiastically. Evelyn's grandmother couldn't hate him any more than she already did.

Lorenzo took Evelyn's bags from her and walked out to

the car. Then he gave Evelyn and her grandmother some privacy. He stood by the open passenger door and waited. Evelyn and her grandmother hugged for a long time before releasing each other.

The town was absolutely beautiful. The well-manicured lawns led to beautifully painted houses. In front of those houses were some of the newest models of all kinds of cars. He looked down the street as far as he could see at Model Ts, Model Ss, roadsters, Rolls-Royces...parked on the street and in driveways. He had been let in on a secret, and he was honored.

He wanted to do something to support this town's success. He had no idea what he could do, or if anyone would even want his help, but he wanted to see this place continue to prosper. Although perhaps the best thing he could do would be to keep his mouth shut about what he'd seen.

Two women walked down the sidewalk, pushing strollers. They eyed him with curiosity. He didn't miss how they looked him up and down, assessing him in that way women had of making a man feel desired. He smiled at them. They whispered to each other and walked on to their destination.

"I'm ready. Sorry to keep you waiting."

Lorenzo hadn't heard Evelyn approach. He turned to see her soaking up the sunlight. She emanated beauty. Her high cheekbones sparkled in the light and her gold eyes looked even more golden as she stared at him.

He needed to say something and stop gawking at her. "It's no problem. I'm happy to be here with you." His voice came out hoarse.

Evelyn didn't respond. She got into the car, her face unreadable. She seemed different. He wasn't sure why, but the lighthearted woman he'd driven here with had been replaced by a woman of coldness. Her grandmother had probably said something to upset her. He wasn't sure if he should inquire, or leave her be.

"Is there anywhere else you want to go? We do have a little more time before we need to head back for your set."

"No, I think we should probably just make our way back to the city."

He hadn't hit it off with her grandmother, and he hoped that wasn't the cause of her change in mood. He didn't want to ask her. He *wouldn't* ask her.

"Did I do something wrong?" The damn question came out anyway.

She sighed loudly. He could see her looking at him in his peripheral vision. He didn't want to take his eyes off the road. The town was busy, with a lot going on, and people were everywhere.

"No, you didn't do anything wrong. It's just something my grand said."

He knew it. "Oh? Are you okay?"

That was a safer question than what he'd almost asked. *What did she say? Was it about me?*

"Yes, I will be. She just has a way of saying things to me that make me feel like a little girl who's too dumb to make her own decisions—a lot like how my mother used to make me feel sometimes."

Lorenzo almost pulled the car over because he wanted her full attention when he said this. "You are not a little girl. You are smart, brilliant, insanely talented, gorgeous and fearless. You are amazing. Anyone who has spent any amount of time with you knows that. Your grandmother knows that. When someone loves you, they can get in a huff when their children don't live their lives they want them to. It's hard to let go of control over your child. I know exactly how you feel."

She let out a breath that sounded like a laugh. "I think that's why Carmichael moved away."

Lorenzo didn't say anything, but he could see why her brother would move. Their grand was intense.

"She's just protective, you know…? She, better than anyone, understands the world we're living in, and she doesn't want to see us get hurt. She tried to keep us in these cocoons, and she's scared to death that she's going to lose us now that we've both gotten out of her reach."

There was silence for a while. Lorenzo wanted to take in all he had learned from Evelyn. He knew that racism had a huge effect on people, especially Black people, but he had been naive to think it was getting better. The KKK had only just started spouting their vitriol in the city. He'd hate to see what would happen once that hatred spread.

He didn't want to see Evelyn get hurt. Perhaps West Eden was the best place for her—the safest place. Not with him, like he'd thought. He wanted to tell her that, but he couldn't get the words to come out. If she stayed in West Eden and didn't work at Blues Moon any longer he'd never see her again. But he needed to think about whether or not he could actually protect her when he had so much he was dealing with himself. He believed he could. But was belief enough?

"You're awfully quiet. Did she say anything to upset you?"

Lorenzo shook his head. "Thank you for bringing me with you. I realize now how hard that must have been for you."

He kept his eyes on the road, trying to ignore the knot in his chest that seemed to grow as he came to terms with how naive he had been. All he'd seen was how beautiful Evelyn was. He'd known she'd been hurt, but he hadn't known it was something he could save her from.

"There's a lot that I want to share…about my life," she said. "I just don't think I'm ready. I'm still trying to process everything that has happened, and I don't think I'm doing a great job."

She adjusted her sweater on her shoulders. Lorenzo

turned to look at her. Her collarbone was so damn sexy. It didn't matter how he felt about her. He had to do the right thing, and that was to let her go.

"You know, West Eden really is as amazing as the legend says. Why would you want to leave and come to Kansas City?"

"Well, West Eden is limited when it comes to catapulting someone's singing career, you know—what with the whole secrecy thing and all. I need to make a name for myself in a well-known club."

Nodding, Lorenzo couldn't think of anything to refute her logic. He had to come up with something to convince her to return to West Eden. That was the only way he could assure her safety.

Lorenzo prided himself on thinking through every possibility, but after visiting West Eden, talking to Evelyn and her grandmother about what it was like for a Black woman in this country, he couldn't deny that he'd missed some things when he'd come up with his initial plan to keep Evelyn safe. He'd thought by simply alleviating her need to travel back and forth to the city alone he could manage any danger she might be in, but he hadn't realized that simply being a Black woman in America was a danger all of its own, that he couldn't manage for her.

They continued to ride in silence.

When Lorenzo pulled the car up in front of the club the doorman opened Evelyn's door and she got out. Lorenzo gave him the keys to pull it around to the garage, then guided Evelyn inside with his hand on the small of her back. His palm tingled from touching her. He was about to tell her he'd have her things sent up to her apartment, but he didn't get a chance.

"Will you help me take my things up?" She smiled.

"I'll take care of it." Lorenzo grabbed a few of her bags and left the rest for one of his staff to bring up.

The club had several patrons. Some sat at the tables close to the stage, some sat at the bar and some danced. He and Evelyn walked to the back, to the elevator.

"Good evening. Sixth floor please." Evelyn said.

The elevator operator smiled and closed the iron gate. He cranked the handle on the elevator, and they jerked as it rose from the ground.

Lorenzo wanted to take Evelyn's hand, to hold her close to him. He used all of his willpower to keep his feet planted where they were…a safe distance from this doll who had walked into his life out of nowhere.

Chapter Twenty-Four

Evelyn

After they dropped her bags off in her apartment, Lorenzo left to return to the club. Evelyn got dressed and made her way downstairs as well.

When she entered from the back, the music thrummed, sending exciting waves of sensation through her. She loved the atmosphere of Blues Moon. It left her feeling so invigorated.

Walking past Lorenzo's office, she saw Lorenzo meeting with Tommy, Jeb and Dred. She wondered what they were discussing, but recognized that it wasn't her concern.

The way the others looked at Lorenzo showed his authority. He'd handed them each a stack of papers and seemed to be explaining something to them. He was the leader of their very capable group. Seeing him in action excited Evelyn.

When he looked up, he saw her staring at him. He smiled like they shared a secret. She looked away and went to her dressing room.

She'd thought long and hard about how different their lives really were. His was embroiled in violence, even though he'd tried to minimize the impact on his life by leaving his family. He had fought for his freedom from the De Luca name, but that didn't mean he didn't still reap benefits from his family's power.

Evelyn, on the other hand, was trying to navigate in a world that devalued her at every turn. How could she and Lorenzo ever be more than what they were: just acquaintances?

She sat down at her vanity to touch up her makeup. A knock at the door alarmed her. "Come in." Her pulse raced, hoping it was Lorenzo.

Yalaina stuck her head in, her full curls swaying. "Hi, sorry to bother you. I just wanted to see how things are going."

"I'm doing well, Yalaina. Thank you. You've been so kind."

"Well, I'm so glad you're here. Getting to hear you sing has been really inspirational. It has also made Lorenzo more open to my singing career. He sees himself as my surrogate guardian, since I've never known my father. And he's overprotective."

Evelyn nodded. She agreed with Yalaina's assessment of Lorenzo.

"Can I ask you a few questions?" Yalaina stepped into the room, leaving the door open.

"Absolutely. Please, have a seat."

Evelyn turned in her seat to face Yalaina as she sat on the sofa. They talked for a little while about the best ways to keep their voices strong, and how to project using their diaphragms. Evelyn really enjoyed talking about singing with the young woman.

"Now, can I ask you a question?" Evelyn said, a bit hesitant.

"Of course." Yalaina's expression was eager.

"I don't want to seem like I'm gossiping, but if I'm going to work here I would like to know a bit more about the boss. He seems genuinely nice…"

That wasn't really a question, but she hoped Yalaina would understand where she was going.

"He is very nice. He's been like a big brother to me ever since my momma moved us here to Kansas City when I was about five. I've grown up with Lorenzo's family. You wouldn't even know they were involved in dangerous things. They just seem like a tight-knit family. I know that walking away was really hard on him. I think deep down he still questions if he did the right thing." Yalaina looked at the door nervously. "Well, I better get going." She got up and walked to the door. "I'm looking forward to hearing you sing tonight." She smiled and walked out.

Lorenzo sat down at the bar as Evelyn wiped her mouth with her napkin. There were so many people surrounding him that she couldn't see his face. She sighed inwardly. That had been the case the entire evening. She'd hoped for a moment alone with him, but he had been busy with his customers, and with Jeb, Dred and Tommy. She'd just had dinner alone.

Looking down, she was fixing her gloves when she felt his warm eyes on her.

"Do you mind if I join you?" he said, with his gorgeous mouth turned up in a slight smile.

"Of course not," she said.

When he stood at her side of the booth she scooted over so he could sit. He slid closer to her than he needed to, considering there was plenty of room on the seat. She didn't want him to move, however. She enjoyed the warmth of his shoulder against hers and the way his thigh just barely touched hers.

"Any plans after your set is over?"

The darkness his gray eyes had taken on seemed to swallow Evelyn.

She shook her head. "No. Do you have something in mind?"

"I do. Can I walk you up to your apartment after?"

She cleared her throat. "Yes."

He placed a gentle kiss on her cheek before sliding out of the booth.

The elevator operator opened the gate to the sixth floor. Lorenzo motioned for Evelyn to step out first. She took a deep breath and smiled at the operator. She noticed how his arms bulged under his white dress shirt. She wondered how hard it was to do his job…

The hallway sconces by each apartment door glowed bright. Evelyn walked to the second of the three doors that formed a circle. She retrieved her key from her pocketbook and opened the door to the apartment. The bright light through the windows took a moment for her to get used to.

She smiled up at Lorenzo as she entered the apartment first. He definitely had gentlemanly ways. "Can I offer you some tea?"

Evelyn placed her handbag on the counter and stepped out of her shoes. Her feet were hurting, and she couldn't take it anymore.

"I would like that." He sat down on her sofa.

She walked over to him with a tray. Sat it on the coffee table in front of them.

"You were busy tonight," she said as she prepared the tea.

"Yes, that's how it usually is. I like to interact with the customers. I feel like they come to Blues Moon not just for music, food and drinks, but also to socialize. I like to be a part of that."

Evelyn nodded as she took a sip of her hot drink. She'd watched as he'd smiled and laughed with so many different people. Men clapped him on the back, and women stared at him like he was a movie star. All the while he'd found her and locked eyes with her throughout the night. It had been like he wanted to let her know that he was thinking about her, that even with all those people vying for his attention his attention had still been on her.

"Is something wrong?" Evelyn had noticed a change in his demeanor.

He sat his cup down on the tray. She did the same. His jaw was clenched, like he was trying to hold something in that he wanted to say.

"Please, tell me," Evelyn said.

He looked at her and then he wrapped his arms around her. He pulled her into his body. His desire, evident in his lust-filled gaze, bewildered Evelyn. Maybe what he desired wasn't her, but just being near a woman's body. She needed to know how he felt about her.

Evelyn pulled away.

Lorenzo ran his hands through his hair. "I'm sorry. I wish I could continue to pretend like you aren't the most beautiful woman I've ever seen and that your scent doesn't make me want to place kisses all over your body, but I can't. Being near you kills me. Because I can't have you, and I'm used to getting whatever I want. I'm trying so hard to be the good guy...but I'm not a good guy, Evelyn."

Evelyn furrowed her brow, confused by his words. "Do you mean you're not a good guy because you have someone already and now you are attempting to...to sleep with me? I'm not the kind of woman who is okay with being a mistress—your secret to keep on the side."

Lorenzo's gaze grew fiery. He stood and started pacing the living room. "What are you talking about? I don't have anyone. I've been single for many years. Ever since..." He trailed off and walked away from her, going farther into the apartment.

"Ever since what?"

He was keeping something from her, and she wanted to know what, but how could she demand he tell her his secrets when she refused to tell him hers?

"It doesn't matter. What made you think I have someone?" He turned back around to face her.

She walked up to him. She stood close, so that she could look into his eyes. "That woman from the other night with the KKK—the woman who slipped in and drugged them all before they knew what was happening—you left with her. And I saw the picture in your apartment. You've known her your entire life."

"That's right. I have known Dred most of my life—as a sister. Her mother and my father were lovers."

Evelyn let out a breath she hadn't realized she was holding. A humorless laugh escaped her. Rubbing her hands together, she looked away from him. She'd assumed that because the woman—Dred—was so beautiful, Lorenzo must be involved with her. She shook her head at her foolish actions. She'd been so jealous and angry. Why...? Why had she felt that way?

Wrapped up in her own thoughts, she was taken aback when Lorenzo cupped her face and stepped in closer to her, so that their bodies touched. Desire radiated off him in waves and suddenly her head spun.

It was a heady feeling to know she turned on such a gorgeous man. He wanted her—and she wanted him too. She was finally ready to be honest with herself. She was a grown woman and she could make her own choices. She'd been so cautious with men her entire life, and now she'd found one that she didn't want to be cautious with. She wanted to give him whatever he wanted.

"I'm going to kiss you now," he said.

Evelyn nodded, too stunned to say anything. She'd allow herself this one moment of weakness. She'd been strong ever since Greenwood. She could give herself this one night to do what she really wanted, without worrying about the consequences of her actions.

Lorenzo leaned down and pressed his lips to hers. The

feather-light kiss soon grew in intensity. She tried to keep up. When his tongue probed, she let him enter her mouth, reaching up to allow him better access.

Wrapping her arms around his neck, suddenly she was off the ground. Her legs clung to his waist and he held her up by cupping one arm under her bottom while the other hand searched her hair. He sat her on the countertop, making her the perfect height for him. Then he hesitated for a moment, breaking their kiss, leaning his forehead against hers, searching her face.

"No, don't stop, please…" She pulled him to her until their lips met, and this time she thrust *her* tongue into his warm, sweet mouth. His mustache and beard scraped her face. She loved how manly he was. She loved that his large, callused hands had found the bare skin under her shirt and were searching her back and sides.

She arched up, hoping he would take off her bra and touch her breasts. She'd never been touched there, and she so desperately wanted to feel his hands on her. There was a pressure building up at her core that she needed to be relieved.

"Please…" she said again.

"Please, what?" His voice rumbled against her mouth.

"Please, I need you."

Those words must have done something to Lorenzo because he shoved up her skirt and ran his hands along her thighs. The absence of his warmth on her back sent a chill down her spine, but she wasn't complaining. She thoroughly enjoyed having his hands on her, no matter where they were.

Her face heated at the thought of him seeing firsthand how much she wanted him and how her body reacted to his touch. But he kissed her, their lips crashing together.

Before Evelyn could register the change in Lorenzo he pulled away from her, growling as he took a step back.

He avoided her eyes. Her skirt was still hiked up around her hips.

"What? What's wrong? Why'd you stop?"

The sudden shift in his actions had left her panting and brought tears to her eyes. She refused to blink, afraid they would cascade down her cheeks like a parade, announcing how badly she'd wanted him to keep touching her.

"We can't. I can't." He ran his hand through his always perfectly neat hair.

"Why not?"

"Because you work at my club, and I'm older than you... more experienced. I'm supposed to protect you. I shouldn't be taking advantage of you in this way."

"You aren't taking advantage of me—and I'm not some damsel in distress who doesn't know what she's doing. I'm fully aware of what I'm doing and very capable of making my own choices."

If Evelyn was the type of woman to use profanity, she would. Lorenzo continued to underestimate her and it boiled her blood. She'd never wanted anyone as much as she wanted him, *needed* him. It scared her and thrilled her. After all life had thrown at her she deserved to have this pleasure, and he'd ripped it away without even considering what it meant to her.

His selfish, self-centered actions made her want to throttle him. She wanted to slide off the counter, but she was so humiliated by his rejection all she could muster was pulling her skirt down to cover as much of her legs as possible.

"Maybe I should leave." He didn't even look at her.

"I think that would be best," she said, focusing on the floor.

Someone knocked at the door.

Evelyn got down from the counter, smoothed her skirt and sweater, and walked to the door. She took several deep breaths to extinguish her tears before opening the door.

The doorman stood there, looking very nervous. He wouldn't look her in the eyes. "Miss Laroque, I have a message for Mr. De Luca. I was asked to bring it up. Is he here?"

"Yes. Come in." She stepped aside.

"Mr. De Luca, I hope you're having a good day, sir. Here you go." The doorman handed Lorenzo a note.

"I am. Thank you for bringing this up." Lorenzo's words came out clipped.

The doorman bowed and said, "Is there anything I can get either of you?"

"No, thank you," Lorenzo said, without even letting Evelyn speak for herself.

She rolled her eyes at the back of Lorenzo's head. He still hadn't looked at her since he'd ended their moment of pleasure. But the more time that passed, the more Evelyn breathed steadier. Perhaps not getting too entangled with Lorenzo was for the best.

"I'm actually going to follow you out," he told the doorman. He glanced back at her and said, "I will see you later. I want to talk about the fundraiser. I hope you'll still help me with it?"

Evelyn didn't intend to speak to him. She didn't know if she'd ever want to talk to him again. She was mortified. She felt led on.

But maybe she'd mistaken his kindness for interest. His fundraiser was important to Evelyn too. She'd have to deal with him just enough to make sure it went well.

After both men left, Evelyn sank to the floor and let the tears fall.

Chapter Twenty-Five

Lorenzo

Lorenzo left Evelyn's apartment completely conflicted. He'd wanted her so badly. He almost hadn't stopped himself. He would have taken her right there on that counter and no amount of knocking on the door would have mattered, but he didn't want her to get hurt. He didn't want to see her in pain.

But that was exactly what had happened.

After he'd stopped touching her and kissing her, the pain on her face had struck him deep. He hadn't been able to look her in the eyes again. He'd thought he was doing the right thing, the noble thing, by stopping before it went too far, but he didn't know what being noble meant.

He wasn't a noble guy. He was a criminal—a man with flexible morals. He'd always been that way, and he hadn't felt the need to change until now.

But it was more than that. Like Evelyn had said, there were two Americas—did he even have a right to pursue her, knowing there would be people who'd try to hurt her just because he loved her. Hell, they might both be put in jail.

He didn't get on the elevator with the doorman; he opted to take the stairs. Just as he was about to go into the stairwell he heard Evelyn's sobs. They were faint, but distinct. He'd heard a woman cry before, but this time he was the cause.

His stomach dropped like he'd been on a rollercoaster. He honestly didn't know what the right thing to do was, so he did the only thing that would ensure she wouldn't cry anymore. He opened the door to the stairwell, climbed it two stairs at a time.

He was taken aback by the tears that clouded his own vision. He immediately blinked them away, opened the door to his loft and resigned himself to not allowing himself to be close to Evelyn, and definitely not being alone with her, ever again.

Blaming his moment of weakness on his exhaustion, he determined he would practice discipline. He had to. The KKK was putting pressure on his club and preying on the young women of his city. He wouldn't stand for that.

And Lorenzo had to prioritize taking care of the threats against Evelyn, even if that meant he had to keep his distance to protect her.

He stripped out of his suit and lay face down on his bed. He still tasted her silky sweet skin, smelled her sweet citrus scent. His fingers trembled at the memory of her thighs. He'd meant what he'd said to her. Being near her, knowing he couldn't be with her, was killing him.

That was his last thought before he drifted off to sleep.

Chapter Twenty-Six

Evelyn

Tears mixed with warm water. As soon as Lorenzo had left, Evelyn had gotten in the shower. Now her tears were finally drying up. What she and Lorenzo had almost done still had her nerve-endings tingling. She'd been crushed by his rejection, but she would never let him make her feel that way again.

It probably was for the best that things hadn't gone any further.

She would keep her position at Blues Moon until she could figure out her next step. She would just have to keep her distance from Mr. Lorenzo De Luca.

She briefly that worried everyone would be able to see her humiliation on her face. But she would *not* feel bad about being a woman with needs and desires. Lorenzo had been sending her signals, she thought. He'd wanted her as much as she wanted him. She wouldn't allow this situation with him to change her plans for herself. She had her grand to think about. She also shouldn't have been so ready to give herself to a man who lived such a different life than the one she lived. They were worlds apart for so many reasons.

What had she been thinking?

He'd saved her from making a huge mistake.

That fact didn't erase the sting of his rejection, though,

and the memory of how badly she'd wanted him, his hands, his lips…his everything.

After she'd dried off from her shower and washed her face, she released her hair from her bonnet. Loose waves fell around her shoulders. She opened the compartment of her toiletry bag that housed her hair pins and began the work of pinning her curls so they would stay in place. She pulled out her makeup bag next, and completed her routine of applying natural-looking makeup with just a touch of pink tones to her cheeks, eyelids and lips.

Looking at the added plumpness of her mouth reminded her of how surprisingly soft Lorenzo's kisses had been…

She rolled her eyes at herself. Then she curled her lashes and applied her mascara.

Satisfied, she'd walked into her bedroom when she heard a knock on the door. She put on her robe, wondering who even knew she lived there, and panicked briefly considering that it might be Lorenzo.

She peeked through the peephole and sighed with relief. She opened the door. "Hey, Benny. What are you doing here?"

"Evelyn, I'm sorry to bother you, but Mr. De Luca asked me to come up and make sure you have everything you need," Benny said gently.

Evelyn's fists clenched at the sound of Lorenzo's name. She stared at Benny and had to remind herself that she was upset with Lorenzo, not Benny. Unclenching, she tried to smile. "I do, and thank you for checking on me. I'll be down just in time for the show."

"You won't need anything to eat before we start?" Benny sounded concerned.

"No, thank you. I'm not hungry."

"All right… You're taking care of yourself, aren't you?"

"Yes, I am. I'll be down in a bit."

Evelyn smiled, trying to convince Benny she was fine.

She didn't know how successful her smile was because she really wasn't okay, but she would be. She'd survived much worse.

"All right, I'll see you in a little bit." He tipped his hat and walked back to the elevator, looking over his shoulder once at her. Sadness filled his eyes.

Did he know what had happened between her and Lorenzo? She would kill Lorenzo if he'd told anyone. She decided that if he had shared their intimate moment, it would warrant his death.

Usually she would want to get to the club an hour or so before she had to sing, but spending only the necessary time there would be best from now on. She didn't want to risk running into Lorenzo.

She closed the door and walked to her newly installed phone. She didn't even know her own telephone number. She dialed.

"Hello, Grand. You were right about Lorenzo."

"I'm sorry, sweetheart, but it's for the best. He will never understand the world you live in, and being involved with him would just hurt you in the long run."

Her grand had repeated the words she'd said before Evelyn had left West Eden. "I know that now."

"I do have some good news. I'm really happy you called. You know West Eden had a baseball field built for the Negro baseball teams? Well, one of the owners called, and he'd heard about your singing. They want you to sing at the baseball game in a couple of weeks."

The fact that people were talking about her talent sent chills of excitement through her. She'd only just started at Blues Moon and word was already out. She hoped jobs would flow her way, so she could move on from the club before she had a chance to humiliate herself in front of Lorenzo again.

As her grand told her the details, she realized the news

was only tainted by one thing. She wanted to tell Lorenzo all about it. She wanted him to come see her sing at the game. But neither of those things would happen.

"I've gotta go, Grand. I'll talk to you later." She moved to hang up the phone, but then put it back to her ear. "Wait—are you coming to the club?"

Her grand's presence there would make it easier for her to avoid any interaction with Lorenzo at all. She ignored the pang of disappointment at not having him to talk to anymore. She'd only just met him, and already she was missing a relationship that wasn't even a relationship. They weren't even friends.

"Yes, I thought you knew? Mr. Lorenzo just called to let me know he's sent a car over to pick me up. I should be there within the hour."

She would arrive just after Evelyn's set started. That would have to do. Evelyn would stay in her apartment until there was only a few minutes before she had to be on stage. She didn't know what she would do about helping with the fundraiser, but she would have to figure something out. Giving back to the community was something that meant a lot to Evelyn.

She went to her bedroom and retrieved her dress. She laid it on the bed. She loved this dress best of all. It had taken several checks from the pharmacy for her to afford it. It was one of her more conservative dresses, floor-length, no slit, and it came with a cape. It hugged her figure perfectly because she'd had it altered. The cream and silver sequined material clung to her like a second skin.

She needed this dress tonight. She needed the confidence it would bring her. If she had to see Lorenzo again, she wanted to look her absolute best.

She realized Lorenzo had had her cabinets stocked, and the refrigerator. She had everything she could want, and she had the man who'd just broken her heart to thank for it all.

Lorenzo made her head spin. A man didn't do all he had done for someone if he didn't have feelings for that person. She was done trying to figure it out, though.

She decided to make some tea, to soothe her throat before she had to perform. The whistle from the tea kettle filled the otherwise quiet room. She'd never lived alone, and although she enjoyed having time to herself, she was starting to feel lonely.

She would ask her grand to spend the night, so she wouldn't have to make the journey back to West Eden late. There was plenty of room. The apartment had two bedrooms, both furnished with modern wood beds and dressers. Evelyn had put her belongings in the larger room. She really didn't need all of the space.

She put one spoonful of honey in her tea and walked over to the window. She looked out at the busy garment district, watching people while she sipped on her drink. She breathed in deeply and let it out slowly. Finally, the tightness in her shoulders loosened, the restless energy in her hands and legs subsided. Hopefully she could put her feelings for Lorenzo out of her mind—or add them to the pain she used as her muse while she sang.

Chapter Twenty-Seven

Lorenzo

Lorenzo had had a fitful dream about Evelyn. He awoke with a start and looked quickly around his room, trying to catch his bearings. There'd been white sheets holding her. She'd screamed for him, but he hadn't been able to get to her. He'd banged on the glass cage he was in until his hands and arms were bloody. She'd cried and screamed as they took her. He hadn't able to stop them. He hadn't protected her.

Sweat dripped from his brow. He cupped his hand over the back of his neck. His sheets were wet with sweat. He looked at his watch. He was late for the club.

He got in the tub and let the hot water soothe his aching muscles. He'd been in knots since leaving Evelyn. Not being able to release his pent-up desire for her had him on edge.

Admittedly, he'd been aroused by her from the moment he met her. He had a lot of built-up energy and he'd almost let it cloud his judgment. But he'd made the right choice. If he'd allowed himself to experience being inside her, the entire world wouldn't have been able to keep him from being with her. He would probably have married her.

That was why he couldn't let himself forget again that being with him would put her in danger—between the bigotry, Jim Crow Laws and his mob family, her life would be in constant danger because of him. He cared too much about her to let that happen. He could and would protect her from afar.

He got out of the tub and grabbed his towel. Stepping on his plush rug, he looked at himself in the mirror. He shook his head. His eyes were bloodshot. He hadn't gotten much rest in the last few days. Usually he didn't need a lot of sleep, but pining after Evelyn really took the energy out of him.

His phone rang in the bedroom. He rushed to get it, almost losing the towel he'd tied around his waist.

"Hello?" He used another towel to dry his hair.

"Lorenzo, we need to meet."

There was something in Dred's voice that made the hair on his arms spike. Something bad was about to happen—or had already happened.

Lorenzo went to his closet, which was really like a second bedroom, and scanned through his suits. When he found what he was looking for—a light brown tweed he'd gotten his last time in Italy—he went over to the bench that was in the middle of the closet and got dressed. He chose cufflinks and a bowtie. He picked a hat, but went back to the bathroom to do his hair first.

Putting on his hat, he walked out the door not even ten minutes after he'd talked to Dred.

He took the elevator down to the first floor. Usually he would walk down the stairs, but his nerves were bad and he needed to stand still a moment to calm himself.

He had to get back to being the cold-hearted, morally ambivalent boss he always had been. He didn't do anything if it didn't fit into the plan that he had for his business and his life. But in just a few days he had started making choices based on what he thought was best for Evelyn. He would still protect her with his life, but that was all he could do. It wouldn't even be safe for them to be friends because he would always want more.

He walked into Blues Moon and was immediately swarmed by Jeb, Dred and Tommy.

"We have to talk," said Dred.

She walked toward Lorenzo's office and obviously expected Lorenzo to follow, which he did.

"What's going on?"

Lorenzo closed the door once they were all in his office. Jeb closed the blinds so no one would be able to see them from the club. Lorenzo could hear Evelyn's melodic voice, and it was all he could do to stay in the room and talk with his friends about whatever had them all riled up. Her voice sounded especially morose and beautiful.

"I infiltrated a KKK meeting tonight, and what I heard was not good." Tommy stroked the light stubble on his chin. He looked disheveled—not at all like his usually impeccably groomed self.

"And?" Lorenzo grew impatient.

"They're coming after Evelyn—and you. They're planning something big. They never said what, but the main cat kept saying the plan was working. He never said what the plan was."

"You didn't interrogate anyone?" Lorenzo watched as Tommy paced.

"I didn't want to blow my cover. I had to get out of there before someone questioned who I was. They were all drinking and smacking each other on the back about this plan. I did manage to lure one of them away from the meeting, but he wouldn't cooperate."

"Tommy, what'd you do?" Dred said. She sat in the chair by the door. "And stop pacing. You're giving me a headache."

Tommy sat in the chair next to her. "I did what I always do. I shut him up."

"Did you kill him?" Jeb asked, completely void of emotion.

"Nah, I don't think so. He was breathing, however faintly."

Jeb leaned against the door. He looked like he was developing a plan in his head. He always looked like that, and he usually was.

Chapter Twenty-Eight

Lorenzo

Lorenzo sat at his desk with his head in his hands. He hadn't had a day like this in a long time. He needed to focus on the problem…the big problem that he and his crew were discussing…but his thoughts kept flitting back to Evelyn.

He couldn't wait to see her. He wanted to talk to her—explain that he cared for her and wanted to do the right thing for her. But he couldn't do that. He had to keep his distance from her.

"Lorenzo, did you hear me?" Dred's glare pierced the air, and it was directed at him.

"No, what did you say?"

Lorenzo needed to tune in to the conversation. They would expect him to have a solution to the problem. Jeb must have proposed a plan, and it would be up to Lorenzo to confirm if that was what they were going to do.

The way Dred looked at him, Lorenzo knew he needed to focus. "I'm sorry. I'm not myself right now."

He stood. Maybe pacing like Tommy would help him get his mind on the task at hand.

"Tommy needs to go deep undercover with the Klan and see what he can learn. If they believe that he is really one of them, they'll bring him in on whatever this plan is," Lorenzo said.

"How exactly is Tommy going to convince them to trust him?" Dred said.

Tommy was probably the most likely to pass as a racist. He had blue eyes, even though his mother was Black and his father was Italian. Tommy looked White, and Lorenzo had faith in his ability to play the role he needed to play.

"I can do it, Boss. I've heard enough racists bumping their gums. I can recite it from memory."

Lorenzo had no doubt that was true. "Who are you going to say you are?"

Tommy smiled. "I'm going to say I'm a farmer from out West and new to the city. I've heard the Klan has started up here, and I want to help. I've had too many coloreds thinking they're as good as me and I'm tired of it." Tommy nodded.

The Klan members Lorenzo had encountered didn't seem that bright, so they'd fall for it. "Be careful. I'll get Malone to bartend while you pursue this plan. But the minute you feel like things are going south, you get out of there."

"I'll be close by, watching. I'll handle it if the situation gets sticky." Dred stood and walked to the door.

"I'll be with her, watching Tommy's back," Jeb said.

"No, you won't. I work alone." Dred's voice had taken on a deadly calm.

"Try to stop me," Jeb said.

They stood face to face, both refusing to relent.

"I need both of you there. Just keep a distance. You're good, but I don't suggest you try to take on the entire Klan on your own." Lorenzo walked over to Tommy and clapped him on his shoulder. "Stay safe, my friend."

"Will do, boss." Tommy nodded again.

"I want to see all three of you back here as soon as the

Klan meeting is over. We can counter any strike they're planning."

All three nodded.

Jeb moved away from the door and Lorenzo left. His heart pounded. He trusted his crew. They'd get the job done and neutralize the threat. Jeb and Dred had specialized training unlike any he'd ever seen. They'd keep Tommy safe or kill every member of the Klan within reach to get him out.

As Lorenzo walked out of his office he smelled the salty pretzels cooking in the kitchen. He loved offering his clients hot, fresh pretzels. They really were the best, and savory food made them drink more. Servers darted about carrying trays, clearing tables, taking orders. The club was packed. Everyone was impeccably dressed in fringe, sequins, suits, bow ties and shiny shoes.

Lorenzo looked at the stage—and almost tripped over his own feet when he saw Evelyn. He had to reach out and grab the bar rail to steady himself. He stared at her, not able to hide it. How did this doll, the most beautiful woman he'd ever seen, keep getting more and more beautiful? It shouldn't be possible.

The cream dress hung on her curves so sensually his body reacted immediately. He tried to stand with his legs farther apart, to hide his growing desire. The sequins seemed to accentuate her full breasts, slender waist and wide hips. He wanted to do things to her she would never forget…

"Mr. De Luca, you're needed at the front door."

Lorenzo turned to see a hostess, her brows knit. She looked frightened. Lorenzo groaned internally. *What now?* All he wanted to do was stand there and watch Evelyn. Her voice filled the room as the band started one of her original songs. She sang about losing everything she cared about in order to learn that what she'd thought was important really wasn't... So much pain in her voice.

With Lorenzo's long strides, he crossed the large club in seconds. He could see through the windows that a crowd had gathered.

"What's going on?" he asked Sam, his doorman tonight. Sam was tall and wide. Lorenzo had to step around him to see the crowd.

"Mr. De Luca, we are at capacity, but this guy is demanding entrance. He said you would want to know he was here."

Lorenzo's eyes fell on the man in an off-the-rack suit. A cop—and a dirty one at that. This cop was on the Ricci family's payroll.

"Do we have business?" Lorenzo's voice rumbled low with annoyance.

"Not yet, but I think you'll want to hear what I have to say, since I'm the only one who can ensure this beautiful club and that beautiful singer of yours remain unharmed."

The man stepped back out of Lorenzo's reach. As if he knew Lorenzo's gut reaction was to pummel the man for his thinly veiled threat against Evelyn. Lorenzo realized that he wasn't even reacting because of his club, but solely because of her.

Sam's arm prevented Lorenzo from getting to the man. "Sir, let me... We don't want you going to jail tonight, but I wouldn't mind taking a load off in a cell."

Sam started advancing on the detective. The man backed up a step and opened his suit jacket. He had a small gun in his waistband.

"You might want to rethink that. Besides, I have information you need and I will tell you everything I know for a price—oh, and I won't kill the both of you."

Lorenzo would have had the gun out of the man's hand before he could even aim it at them, but he decided he'd let the man talk first, before he handled him. It was always best to get your enemy talking before you shut them up.

"Well, let me invite you in," Lorenzo said, without a shred of kindness in his voice.

He gave Sam a look. Sam nodded almost imperceptibly.

Lorenzo's hands balled into fists as he led the man into the club and back to his office. Evelyn's voice still filled the air with sweet harmony.

Lorenzo took a deep breath and opened the door to his office. "After you," he said.

The man walked in and made himself comfortable on top of Lorenzo's desk. The shades were still drawn from earlier. Good. If Lorenzo did have to put his hands on this man, he didn't want his customers to be witnesses.

"What information do you have, Mr....?"

"Detective Brown," the man said, taking a cigar from his pocket and a lighter.

"Detective Brown."

"The Klan is going to make a move on you unless you agree to their terms. They have a price on Miss Laroque as well, for incentive."

Lorenzo stood silent by the door, staring at Detective Brown with such vehemence he struggled to keep his fists at his sides. "And what are those terms?"

"You have to join their ranks, and you have to segregate your club and serve only White customers."

Lorenzo laughed. "I don't like ultimatums. Now, let me inform *you* of something. You might want to be careful, coming into my establishment and threatening me."

"I'm aware of who you are, Mr. De Luca. You can try all you want to act like you're above being a criminal, but you're not. That's why I wanted to come and share this information with you, see how I can help you make the right decision. Your family is powerful, and the Klan just wants to help keep it that way. You don't want them as enemies. They're not as refined as you and me."

Lorenzo frowned. He wouldn't describe the detective as "refined" in any way—from his store-bought cheap suit to his sheer stupidity. He was aware that he relied on the dirty cops on his father's payroll to ignore his speakeasy, but deep down he hated corrupt police officers.

"Here's what I'm going to do, Detective Brown. For your generosity, I'm going to let you walk out of here with both of your legs, if you can do one thing for me."

The detective's expression didn't change, but Lorenzo could tell his breathing had picked up in speed.

"Go on."

"You are to leave my club and never show your face here again. If I do see your face again, Detective Brown, I won't be so generous."

The detective shook his head. "You're a fool. You'll regret not taking me up on my offer."

Lorenzo took one step toward the man.

Detective Brown got up and walked around Lorenzo, giving him a wide berth.

"I didn't say I wasn't going to take you up on your offer. I just don't like being threatened in my place of business," said Lorenzo. "I'm actually working on getting word to the Klan that I want to talk. Maybe you can do me a favor and share that with them? Ask them to come by on Monday evening for a chat about how we can move forward in a way that will benefit my family and the Klan."

"I can share that with them. I'm glad you've come to your senses."

The detective left without saying another word.

Anger pulsed through Lorenzo like a tornado.

Chapter Twenty-Nine

Evelyn

A cloud of darkness seemed to shadow Lorenzo's remarkable features. His grayish green eyes darkened and focused on Evelyn. She wanted to shrink under his unyielding gaze, but she held her head high and took a deep breath. She wasn't even sure why she'd sought him out.

Evelyn had just finished her first set when she'd seen Lorenzo enter with a shorter man. Lorenzo had seemed angry when he and the man had disappeared into the office. The shorter man had left just moments before, and Evelyn found herself at Lorenzo's office door.

Evelyn asked, "What happened?"

Lorenzo's eyes softened some, and the set of his jaw slackened. She had to fight the urge to go up to him and place her hand on his cheek—Lorenzo, the man who'd humiliated her and rejected her.

"Nothing. Sometimes the best action is inaction, but that doesn't make it easy."

"Oh…"

She walked over to him, needing to be sure he was okay. She hadn't seen his emotions so close to the surface before. He usually held himself in check in a way so that it was hard to tell what he was thinking.

His lips parted—not like he was going to say something, but for another reason. She licked her own lips, possibly for the same reason. He brought his hand up and placed it on her cheek. The feather-light touch sent chills down her back. She had been so worried about him, but he was so tender in that moment she almost forgot why she was angry with him.

When Cook cleared his throat, Lorenzo pulled away from her. She couldn't face Cook—not with her emotions burning her cheeks. She needed a moment to collect herself.

"Everything is fine, Evelyn. You should get some rest before your next set."

His voice gave nothing away to show he was feeling as confused as she was. He was dismissing her again. Feeling foolish, she walked to the door.

"Is it possible for us to talk about the fundraiser after you finish singing? We have to get going if we're to help the families that are having a hard time in the city."

Evelyn couldn't be cruel. She enjoyed helping others, and she wouldn't allow her pride to keep her from doing what needed to be done.

Without turning to face Lorenzo, she said, "Yes, I am available after the set."

"Great. Everyone will meet in my apartment for breakfast right after you're done singing. I'll see you there."

Unable to help her disappointment that she and Lorenzo wouldn't be alone, she nodded and turned to leave his office. She hated how her emotions were all over the place where he was concerned. How had she gone from not being able to see herself with anyone, let alone a White man, to hoping for moments to be alone with him?

"Night, Miss Evelyn," Cook said as she passed.

She didn't want to talk because if she did she was certain her voice would quiver, giving away her fragile state. She nodded, her gaze glued to the ground.

Once in her dressing room, she shut the door and let

out a breath. Tears welled in her eyes and she let them fall. She would need to rein in her emotions or she would have to find other employment sooner than she'd thought. Lorenzo certainly seemed to be able to turn his on and off.

But she wasn't made like that. When she did allow herself to care for someone—which was extremely hard to do, given what had happened to her friends and family in Greenwood—she couldn't just pretend that there was nothing between them.

After a few moments, the tears slowed. She wiped at her cheeks and walked over to sit at her vanity. She pulled out powder, mascara and rouge from her makeup bag. She busied herself putting her face back together, even if her heart was in pieces.

A knock came just as she'd finished trying her best to cover up the splotchy patches of red on her cheeks and the streaks of mascara from the trail of tears. Her eyes were still red and a little puffy.

Sighing, she got up and crossed the room. "Who is it?" She wasn't going to open the door if it was someone she didn't want to see her upset—like Lorenzo.

"It's me—Cook."

She opened the door but couldn't meet his eyes. "Is something wrong?"

"Well, technically, no, but I wanted to make sure you were okay. Whatever happened with the boss man seemed pretty intense." He walked in and stood by the table. "Boss is a good guy, but he seems not to know exactly what to do about you. He's never been like this over a dame—I mean a woman before."

The big, burly man smiled, and Evelyn could see he was missing some teeth. He reminded her of Santa Claus, right down to the rosy cheeks and big belly. His beard wasn't white, it was gray and brown, but he had a jolly temperament that Evelyn found endearing. His cooking made her feel at home too. She wanted to introduce her grand to him.

She groaned loudly, remembering that her grand should arrive any minute. She would know immediately that something was wrong.

"Everything all right, Miss Evelyn?" asked Cook.

Evelyn smiled. "Yes, I just forgot my grandmother is going to come see me sing tonight. She should be here any time now."

"Did you tell Jeb or the boss?"

"Lorenzo knows, but I don't think he told Jeb."

"I'll go tell whoever's at the door. I think it's Sam tonight. He'll make sure she gets the best table and free drinks of her choice. I'll bring her out a nice spread too."

Evelyn touched Cook's arm. "Thank you so much."

The man reddened even more, which Evelyn hadn't thought possible, and left the room. Evelyn shut the door behind him, trying to think what she could do about her eyes.

She walked to her vanity again and stared at her reflection. She closed her eyes, unable to look at the puffy redness any longer, then put one more layer of powder on and hoped she could blame her appearance on being on stage under the spotlights. She didn't like lying to her grandmother. She actually hadn't ever lied to her before. Thanks to Lorenzo, she would have to figure out something to say.

Deciding there was nothing else she could do, she left the dressing room and headed to the stage.

Benny was walking toward her. "I was just about to come get you," he said.

"I beat you to it." She tried to smile, but the action didn't ring true with how she felt.

"Are you okay?" He tilted his head, as if trying to get a better look at her.

She avoided his eyes. "Yes, I'm wonderful."

"We can wait a little longer if you need to lie down or eat something."

She had no appetite at all. "No, thank you. I'm okay— really. And I'll feel even better once I'm back on stage." She looked at him in an attempt to sound convincing.

Benny smiled and took her arm. He tucked it around his own, and they strolled on stage together.

Chapter Thirty

Lorenzo

Lorenzo slumped in the chair. When Evelyn had appeared in the doorway, he'd almost lost his resolve to stay away from her. He'd stood frozen in place, not allowing himself any closer to her for fear of what he might do.

He hadn't anticipated her coming to stand right in front of him, inspecting him. The genuine worry on her face had leveled him. And before he'd known what he was doing, he'd cupped her face, touched her soft skin, and her intoxicating sweet smell had enraptured him.

After Cook had interrupted them Lorenzo had been able to gather himself a little, and even though sending her away was the last thing he'd wanted to do, he'd done it anyway.

"Boss, Evelyn's grandmother is here. Would you like to greet her?" Cook said, standing in the doorway.

Lorenzo smoothed his hair and walked toward the front of the club. Evelyn was in her zone on stage. She probably hadn't noticed her grandmother waiting by the door to be seated.

Lorenzo approached with hesitation, since Delphine didn't like him and hadn't bothered pretending when they'd met so briefly.

"Delphine, welcome to Blues Moon. We have a special table waiting for you. I wanted to come to greet you personally. I know Evelyn will be very excited when she sees you."

"Mr. De Luca, thank you for sending your fancy car and driver to retrieve me. Have you thought about what I said when you visited our little town?"

"Yes, I have, and I believe you were right."

Lorenzo held out his arm for Delphine and led her to her table. She'd told Lorenzo how dangerous an interracial relationship would be. She spoke from experience, she'd said, and in no uncertain terms she did not want that for her granddaughter. She also didn't approve of Lorenzo's less than scrupulous methods of making money.

"It's a shame you won't be able to visit us again."

Delphine's smile wasn't sweet. And her words pierced Lorenzo even though he had no intention of returning to West Eden. He hated knowing he couldn't even if he wanted to.

"It is a lovely place. And I am still humbled by Evelyn bringing me. As I told you, some of my customers live there and have spoken privately to me about it. I'm glad I finally got to see it. But I don't want to keep you. Please let my staff know anything you need and order whatever you like. Your bill is on the house."

Lorenzo held his hand out to help Delphine sit. After she'd gotten comfortable he walked toward the bar, to see if Tommy had returned yet. He sighed loudly when he saw Tommy's replacement still tending bar.

It had been at least an hour since they'd left, and he wanted to know they were all okay. With Jeb gone, Lorenzo had to cover and make sure the club ran smoothly. He was used to zoning out, listening to the music and looking at the numbers. He interacted with his customers, but Jeb was really the front man. Lorenzo preferred to interact on his own terms.

"We're going to take a brief break…" Evelyn's voice floated through the room.

The crowd groaned audibly.

Evelyn's face lit up when she saw her grandmother. It made Lorenzo's heart skip to see her so happy. *He* wanted to put a genuine smile on her face like that. *He* wanted to be the receiver of her warm embrace.

He shut his eyes for a moment, and took a breath before turning away from her and her grandmother. He sat at the end of the bar sulking—something he didn't ever do. He was someone who got what he wanted. Usually he didn't stop until he got what he wanted. But he had to remember that he was the one who had stopped anything happening between them, and that it had been the right thing to do—no matter how much he ached for her.

Chapter Thirty-One

Evelyn

With her grand in the audience, Evelyn sang until she thought her heart would explode. She had so much pain to draw from that she could have kept going all night, but Benny suggested that she take a break and have something to drink with her grandmother.

The band continued to finish the set while Evelyn sat down at the table with her grand. She saw Yalaina walk on to the stage. She hadn't heard the young woman sing, so she was excited to hear her and enjoy the music with her grand.

"So this is Blues Moon." Her grand smiled, but worry lines creasing her forehead.

"Yes, what do you think?"

"It's nice, baby, and of course your singing brings tears to my eyes…" Her grand touched her gloved hand.

Evelyn had to have her emotions close to the surface, so that when she sang she could make the audience feel it, not just hear it. She'd tried to convince herself that was why she felt so strongly for Lorenzo. She was just full of emotions from singing so much lately. The feeling would pass.

"You should stay at my apartment for the night. I would worry about you going back so late."

"That sounds nice, sweetheart. And I'll come by to see it. But I really need to get back. I have a doctor's appointment in the morning." Her grand squeezed her hand. "Everyone in West Eden has heard rumblings about the KKK setting up in the city, and we worry about your safety. It'll be nice to see where you're living so I can put my mind at ease. I haven't really seen you these last few days, since you started here. You look like there's something wrong. What's going on?"

"I'm fine, Grand. I have a meeting right after my set, but I'll show you my apartment, and then you can get home and get some rest."

"Stop trying to avoid my question."

Evelyn sighed. "I have everything I need right here, really. Lorenzo has been so generous…" Saying his name was like a dagger to her heart. She had to get past this infatuation she felt for him.

She searched the club for him. He was at the bar, and their eyes met. He was staring at her. She wondered how long he'd been watching her. What must he think of her? She'd almost given herself to him so willingly. She'd never wanted anything more than she'd wanted him to make love to her.

He stared at her without even trying to hide it. What did he want from her? His steely gray-green eyes sent shivers through her body. She shook her head at the memory of his callused palms on her thighs and averted her gaze.

"Are you cold, sweetheart?"

Her grand's worry lines seemed to be set permanently.

"No, I'm okay. I'm going to get back on stage. This is the last set, so we can go to my apartment after. Order some food—I'll have Cook put it on my tab."

"Your boss has already taken care of my bill. He didn't tell you?" Her grand arched an eyebrow.

"No…"

Evelyn chanced one more look in Lorenzo's direction. The corner of his mouth tugged up. That smile set fire to the ice she'd formed around her heart. But she was determined not to let a man she'd just met have this much power over her.

Evelyn returned to the stage as Yalaina finished her song. She was an excellent singer. She and Evelyn were very different in their sound, but Yalaina had a beautiful voice.

"You did amazing," Evelyn said with a big smile.

"Thank you. That means a lot from you." Yalaina squeezed Evelyn's arm and then walked toward the back of the club.

Evelyn knew Lorenzo spent the entire set watching her. Even when someone would come up to talk to him, he never took his eyes off her.

But there were at least four gorgeous women who leaned against the bar next to him and gently touched his shoulder, or his knee, or his chest. Evelyn sang through her fury. She wasn't even sure why she was so angry, but her emotion fed the more up-tempo songs that she'd written recently.

The night came to a close, and Evelyn couldn't have felt happier, knowing she could retire to her apartment with her grand. But first she showed her the dressing room.

"Wow, this is all for you?" her grand asked.

"Yes, Lorenzo did all of this. I told him it was highly unnecessary."

Her grand harrumphed. "Let's go upstairs. I'm pretty tired, and I don't want to keep that driver out too late."

"I can't wait for you to see it. It's really lovely."

Evelyn took her grand's hand and led the way through the back, hoping they wouldn't run into Lorenzo. They got all the way to the elevator without seeing him, so she started to relax.

The ding of the elevator bell shattered the silence. Evelyn got on first and asked the attendant for the sixth floor. It was such a pleasure to see her grand. Having her at Blues

Moon, letting her see what Evelyn did to help pay for her care meant the world to Evelyn.

When Evelyn had first entered the club, her breath had been taken away by the beautiful red linen and chandeliers, the people dressed in the most expensive clothing, and the cars that lined the street. Her grand seemed genuinely impressed as well.

They stepped off the elevator and Evelyn walked to the door. "Here we are."

She smiled brightly as her grandmother stepped inside, to see the backdrop of the city shining through the oversize windows. To Evelyn's amazement, her grand gasped.

"How much does this cost, Evelyn Anne Laroque?"

It was never a good sign when her grand used her entire name.

Evelyn set her bag down and took her grand's coat. She hung it in the hall and ushered her into the living room. "Please, sit down. Let me make you some tea. The apartment is part of my contract. I don't know how much it costs. It's a job perk."

Evelyn busied herself, intentionally not completely answering the question. One, because she truly didn't know how much it cost, and two, because she didn't want to admit that Lorenzo allowed her to stay in the apartment for free.

Oh, and should she mention he lived upstairs?

No, she definitely wasn't going to say that.

Thoughts of Lorenzo filled her mind. She couldn't help but wonder what he was doing and if he thought about her as much as she thought of him. He had stared at her so intensely. Why would he do that if he didn't want her?

She set two saucers on the coffee table with teacups. She brought out a container of honey and one of sugar. She'd found them in a cabinet. Lorenzo had thought of everything.

"I'm going to change out of this dress, but please make yourself at home. I have to go to my meeting, but I'll take you down to the driver who's taking you home."

Evelyn went to the bedroom to change her clothes. She heard a knock at the door. If she were a cursing woman…

She threw on some linen pants and a long linen shirt. Walking out of her room, she heard him. Lorenzo's voice filled the apartment. The deep baritone sound thrummed through her.

She stopped in the hallway to compose herself. She took a deep breath and his masculine spiced scent filled the air. *Oh, God…*

"I want to make sure you all have everything you need."

"Well, Mr. De Luca, I hope you didn't go out of your way. We're just fine," Evelyn's grand said.

"It's no problem. I live on the top floor of the building. I'm heading up now, but thought I'd stop in to make sure you all were okay. I also wanted to see if Evelyn wants to walk up with me to our meeting."

Evelyn couldn't see them, but she knew the silence meant that her grand was digesting what Lorenzo's proximity to Evelyn's apartment might mean.

Evelyn walked into the room, her skin warm and her palms sweaty.

"Lorenzo, to what do we owe this honor?" Evelyn's voice had taken on a high pitch. She was aware it had only been a few hours before that she'd allowed him to explore nearly every inch of her before he'd rejected her.

He smiled. Evelyn did not return his warm expression.

"I'm heading up now, and thought I would check to make sure you don't need anything—and see if you want to walk up with me to our meeting."

"We don't need anything. And I'll be up to the meeting in just a moment. I need to see my grand to her driver."

Evelyn's clipped tone came out harsher than she'd meant it to, but she couldn't feel bad about it.

"Well, okay… I will see you in a few minutes, then."

He tipped his hat, then turned and walked to the door. Evelyn followed him.

He opened the door, but turned to look at her. "We have to talk about earlier." His eyes peered into her.

"No, we don't." She grabbed the handle of the door to encourage him to leave.

"Please, I want to explain. I don't want us to be distant with each other when we were just starting to get close."

"We are employer and employee. That is as close as we need to be. Now, please leave. I will be at the meeting on time."

Chapter Thirty-Two

Lorenzo

Lorenzo had to step back so the door wouldn't hit him in the face. He wasn't sure what he'd expected Evelyn's response to be. He hated that she was so angry with him, but maybe it was for the best. Although he would continue to watch out for her—protect her.

He ran up the stairs to his apartment with so much on his mind. He just wanted to escape for a little while from the torturous thoughts of how much he wanted Evelyn but couldn't have her.

Tommy, Dred and Jeb sat in his living room. They'd cleaned themselves up in his spare bathroom. Tommy's hair was wet, and Dred's skin glowed dark brown under the moonlight. She stood looking out of the window. Lorenzo didn't miss the way Jeb watched her.

"So, give me the rundown."

Lorenzo went to his bar cart and poured himself a glass of whiskey. He drank it all in one gulp. He ran his hand through his hair, poured himself another glass, then sat down on a chair.

"It's worse than we thought. They're planning to make a move on Blues Moon—to 'send a message.'" Dred rubbed her temples and closed her eyes.

Lorenzo took a moment before responding. He wanted

to weigh his options before telling them what the plan was going to be.

"I got it covered," he said at last. "I let the detective who so generously stopped by here know that I'm interested in joining the KKK. They'll show up and expect things to be amicable, but what they will find is their secrets outed for the entire city to see. They'll be caught off guard, and I will give them an ultimatum: disband or I will shatter their lives."

"Are we doing things the mob way?" asked Tommy.

Tommy had a glass of brown liquor of his own that he stared into. Although he was a bartender, Lorenzo hadn't seen him drink but a handful of times in the six years they'd known each other.

"No, we will do things my way."

Lorenzo had decided that he would take the heat from the Klan alone. He wouldn't involve anyone else.

He had reporters who loved to cover his club. The one thing about the Klan was that they were cowards. They were also doctors, and lawyers, and held other positions in the city. If their identities got out their anonymity would be ruined and they wouldn't be able to continue to terrorize the citizens any longer. Not to mention Lorenzo had forged a friendship with some of the up-and-coming officials in the city who believed that the only way the city would thrive was through desegregation. Some of those officials had vowed to help Lorenzo get the Klan members put away.

Dred stood immediately. Tommy and Jeb followed.

"We need to get things in place if my plan to ambush the Klan is going to work. As soon as things are ready, let me know," Lorenzo said.

Jeb, Dred and Tommy nodded as they left.

After the door had closed behind them, Lorenzo sat down just as his phone rang. He answered it. "Hello?"

"Tell me about your new singer."

His mother's voice was a relief.

"What have you heard?"

"She's beautiful, a Negro and one of the best singers people have ever heard. You need to hold on to her—but more importantly you need to keep her safe."

Lorenzo loved his mother for her kind heart.

"There's talk that there's a hit on her," she went on. "I don't think you have the manpower to go against the Klan."

"I've got it handled, Mamma."

"I think it would be a good idea to get her acquainted with the family...you know, so people will know she's protected."

"I don't think—"

"Lorenzo, I know you see our family as a threat to protect her from, but her association to us could benefit your plan. Bring her by the hotel. Introduce her to people. Get the newspapers to cover a story on you and her."

"Wait—you want to make it seem like she's my girl-friend?"

"We could use that to our advantage. I hear she's bringing in large crowds every night. Your father has mentioned that the family could get into the music business with this young woman if she's everything everyone says she is. She's too much of an asset to let her get harmed or go to another club."

Lorenzo knew there had to be a reason his father was interested in Evelyn.

"This could be good for the family, Lorenzo. This could be your way to go completely legal. I know that you have declined to be the next Don, so you're going to have to figure out another way out of this life if you are going to..." His mother trailed off.

"I don't plan to use Evelyn and exploit her talent."

"You'd be helping her build her career."

Lorenzo's mother had a point.

"Let me think this through. I'll let you know."

"At least bring her by the hotel. We have to put her under our protection. She's an asset. Your father's interest in her may not be centered around her safety, but mine is. I'm worried about you and her. I couldn't go on if something happened to you like what happened to Vinny. You have to choose her safety over your own past, son."

Lorenzo's mother sighed as a knock at the door drew his attention away from his conversation with his mother. "I have to go."

"Please consider what I said. I would love to meet her."

"Okay."

Lorenzo wanted Evelyn to meet his mother. He thought of them both as amazing women. He knew they would hit it off.

Lorenzo stood and strolled to the door. He almost couldn't contain how happy he was to see the golden glare of Evelyn.

"Are we still meeting? I'm sorry I took so long. My grand wanted to chat before she left."

"Yes. Well, not exactly. Tommy, Jeb and Dred have something to handle." Lorenzo gestured for Evelyn to come in.

She looked up at him through lidded eyes. She pulled up her gloves as she stared at the table.

"But I'm happy you came. We can get started discussing the fundraiser and then you can get some rest."

"Okay," Evelyn said.

Lorenzo breathed a sigh of relief.

Chapter Thirty-Three

Evelyn

Evelyn sat frozen. She hadn't expected to be alone with Lorenzo. She wasn't sure if she should stay. But she didn't want to leave. She'd feel like she was running from a challenge.

She thought back to the night of the massacre, and how she'd accused her mother of running scared. Images of the fire burned through Evelyn's head. Her family had almost made it out. For Evelyn, that had been the worst part—thinking they were safe, and then having their entire lives shattered in minutes.

"Evelyn? Evelyn, are you okay…?" Lorenzo's voice trailed off.

When Evelyn opened her eyes, she saw his gray-green ones etched with concern. "Oh, Lorenzo!"

She threw her head in her hands and wept. He pulled her from the chair and sat cradling her on the floor. He caressed her hair and her back as she cried.

She wasn't sure how long they sat like that, holding on to each other, but she didn't care. In that moment what she wanted—needed—was comfort, and she wanted that comfort from Lorenzo.

"I want to tell you what happened," Evelyn said.

"You don't owe me anything," Lorenzo said.

"I know, but I think I should tell someone finally. I've

never told anyone what happened that night…not even my grand."

Lorenzo held her tighter. He took one of her hands in his. He slid down her glove and took it off.

Evelyn tensed, and then she relaxed back into him. Her hands shook. She couldn't hold back the tears. Memories from that night in Greenwood crashed into her again and a sob escaped. She covered her mouth and closed her eyes. The tears still fell.

Lorenzo scooped her up in his arms and positioned her on his lap. He held her, not saying anything, just holding her in his tight embrace. She breathed into his neck, letting his scent soothe her. The sobs eventually stopped and so did the tears. What must he think of her now? She'd tried so hard to hide this side of herself.

Lorenzo whispered in her ear. "Please tell me what happened to you? These scars are old. You must have been a child… Please, you can trust me."

Lorenzo ran his hands through Evelyn's hair. The repetitive motion was calming. She eased off Lorenzo's lap to sit next to him. She took a deep breath and looked into his eyes.

"When I was seveneen, there was a massacre in Greenwood—right outside of Tulsa. Greenwood was a very affluent area for Black people. Black-owned businesses flourished there—everything from hotels and banks to hospitals and movie theaters. My family had only been in Greenwood about a year before the massacre. We moved there so my mom could continue to practice medicine. She was a leading physician in her field, Black or White. One night my momma came home from the hospital frantic. She seemed out of her mind at first. She was so unlike herself we thought she was sick or something. She told us a horde of angry White men was heading for Greenwood and they were out for blood. They were saying a Black boy attacked a White woman. The courthouse wouldn't let the men get to the boy, so they turned their hatred on our town."

Tears started streaming down Evelyn's cheeks again. Lorenzo wiped them away with his thumb. He kissed Evelyn's hands and looked into her eyes. She didn't know what she was supposed to feel in that moment. She was telling a White man about how a White mob had destroyed everything she loved, changed her life irrevocably, and yet all she wanted was for Lorenzo to keep holding her.

"They set fire to our buildings, to our homes, after they shot and killed entire families and stole whatever they wanted. They burned down the entire town. My mom had made us pack up and leave as soon as she'd gotten home. We were driving out of town when a group of men stopped us. They pulled my mom and dad from the car."

Another sob escaped. Lorenzo rubbed Evelyn's back.

"My dad and mom fought back, but they were both shot dead. The men set my parents on fire, and I ran to my mom and took her hand."

"That's how you got these scars?"

Evelyn nodded. "It was so much chaos. Military planes were flying over, dropping bombs on the town to target the people. I didn't notice, but a group of Black men came and killed the rest of the White men. I managed to escape that night, but I will live with these scars forever."

And Evelyn didn't mean the scars on her arms.

When she was done talking, she noticed tears in Lorenzo's eyes. He cupped the back of her neck and pulled her lips to his. It was the softest kiss Evelyn had ever had.

"I'm so, so sorry. That never should have happened to you…to any of you. I'm just…"

Behind the tears, Evelyn saw rage in Lorenzo's gaze. She reached up to touch his cheek. "It's in the past, Lorenzo."

"I know, but…" He stopped before finishing his thought.

"I just want to make sure no one ever hurts you ever again."
He covered her hand with his.

"You know what the worst part of it is?" she said.

"What?" Lorenzo asked.

"It's like it never happened. No one was ever prosecuted
for the murders or the destruction. The papers reported on
it only briefly, and then nothing. It's like Greenwood never
existed—like *we* never existed."

Chapter Thirty-Four

Lorenzo

Lorenzo continued to run his hand up and down Evelyn's back. Hearing her tell of the destruction of her home, of an entire town full of successful businesses and families, made him want to hurt someone. He wanted to get revenge for all of those people…for Evelyn. He wanted those men to pay with their lives.

Suddenly he understood his father better than he ever had before.

Evelyn got to her feet and held her hand out to Lorenzo. He took her hand and stood up. She led him down the hall to his bedroom. His mind raced. He wanted her. He wanted her so badly. But he couldn't shake the fact that being with him would put her in even more peril.

"Evelyn, I don't know if this is a good idea…"

Evelyn shut the door when they were both inside the room. The dim light from the lamp next to his massive bed glowed gold, casting shadows on the wall. Evelyn walked toward him. Looking at her beautiful eyes, lush lips and glowing skin made him hard. *Oh, God.* He didn't think he could be strong enough to fight his desire for her.

"Lorenzo, don't think. I've been through so much, and I know you have too. Let's just comfort each other. Can we do that?"

Lorenzo nodded and scooped her up. He laid her gently

on her back on his bed. He pulled her shirt over her head and took in her beautiful body. Leaning down, he kissed her neck and caressed her breasts. He pulled her bra from her shoulder and kissed her collarbone. Oh, how he relished her soft skin and the seductive curves of her body. He wanted to pleasure her pain away.

He kissed a path down her stomach to the waistband of her pants. He stood and pulled them off, leaving her pink silk underwear on. He positioned himself between her legs and took one of her feet in his hand. He massaged her delicate foot and kissed a trail from her ankle all the way up her leg, kissing her core through the thin layer of fabric.

Evelyn gasped. "Oh, Lorenzo…"

Her desire fueled his own. His erection pushed painfully against his pants. He still had on his suit from the club. He continued to kiss her through her underwear, savoring her scent and her wetness. He put pressure on the bud that hardened almost immediately as he continued to kiss her in her most sacred place.

Evelyn started to move her hips. Lorenzo pulled her underwear off and tossed them on the floor. He sat back and took in her beautiful body.

"Why do you get to see me, but I don't get to see you?" she said, lust evident in her voice.

Lorenzo stood and took off his suit jacket. He then took off his bow tie, unbuttoned his shirt and slid it off. Evelyn sat up and ran her hands along his chest. She traced the outline of his muscles.

"Let me."

She took his belt off and unbuckled his pants. There was no hesitation in her movements until she pulled his underwear down.

"Oh, my," she said. "It's… Is that going to fit inside of me?" Her gaze met his, full of concern.

"I won't hurt you. I promise."

Lorenzo crawled onto the bed between her legs. He took one of her breasts into his mouth. Her breasts were more than a handful and he loved them. He spent time sucking, tugging, kneading her nipples, before finally moving down her stomach and kissing her mound of hair.

He slid two fingers inside of her as he took her bud into his mouth and sucked hard. Her back arched off the bed and she screamed his name. He laughed, enjoying seeing her overwhelmed with pleasure. He increased the speed of his fingers. She clung tightly to him. Her wetness slicked his skin and he wanted to sheathe himself inside her. His erection throbbed.

But before he would allow himself to experience her, he wanted to make sure she was ready. He refused to hurt her. He thrust his tongue inside of her, lapping up her wetness. She writhed under him. He held her thigh to the bed, so she was still from the waist down. Then he pushed his tongue inside of her, over and over, until he felt thunder rip through her and his mouth was full of her wetness. She was ready.

He pulled his fingers from her and licked them. Then he licked his lips. Holding one of her legs, he pulled protection from his drawer and positioned himself at her entrance.

"Are you sure this is what you want?" he said, gazing into her eyes.

"Yes," she said, and she pulled him to her and kissed him passionately.

He pulled back reluctantly. "It might hurt a little at first, but I promise I will please you."

She nodded and lifted her hips off the bed to encourage him to enter her. And he did. He closed his eyes at the sensation of her clinging to his erection. He worried that he would finish right then and there, just after one thrust inside of her warm, tight cove. He held on to his release with all his might. He'd never felt anything like it.

His heart beat fast in his chest and his senses were consumed by Evelyn. All he could see was her beautiful body, connected to his in the most intimate way. He smelled her sweet scent and tried to hold on so that he could please her the way she deserved.

Her body tensed as he pushed inside of her, over and over, but eventually she relaxed, which allowed him to go deeper. She yelled his name as he let out unintelligible sounds of his own. Her back arched and her hips moved in rhythm with his thrusts. He lost himself in his magical experience with Evelyn, where time no longer existed and all that mattered was the way her body felt as she climaxed repeatedly around his shaft.

Evelyn had fallen asleep in his arms, and before he knew it dreams were taking over for him too.

Lorenzo woke first. Evelyn was wrapped around his body and he held her tightly against his chest. He looked over at the clock. They'd been asleep for several hours.

It had been a long time since Lorenzo had spent the night with a woman, and this was the first time he'd had a woman stay in his bed. Now he didn't know if he could ever let Evelyn go.

Evelyn stirred in his arms. "Good morning," she said.

"Good morning. How do you feel?"

"I'm a little sore, but I feel wonderful."

"Can I see it?" Lorenzo said.

"See what?" Evelyn turned to look up at him.

"Greenwood?"

"There isn't much there. They started rebuilding, but so many of us died that night, and the ones that could leave did. My friend Erin was murdered that night—but her grandmother is still there. Miz Minny was like a grandmother to me too. I've been meaning to go back and check on her, but I've been...afraid."

"I will take you. I won't let anything hurt you."

"I'm not afraid of anything hurting me. I'm afraid of what being back there will do to me. Your offer is sweet, Lorenzo, but I don't know if it's a good idea. How can you leave your club?"

"Jeb will handle things."

Evelyn took a deep breath and sighed. She looked away from Lorenzo. "What about the fundraiser?"

"We'll get it done. I believe that you walked into my club for a reason."

Evelyn turned back to face Lorenzo. "Yes, I did. I wanted to sing."

"No!" Lorenzo laughed. "I mean, I think that there's a reason we met, and it's bigger than you or me."

"Lorenzo, I—"

Lorenzo cut in, "No, Evelyn, I need to say this. There's something about you that makes me want to be a better man, and that's not even the craziest part. I'm starting to believe I might be able to *be* better."

"What makes you think you're not already a good man?" Her brows furrowed with frustration.

"Because I know me."

"I don't think you give yourself enough credit. From what I've seen, you're one of the best men I've met." Evelyn looked away shyly. "I'm sorry for how I reacted to you not wanting things to go too far between us initially. You were right. We shouldn't have gone down that road with each other."

For a moment Lorenzo had thought he could finally move past what had happened to Holly. That he could love Evelyn in the way she deserved. But in the short time he'd known Evelyn, he'd realized how little he knew about falling in love.

He recognized that what he'd had with Holly didn't have anything to do with what he had with Evelyn. He'd been a kid. The man he was now wasn't the same as the boy who had been trying to mimic the actions of his father.

Evelyn stood up. "I should get dressed." She pulled the covers around her and stood up. She picked up her clothes. "May I get cleaned up?"

"Of course. I'll have some of your clothes and toiletries brought up."

Lorenzo pulled on his pants and picked up the phone beside his bed as Evelyn disappeared into the bathroom. Then he got dressed in his other bathroom and started cooking breakfast.

Chapter Thirty-Five

Evelyn

After returning to her apartment, Evelyn had a few hours to rest before she had to get ready for the club. Her head spun with the possibilities for her and Lorenzo. She wanted to believe that there was a chance for them to be something real, but as soon as he wasn't touching her reality hit her. She and Lorenzo lived in two different worlds and nothing would change that.

She didn't go back to Lorenzo's apartment, like she'd thought she would. She needed time to think. He knew her past, but she still didn't know his. And what really kept them apart was the future. There wasn't any future where they could be together safely. Between his family, the KKK and his illegal businesses, Evelyn would be in constant danger.

She pulled a short black flapper dress and a feather and rhinestone turban headpiece from her closet. She pinned her hair, slipped on the dress and put on the headpiece. She chose black gloves with rhinestones. She'd just set them on her dresser when a knock sounded at her door.

She grabbed her gloves. She wasn't expecting anyone, and she approached her door hesitantly. She smiled with relief, put her gloves on the table and opened the door for Lorenzo.

"Hey, sorry to bother you… I'm not really sure why I'm here."

Evelyn laughed. "Don't you think you should have thought about that before you came down?"

"Well, it's obvious how much I enjoy your company. I keep showing up at your door uninvited."

They both laughed.

"Please, come in." Evelyn stepped aside and waved him in. "This is a perfect opportunity for me to learn more about you. I feel like we talk a lot about me, but I don't know very much about you."

Lorenzo

Lorenzo had been expecting this, but it still shook him. How was he going to explain that his first and only girlfriend had been murdered because she was in the wrong place at the wrong time when some goons had come looking for Lorenzo?

He walked over to her window and stared out like the answers might be out there in the darkening sky. "There really isn't much to tell."

"Oh, you're not being fair. I thought we were going to get to know each other."

Lorenzo sighed and sat down in the chair. "Okay, let's see… I grew up in a very protective family. My cousins and I played in the backs of speakeasies. We grew up with guns in our hands, learning to shoot before we got out of training wheels on our bikes. Where I come from, family and respect are the only things that matter. My father's business is very lucrative, but very dangerous. I lost someone when I was younger, and that changed how I thought about the world."

Lorenzo looked out of the window, remembering Holly. She'd been innocent…like Evelyn.

"What happened to your friend? If you don't mind me asking."

Lorenzo's brow creased and he ran his hand through his hair. "That's a story for another time. We better head downstairs now, before Benny sends out a search and rescue party." Lorenzo stood, holding his hand out to Evelyn.

Evelyn took it and said, "I'm sorry if I've upset you."

"You didn't." Lorenzo turned to look at her. "Really. I'm just still not able to talk about what happened. It's hard to put into words what I lost that day."

Evelyn stepped in closer to Lorenzo and put her hand on the side of his cheek. She gazed into his gray-green eyes. "I understand. But I want you to know that when you are ready to talk, I'm here to listen."

Lorenzo leaned in and pressed his lips to hers. The kiss brought him back to the present. He let his lips linger against Evelyn's. She smelled like candy and tasted just as sweet.

His heart beat erratically in his chest. Whenever he was close to this dame he teetered on the line between having a heart attack and playing things cool. Her soft touch had saved him from spiraling into past nightmares.

Leaning his forehead against hers, he rubbed her arms and took her hands in his. He enjoyed seeing all of her. Running his fingers along her scars and kissing them was quickly becoming one of his preferred things to do. She was beautiful. Her scars were beautiful. He wanted all of her.

"I'm glad I got to spend this time with you. Are you ready to head downstairs?" Lorenzo said, pulling away to step back.

Evelyn nodded. Lorenzo took her hand again and led her to the door. She grabbed her gloves from the table by the entryway and slipped them on. He wondered if she would ever feel confident enough to let her scars show, but relished the fact that they shared this secret and that she hadn't tried to put her gloves on in front of him. He felt that in some way that was something significant in what they were becoming to each other.

Lorenzo's head spun at how quickly things had changed between him and Evelyn, but he wasn't complaining.

They rode the elevator downstairs in silence. The operator smiled when he saw Evelyn, and quickly became stoic again when Lorenzo got on the elevator. Lorenzo tried not to be annoyed by that. Everyone seemed to like Evelyn. But what wasn't to like? She was beautiful and smart, talented and humble,

The sounds of music and people laughing and talking filtered out to the hall, where Lorenzo now stood with Evelyn. "Thanks for letting me show up on your doorstep with no real reason," he said. "I hope to do it again soon."

Lorenzo held his breath for Evelyn's response. Being shot down was not something he wanted to happen in front of people, so he'd decided to try and set up their next date before going inside the club. His heart raced as he realized just how much he wanted to see her again, alone, so he could really enjoy her smile and their light-hearted banter.

He had ensured that the women he'd been involved with in the past didn't hang around long, so no attachments could be formed, but with Evelyn he wanted a connection to her. He needed it.

"I'd like that," she said with a bright smile.

Lorenzo leaned down to kiss her gently on the mouth. He played with her plump bottom lip, nibbling it before pulling back from her.

"I need to go to my winery next week—want to come with me?" Lorenzo said.

"Sounds good."

Lorenzo was taken aback at how agreeable Evelyn was being. She'd turned him down so much and even run away from him. He'd been expecting her to decline his invitation…

Chapter Thirty-Six

Evelyn

Evelyn clutched a cup of coffee in one hand and the newspaper in her other. She sat in what had quickly become her favorite chair by the window. She often melted into this high-back green velvet chair after a long night of singing.

She and Lorenzo had managed to get along well all week, and Evelyn felt rested after having had the previous night off. She'd even ventured out to see a bit of the city. Now she sat in her apartment, waiting to go to Lorenzo's distillery and winery.

The fundraiser was to be the next evening, and she was the star of the show. They'd spent the last few days getting things ordered for the big party. They hadn't been alone, and Evelyn was very confused about the disappointment that had settled in her stomach.

She'd opted for a three-quarter-length green dress that clung to her curves. Her pearls hung down low and she fiddled with them as she got up from the chair and paced her apartment, waiting for Lorenzo. This would be the first time it would be just the two of them since the night they'd made love.

Since the night her grand had come to the club, she had tried to insist that Evelyn try spending time with other young men before settling on one, but Evelyn didn't have the time or the desire to spend time with anyone other than Lorenzo.

Evelyn had hired back her grand's nurse, and things had been doing remarkably well. Evelyn had even started singing from a place other than pain and anger. She envisioned her night of passion with Lorenzo while she was on stage, and that had produced a seductive, sultry sound for her new songs that she absolutely loved.

The crowd danced and writhed along with her, and Lorenzo had spent every evening staring at her for nearly the entire set. The only time he wasn't watching her was when he met with Jeb, Dred and Tommy on occasion.

The knock at the door shattered the silence of her morning.

"Hold on. I'll be right there."

She grabbed her gloves and slipped them on. She took her coat from the closet and put her purse on her shoulder. Opening the door, she gasped.

"Hello, gorgeous." Lorenzo stood there with a bouquet of pink roses. "Pink roses symbolize grace, happiness and gentleness. You are the epitome of all that." He handed her the bouquet.

"Thank you, Lorenzo. There you go again. sounding like a salesman."

They both laughed.

Evelyn put down her purse and her coat so she could go get a vase and water. She placed the flowers on the table next to her favorite chair. Lorenzo still stood by the door.

"Do you want to come in for a cup of coffee?"

Evelyn's heart raced. She wanted to be alone with him again. Images of their night together had consumed her over the last week.

"I do want to, but we should really head out if we're going to get back in time to set up for tomorrow night."

Lorenzo wore a three-piece light gray suit with a striped

tie. The way his chest bulged under the rich fabric sent heat to Evelyn's most intimate place. She wanted him to take her on top of her counter right then.

"Of course," Evelyn said, grabbing her coat and purse again.

They walked to the elevator and rode down in silence. Evelyn stared in front of her. When she did risk a look in Lorenzo's direction, he was staring at her with heat in his gray-green eyes.

Jerry stood by Lorenzo's Rolls-Royce with the door open. Evelyn got in first, and Lorenzo climbed in after her. October in Kansas City was cold, and Lorenzo seemed to notice Evelyn shiver. He slid close to her and wrapped his arms around her.

The car was already running, so it was warm, but Evelyn wouldn't turn down a chance to be close to Lorenzo. He slid her gloves down, placing kisses on her scars before pulling the gloves back up. They stared into each other's eyes for a long moment. Then the car pulled away from the club and headed to the road that would take them the twenty miles outside of the city.

Lorenzo had told Evelyn how close to West Eden his distillery and winery was. She'd been amazed at the coincidence. She'd never traveled past the road to West Eden, but she was finally going to get to see what was just beyond her town.

"It's been a busy week," Lorenzo said.

"Yes, it has."

"Are you looking forward to the fundraiser?"

"I am. I think it's amazing what you've done."

"I couldn't have made it happen without you. Thanks again. You have an eye for detail that is simply remarkable."

Evelyn smiled, not sure what to say. She turned her gaze out the window. Sometimes it felt like she and Lorenzo were in an alternative universe. Like when they were together anything was possible. She hated going back to reality, where everything was meant to keep them apart. Perhaps they would find a place where they could be together...

"What's on your mind?" he asked.

"Everything...and nothing," she said, smiling shyly.

"I've wanted to be alone with you every moment of this week," he said.

"You have?"

"Yes, but I'm trying to give you space. I don't want you to feel pressured into anything that you aren't ready for."

Evelyn considered this. Was she ready for a relationship with a man who was known to be lethal? She'd already realized that no matter what Lorenzo's past might have been, the man he was now was good. Everyone had a past.

"I'm going to kiss you," Lorenzo said.

Evelyn nodded.

Lorenzo's mouth was warm against hers. She lost herself in his savory scent and the taste of his sweet breath. They kissed for a long moment. Evelyn wasn't even sure where they were.

"We're here, boss." Jerry shut the car off and got out.

Evelyn looked around, startled. She hadn't even noticed that they'd pulled up outside of a huge brick building in the middle of an open field. There was a fence that surrounded the perimeter.

Jerry opened the door and Lorenzo exited first, holding his hand out to help Evelyn.

"This is amazing..."

Evelyn took in the beauty of the distillery and winery. She hadn't expected it to have huge gardens with flowers of all kinds and trees. She saw rows and rows of grapevines in the distance.

"This is magnificent!"

"It's one of my favorite places to come when I need a

break from the hustle and bustle of the city. Come with me. Let me show you around. I wish it were warmer—we'd have wine and dinner in the vineyard—but I have a surprise inside that might make up for us not being able to."

Lorenzo took her hand and led her up the massive steps to the front door.

Chapter Thirty-Seven

Lorenzo

Lorenzo wanted everything to be perfect. He'd asked Evelyn to have a seat and then he'd gone to get everything ready. This was his chance, even if just for a moment, to be the kind of man Evelyn deserved. He would spoil her with delicatessens, some of the freshest seafood money could buy and the best wine from his winery. He couldn't wait to get their first course out to her.

He'd just finished plating the Waldorf salad when a car door shutting outside drew his attention. Then Dred slipped into the back through the kitchen, where Lorenzo was getting the tray ready to carry out to Evelyn.

"What are you doing here?" Lorenzo tried to assess Dred's mood. It wasn't like her to pop up when he was entertaining someone.

"I'm sorry, but I wanted you to know that everything is set up for our ambush on the KKK. That detective must have run right back to them and told them what you said. I've also come to let you know the Ricci family had something in the works for tonight, but Jeb, your father and I took care of it. You and Evelyn are safe, so have fun, okay?"

She smiled. Something she never did.

Lorenzo hugged her. "Thank you."

He loved how she was always looking out for him, and it seemed that she approved of his pursuit of Evelyn, which meant a lot to him. She was his closest family at the moment, since he was still keeping his distance from the De Lucas, with the exception of the ambush.

She shoved him away. "Now get out there. You shouldn't keep a lady waiting, I hear. Or something like that."

They both laughed and Dred slipped out as Lorenzo grabbed the tray with the salad and the first glasses of wine and carried it out to Evelyn.

"Lorenzo, I hope you didn't go to any trouble." Evelyn's eyes lit up when she saw the first course.

"There isn't any amount of trouble I wouldn't go to for you."

Lorenzo sat. When he looked at Evelyn, one eyebrow was arched.

"Okay, I know. I sound like a salesman again." They both laughed. "I'll try to keep those comments at a minimum, but I make no promises."

They ate in silence for a moment, just enjoying each other's company.

"This wine is delectable. How'd you make it?" Evelyn closed her eyes, seeming to savor the notes of the wine.

"We pick grapes right before they're ripe and press them with citrus, and then we interrupt the fermenting process to allow just a touch of sweetness."

"Wow, it's amazing... Really."

She stared at him for a long moment. Her eyes were so golden and her rose-colored lips begged to be kissed.

"How'd you get into all of this?"

"When word started circulating that alcohol was going to be outlawed, I managed to buy the winery at a knockdown price. My business was doing well, and I didn't want the place to just sit. It was too beautiful. Then I started learning about how to make other kinds of liquor, which led to me getting involved with the distillery and some speakeasies. I fell in love with music all over again. My family had a few bars when I was younger, and I saw how it brought so many different kinds of people together. I wanted to do that too. It just made sense to open Blues Moon."

"Wow, it seems like you've always known what you wanted to do."

"Not always. There was a time when I questioned everything I was and everything I knew."

"Really? Why? You seem so sure of everything now."

"You should know that the only person I've ever been in a serious relationship with was murdered." He looked at Evelyn. "Because of me."

"Oh, my… Lorenzo, I'm so sorry."

"It's something that I still struggle with to this day. Although it was almost ten years ago now. I care so much for you, Evelyn. I never thought I'd feel this way about anyone else. I told myself I didn't deserve to feel this way ever again."

"Ten years ago? You couldn't have been but a teenager when it happened. It couldn't have been your fault, Lorenzo."

"It was. If she hadn't been with me they wouldn't have killed her. The Ricci family did it, as retaliation for what I did."

Evelyn waited. It must be obvious to her that he struggled to share this with her.

"My father wanted me to kill one of the Ricci family's future Dons. He was a kid the same age as me. I went to his house and I was going to do it. My father had told me that the Riccis kidnapped one of my cousins when she was just thirteen years old and tortured her before they killed her. It was just another tragedy in the ongoing war between our families, but when I saw the kid come out of the house I didn't want to kill him. I couldn't. So I shot him to make it seem like I was trying to kill him. I didn't want my father to think I was a coward, and that I didn't take my future as a boss seriously, but I was only seventeen years old. I shot him in the leg."

Tears clouded Lorenzo's eyes. "I've never killed anyone. I didn't think I could until I saw Simmens hurting you. I lost it, and I would have killed him if you hadn't stopped me. That scared me…that I could get that angry, just like my father."

"Oh, Lorenzo."

Evelyn pulled him into an embrace. He breathed heavily against her neck. She held him and ran her hands up and down his back.

"You were just protecting me. And when you shot that kid you were just trying to do what you thought was right. We've all done things in the name of what we believed was right at the time. You can't hold the decisions of your past against who you are today. Eventually you're going to have to allow yourself some happiness."

Lorenzo pulled away. "Being in my life is a risk. It's dangerous for anyone to get close to me. I've distanced myself from the mob, but once you're known in this world there really isn't a way out. I knew that back then, and I still let her fall for me."

"You're easy to fall for," Evelyn said.

"I've never told anyone what really happened that day. I've never admitted that I didn't want to kill him. I think my father knew, though, because I'm an excellent shot. I have been since I was ten years old. If I'd wanted to kill that kid I could have—easily. But my father has never asked me outright about what went wrong and why the kid wasn't dead. It wasn't long after that when my grandfather and father took care of the Ricci bosses. The war went cold, but now the younger Riccis are preparing to retaliate after all these years. And even though I've stepped away from my family, that doesn't matter. The Mafia never forgets."

Lorenzo drank the rest of his wine and poured some

more from the bottle that he'd placed in a cooling bucket next to their table. He took a deep breath and leaned back in his seat.

"Her name was Holly. We were just kids, but we thought we were in love. We'd known each other since we were ten years old. Our fathers were close friends. Her family wasn't involved in the mob, though. They were good people—religious-like, you know?"

Lorenzo blew out a breath.

"We were going to get married that summer. I would be turning eighteen and she had just turned eighteen. We couldn't wait. Our families didn't exactly approve, but they didn't object either. We'd been in each other's lives for so long it just made sense, I guess. Now that I look back, I'm not sure that we were in love as much as we were best friends... One night, after a particularly ugly clash with the Ricci family, Holly and I were walking downtown. We had nowhere to go. We were just walking around and talking. It was warm that fall night, and we wanted to enjoy it before the weather turned, like it does in Kansas City. Anyway, I heard some men walking up behind us, and before I could turn to see what was going on out of nowhere, Dred jumped from a fire escape above where we were standing. She swiped with her leg and one of the men—the man pointing his gun at me—fell backward. Jeb appeared, but the other man shot Holly before Jeb could knock him out. She was shot in the chest. The guy who shot her was so young...like us. Jeb was going to finish him off, but the kid managed to wrestle free and took off running. There were too many people on the street for Jeb to get a clean shot."

Lorenzo took another breath, trying to keep the memories at bay.

"I knelt down next to Holly. She looked up at me with pleading eyes. She couldn't speak because she was bleeding internally. She died right there in my arms."

Lorenzo exhaled when he was done. Had he said too much? He didn't want Evelyn to live with his burdens. But once he'd started, he just hadn't been able to stop. He'd never confided in anyone like this before. Now he was having second thoughts.

"My God. Why were they trying to kill you?"

"For what my father and uncles did…for what my father made me do. That's how it goes, you know? One family kills a member of the other family, and then there's retaliation. It is a never-ending fight."

"And that's why you didn't want to let things go too far with me?" Evelyn said, as if to herself rather than to Lorenzo.

"Yeah." Lorenzo stood to go get the main course. "I'll be right back."

He picked up their plates. He felt a sense of relief. At least now Evelyn would know why she should stay away from him. He wanted to be with her so bad his throat closed at the thought of never being with her again, but it was for her safety, and nothing else mattered.

When he returned, he found her in the small office at the front of the winery, looking out of the window.

"Is everything okay?" he asked.

Evelyn turned to look at him. Her eyes were damp and she swiped at a tear that fell down her cheek. She nodded and walked toward the table. Lorenzo met her halfway and engulfed her in his arms.

"I won't let anything hurt you. You don't have to worry."

She pulled away and looked at him. "I'm not worried about that. I'm worried for you. How will you ever be safe if you stay in this city? In this business? You can't choose your family, Lorenzo. Sometimes you have to live the life you've been given, and that means doing what you have to do to survive."

"I know, and I've tried to distance myself from my family."

"But does the other family care about that? Isn't it all about revenge anyway?"

Lorenzo didn't say anything.

"I don't want anything to happen to you," she said, concern etched in her gorgeous features.

She grabbed handfuls of his suit and pulled him to her. She kissed him in a way that personified everything she'd just said. Her kiss was full of emotions, from fear, to longing, to lust, to something much more.

Lorenzo wrapped her in his arms and caressed her curves. Her body felt so right against his. His arousal was instant. He swooped her up and then knelt down to place her on the carpeted floor of the small office. He was so glad they were alone. Having Jerry return to Blues Moon had been the best idea.

Lorenzo brushed her hair from her face and kissed her again. He slid between her legs and let his arousal push against her through his pants. Her breath hitched.

"Is this okay?" Lorenzo said.

"Yes..." she said on a breath.

Her intoxicating scent and her melodic voice shattered Lorenzo's resolve. He pulled her stockings and panties off and played with her center like he'd done in their first intimate encounter. He didn't want to hurt her, so he took his time getting her ready for him.

She moaned and panted through her orgasms. When she'd had three, Lorenzo entered her, and as their bodies connected he knew it would be the biggest effort of his life to withdraw before he came. He couldn't risk her getting pregnant, even if he knew he wouldn't be able to let her go...

Chapter Thirty-Eight

Lorenzo

Lorenzo knocked on Evelyn's door. He was just about five minutes early, but he couldn't wait any longer. He was both nervous and excited to take Evelyn to the fundraiser. He wanted to be seen with her. He wanted people to know that she was his to protect and that messing with her would most assuredly result in them coming to harm. He had given his father's proposition some thought, but he refused to use Evelyn in any way. Her career was hers. He would only help her if she asked him to.

Knocking again, Lorenzo felt fear rising in his chest.

When Evelyn finally opened the door he saw she'd donned a blue dress that clung to her curves like a second skin. The feathers on it gave her an otherworldly appearance. She'd pinned her hair so that it fell into curls over her right shoulder. That long, thick black hair called to Lorenzo. He wanted to run his fingers through it. Grab a handful of it and secure her mouth to his.

He stood enthralled by her beauty. "You look stunning." Lorenzo couldn't take his eyes off of her.

"Thank you," she said, avoiding his gaze.

"Are you ready to go? We'll need to go out the back entrance so we can enter the fundraiser through the front. There will be reporters outside."

Evelyn nodded. She pulled on navy silk gloves that went

all the way to her elbows and a brown fur cape. Her earrings hung from her delicate ears like small chandeliers. She couldn't have been more beautiful.

Lorenzo smoothed his classic gray three-piece suit. He'd chosen navy shoes and a navy and gray bowtie. He'd had Jeb inform some reporters about the fundraiser and tell them that he'd be arriving with his new singer and possible love interest. He told himself the "love interest" part was just to protect her.

"After you," she said, motioning toward the door.

Lorenzo stood in the hall while Evelyn turned out the lights and grabbed her pocketbook from the table. It was small and navy. It matched her dress perfectly. He tried to focus on anything other than Evelyn's plunging neckline and the curve of her breasts as she walked toward him.

His mouth watered at the thought of kissing her soft skin. He swallowed and took a deep breath. He offered Evelyn his arm as they approached the elevator. The attendant waited for them to get on before closing the gate and taking them down to the first floor.

Walking into the foyer of the club, Lorenzo directed Evelyn to the back door that led to the street. There was a red carpet leading around the building to the front of the club, where they would enter, in front of all the reporters.

Lorenzo walked uncomfortably as his pants had tightened due to his growing desire for her. Her eyes were traveling down the length of his body. He worried that she could tell he was aroused. He needed to divert his attention—and hers.

"Have you been to many fundraisers?"

Evelyn's gaze fell on Lorenzo's face once again. Her brow creased. "Just one in Greenwood. My aunt used to sing at a lot of events like this. I wasn't really old enough to go, but she let me come with her once."

"That must have been exciting."

Evelyn smiled, then looked at the growing crowd of patrons waiting to get into Blues Moon, and the roped-off area where the reporters stood, cameras flashing. They walked toward the entrance so the reporters could see them entering Blues Moon.

"Why are there so many reporters? I thought it would just be a few."

The fear in Evelyn's voice made Lorenzo's heart sink.

"Nothing to worry about. They're always looking for a story. There are usually famous people at these events."

Evelyn looked at Lorenzo with a grief-stricken expression. But he couldn't be prouder to have her on his arm. The stars in the sky shone down on her like a spotlight. The city bustled with patrons flitting around, waiting to be let into the fundraiser.

"Mr. De Luca, can we talk to you? Can we meet your date?"

Lorenzo continued to walk, ignoring the prying questions of the reporters who lined the path to the door. A few of Lorenzo's security guards came out to ensure the reporters stayed back and Lorenzo and Evelyn could enter Blues Moon easily.

"Mr. De Luca, is it true that you're involved with your new lead singer? Is this her?"

Evelyn looked at Lorenzo with wide eyes.

He reached out and took her hand in his. "You don't have anything to be worried about while you're with me."

Then, out of the corner of his eye, Lorenzo saw something go up in flames. He turned to see a large cross ablaze. A signature KKK move. Smoke filled the air instantly. The reporters turned to see what was going on. Their cameras flashed and Lorenzo took that moment to get Evelyn inside of the club. He had to get her away from this chaos.

Sam opened the front door of Blues Moon. "Mr. De Luca and Miss Laroque, are you okay?"

"Yes, Sam."

Lorenzo offered Evelyn his hand and helped her climb the stairs. The air had turned cool. He was glad Evelyn had on a cape, which made her look regal.

Chapter Thirty-Nine

Evelyn

The clicking of cameras and the blinding flashes that had followed made Evelyn's head spin. She was thankful for Lorenzo's arm. She clung to him like her life depended on it. She had anticipated strange looks from the other guests. She had mentally prepared herself for glares from women and men of all races. But she hadn't planned for the reporters and the burning cross that stood at least six feet high.

Her heart threatened to beat right out of her chest as Lorenzo wrapped his strong arm around her, pulling her into him as she shook.

Just inside the club, Lorenzo turned to her with his hands on her shoulders. "Are you okay?"

"I'm…f-fine," Evelyn stammered. She tried to smile, but her legs were weak, and she feared she would pass out at any moment.

Lorenzo, seeming to realize she was unsteady on her feet, wrapped his arm around her again and directed her to a seat at the bar. "Tommy, get her some water, please."

Tommy obliged, handing Lorenzo a glass.

"Here, take a sip." He turned to Tommy. "Stay with her. Keep her safe. I'll be right back."

Lorenzo sprinted out the door toward danger.

Evelyn couldn't breathe while he was gone. Every second felt like an eternity without him, not knowing if he was okay…

When he finally ducked back through the door, Evelyn let out a labored breath of relief.

He stood in front of her with his hands resting on her thighs. "We can leave. You don't have to stay after all of this."

"If we leave, then they win. They're trying to scare me. I won't run." She shook her head. "No, no. I want to stay. I want to sing—show them that a little fire doesn't scare a survivor of Greenwood. You said a lot of these people have come just to see me. We can't disappoint them."

The club gleamed, with newly installed white marble floors, crystal chandeliers hanging low from the ceiling and beautiful black poker tables. The grandeur of the club was not lost on Evelyn, even though she was struggling to keep her breathing steady.

She took deep breaths as Lorenzo leaned in. He took her hands in his. "Look at me, Evelyn. It's okay. You're okay."

He cupped the back of her neck. He pulled her lips to his and kissed her gently. The warmth and sweet taste of his mouth helped to calm her pounding heart. She lost herself in the kiss as Lorenzo's tongue entered her mouth. She forgot where she was for a moment and grabbed a handful of his suit jacket, anchoring him to her.

"Boss, you might want to look up," Tommy said.

Evelyn felt Lorenzo pull away from her reluctantly. A look passed over his face.

"This must be Evelyn."

The man who could only be Lorenzo's father didn't smile at her.

"Nice to meet you, Mr. De Luca."

Evelyn stood on wobbly legs to shake his hand. She tugged at her gloves to make sure they completely covered her scars. She still couldn't believe that Lorenzo had seen them and simply acted like they were a beautiful secret she was keeping from everyone.

"Lorenzo, we need to talk." Lorenzo's father didn't acknowledge Evelyn again as he focused on his son.

"What are you doing here?" Lorenzo said.

"I'm here to congratulate you, of course." Lorenzo's father placed a hand on Lorenzo's cheek.

"Please, come this way," a waitress said. "Your table is ready."

"I'll only join you for a few moments, son."

Lorenzo's father smiled, showing his bright white teeth. Mr. De Luca looked like an older, plumper version of Lorenzo. They had the same perfect hair, sculpted face and long dark lashes. But Lorenzo's eyes were lighter than his father's, and Lorenzo was all muscle where his father was rounder from living an opulent lifestyle.

Walking through the club, Evelyn tried to ignore the stares. She tried to ignore how Lorenzo's father had dismissed her. She stood tall and held her chin high. She gripped Lorenzo's arm tight.

He looked down at her with an arch in his brow. "Are you okay?"

Evelyn loved when he asked her that. She nodded in response, but she really wasn't okay. She wanted to get out of there and get back to the safety of her apartment, where she and Lorenzo could be alone and away from the prying eyes of strangers.

The chandeliers blinded Evelyn. They were like white snow on a sunny day. Evelyn rubbed her forehead with the back of her glove, feeling a little faint. She was thankful to get to the small table with two chairs right in front of where the band was playing.

"I'll grab another chair."

The waitress returned shortly, and the three of them sat down.

The other tables were all full and there were patrons standing around the dance floor, listening to the music and watching Lorenzo and Evelyn.

Benny was playing and she couldn't wait to join him—if for no other reason than to get away from Lorenzo's father. The music was upbeat, but Evelyn felt an instant calm when she sat down and focused on the rhythm. She found herself tapping her foot.

"So, son, you weren't going to invite your own father to the biggest event in the city?"

"I didn't know you'd be interested."

"Well, I won't be staying long. But I will always be interested in you and your well-being. Besides, I love a good party. I've come to tell you that I believe you should consider rejoining the family. Can't you see how much your family has missed you? I've heard some upsetting things have happened and more are in the works. Nothing will prevent me from protecting my son. Not even his own stubbornness."

Lorenzo squeezed Evelyn's hand under the table. "I appreciate the offer, Father."

And, truth be told, after the burning cross Evelyn was worried that the KKK might feel emboldened and make a move.

Mr. De Luca shook his head. "You are definitely stubborn, but you should know that sometimes our own vices are what lead to those we care about dying."

Lorenzo's father looked at Evelyn with growing disgust in his eyes.

"Well, I guess I'll be going." He stood. "Think seriously about the choices you're making, son."

Lorenzo's father's eyes roamed over Evelyn once more before he left, but Evelyn was determined not to let the KKK or Lorenzo's father ruin this night Lorenzo had worked so hard to put together. She would have a great time and show everyone that she was a lot stronger than anyone gave her credit for.

It took a while, but eventually Evelyn started enjoying the party. She felt so regal, being the star of the show and being with the owner of the club. This was more than she could have hoped for when she'd set out for Kansas City.

Evelyn continued to listen to the music, swaying with the rhythm.

"I'm glad you're starting to enjoy yourself," Lorenzo said after sitting silently for several minutes. "I'm sorry about my father."

"It's okay. He doesn't approve of me. I'm not surprised. But I am enjoying myself. I hope you are too."

She just wanted to listen to the music and be with Lorenzo as the smell of expensive perfumes, liquor and meat filled the air.

When it was time for her to perform, she didn't hesitate. She smiled at Lorenzo and left him at the table. She took her place center stage to a standing ovation and cheers from the large crowd. Blues Moon was always packed, but this was an even larger crowd. They hardly had room to move.

The notes of her latest original song coasted on the air, parting the silence like a sharp knife.

Once she started singing, the crowd stood frozen.

She closed her eyes and let all the built-up emotion of losing her family, her guilt at falling in love with a White man, and the overwhelming pleasure he'd given her when they'd made love spill from her lips.

Evelyn sang for an hour as people filtered in and out of the fundraiser. She couldn't imagine how much money had been raised. When her set was over, she returned to the table, where Lorenzo greeted her by engulfing her in his arms. She inhaled his savory sweet scent. He looked down at her and pressed his lips to hers. Cameras flashed. She didn't care.

After their kiss, he pulled her down into the seat with him. The waitress brought over two full glasses of brown liquor. The sweet, strong smell took Evelyn's breath away.

"You don't have to drink that," Lorenzo said.

"I know, but I don't want to be rude."

"I don't want you to get sick."

"I won't." Evelyn picked up the glass with her free hand and took a large sip.

"Be careful. Tommy's special drinks can be tricky. It tastes sweet, but it will knock you out."

Evelyn smiled. The brown liquid blazed a trail down her throat straight to her chest. The room was suddenly warm, like someone had turned up the heat. Evelyn unhooked her fur cape.

A waiter was there instantly, to take it from her. "May I take your gloves, miss?"

The young man couldn't be much older than Evelyn.

"No, thank you." Evelyn pulled them up farther on her arms, as if to assure him that she wanted to keep them on.

The lights on stage where the band played were dimmer. Evelyn started to relax a little.

"What do you think of the transformation of the club?" Lorenzo asked.

"This is grand. It reminds me of the hotel in Greenwood, but this is bigger," Evelyn said.

Seeming to notice her anxiety, Lorenzo asked, "Do you want to leave?"

"I'm fine."

She wasn't fine. She was scared to death of what the KKK was planning and she was faltering under the scrutiny of all the people at the fundraiser. It seemed like all eyes were on her and Lorenzo.

"I'm going to take you back to your apartment," he said.

"No, really. I want to stay."

Lorenzo and Evelyn ate sauteed vegetables and cured meats that Cook sent to their table. After they were finished, Evelyn just wanted to lie down. The events of the night had finally hit her. Her eyes grew heavier with each passing second.

"I can take you to your apartment now. I'll come back in the morning and check on you. The fundraiser is nearly over now anyway. And, thanks to you, it was an amazing success. I'm not sure of the exact numbers, but I think we will surely be able to renovate a couple of buildings and devote them to helping families in need."

Evelyn smiled and nodded.

Lorenzo helped her to her feet and motioned for the waiter to bring her cape.

While they waited at the elevator, an older gentleman walked up.

"Good evening," Lorenzo said.

"It looks like it's going to be good for you." The man smiled slyly. "When you're done with her, you think I can have her next? How much does she go for?"

"Excuse me? I beg your pardon?" It took Evelyn a moment to register what the man was implying. The events of the evening had her reflexes completely messed up.

Lorenzo moved Evelyn behind him. "If you say one more word that might suggest that you are disrespecting this beautiful woman, it will be the last word you say."

The man held both hands up. "Excuse me—I thought…"

"I know what you thought, and if you think it again I'll smash your face."

"Lorenzo, it's okay." Evelyn took Lorenzo's arm to keep him from pummeling the man. She turned her ire on the man. "If he says anything else to dishonor me, I'll punch him myself."

That made Lorenzo laugh. Evelyn was relieved. She

didn't want Lorenzo to get into a fight because of her—not tonight. She had other things in mind for his hands.

The stranger turned and walked away.

The elevator doors opened and the operator asked, "Did you have a nice time at the fundraiser, Mr. De Luca? Miss Laroque?"

"Yes, we did," Lorenzo said as he guided Evelyn onto the elevator.

When the gate opened to the sixth floor, Evelyn held on to Lorenzo. The crystal sconces that lined the walls next to each door glittered like ice, causing her to close her eyes.

Lorenzo opened her door for her. He took Evelyn's hand and led her down the hall to her bedroom. His touch sent a shiver up her spine. She took a deep breath, taking in the scent of him.

"Do you need anything before I go?" Lorenzo turned to face her.

Evelyn fell silent. She wasn't sure what she wanted to say. She stared into his gray-green eyes of steel and reached up to kiss him. The kiss was hesitant. Lorenzo was holding back.

"Stay with me," Evelyn said against his lips.

He placed his hands on her shoulders and took a step back from her. "Evelyn, you've had a traumatic night. I don't want you to make a choice you will regret."

"I won't regret being with you. I don't want to be alone after everything that's happened."

Chapter Forty

Lorenzo

Lorenzo stared down into Evelyn's golden eyes. Her full pink lips called to him. His mouth watered at the idea of having her tonight, but he cared too much for her to let her make a decision she might regret later. It would kill him if she regretted being intimate with him again. He had to know she was sure.

The floral smell in her bedroom made Lorenzo's head spin a little. He took a deep breath, trying to muster the courage to do the right thing, the noble thing.

"I know what I want, Lorenzo. I've always been very decisive. And right now what I want is you. After what we accomplished tonight I can't imagine anything I want more than to be with you right now."

Evelyn let her cape drop to the floor. She stepped out of her heels and closed the distance between them. Her hands were in his hair and her lips pressed firmly against his before he could think what to do or say.

Their tongues intertwined and Lorenzo caressed her round bottom. His desire throbbed painfully in his pants. But this was not why he'd brought her to her apartment.

He pulled away from her again.

He didn't want to leave her. But he didn't feel right about going back to the fundraiser without her. He would spend the night on the couch, watching her to make sure she was okay.

"I can stay with you," Lorenzo said. "Let me make a call." He walked over to the gold and white phone. "Tell Jeb to handle things for me."

After Lorenzo had hung up the phone, he went to the radio and turned it on.

"Dance with me?" He took Evelyn's hand and pulled her to her feet.

She fit so perfectly in his arms. Her soft skin had him transfixed. He wanted to hold her forever. He knew that if he rejected her he would push her away, so he needed to figure out a way to show her how much he wanted her without going all the way.

He wanted a future with her, not one night.

The realization that she'd gotten into his heart took his breath away. He tried to take slow, steady breaths as they danced. Her soft hair brushed against his chin as she nestled into his neck.

"You're such a mystery, Mr. De Luca."

Lorenzo laughed. "Please don't call me that. That's my father's name."

Evelyn laughed. "Your father is intense."

"Your grandmother is intense."

Evelyn laughed again. "Yes, she is."

The musical sound of her laughter filled the air and made Lorenzo smile. "Aren't you worried about what people will say if we both don't return to the fundraiser?" he asked.

Evelyn held on to Lorenzo tighter. "For the first time in my life, I don't care what people are going to say about my choices."

"I don't want anyone to get the wrong idea," he said. "You're important to me. This…whatever this is between us…is important to me."

"Then we have to be strong. Choosing each other is not going to be the easy choice."

Evelyn was wise beyond her years. And she'd waltzed into Lorenzo's life and completely changed everything.

About an hour later, a knock on the door stirred Lorenzo and Evelyn from their reverie. They'd been dancing and talking. When Lorenzo opened the door, Jerry stood there with two trays of dessert—one for Lorenzo and the other for Evelyn.

"Cook asked me to bring this up. I hope I've gotten everything you will need, sir."

"I'm sure you did, Jerry. Thank you for your help."

Lorenzo closed the door, ignoring Jerry's arched brow. He would worry about explaining spending the night with Evelyn in the morning, when he was sure Dred, Jeb and Tommy would have lots of questions about how he'd spent the rest of his evening.

"Here you go." Lorenzo walked back into the room and placed Evelyn's tray on the table.

Evelyn took the lid off. "Oh, Lorenzo, you shouldn't have." She took her finger and dipped it into the chocolate mousse.

"I had this made just for you. I didn't want you to miss out on it."

Evelyn walked over to Lorenzo and wrapped her arms around his neck. "Thank you, so much. This night has been wonderful."

"Even though you drank strong liquor and a man thought you were a night worker?" Lorenzo said with amusement in his voice.

"Yes."

Evelyn reached up and kissed Lorenzo, softly at first. Lorenzo picked her up in his arms, careful not to break their kiss, walking to her room. He laid her on the bed. He took off her gloves and kissed each of her hands. He slowly unpinned her hair and ran his fingers through it.

Evelyn pushed Lorenzo's jacket from his shoulders. He

took it off and let it fall to the floor. She unbuttoned his shirt, sliding it down his arms. It fell on top of his jacket. Lorenzo leaned in and kissed Evelyn's chin, then her slender neck, before making his way to her collarbone.

"Evelyn," he said against her skin. "I don't know if I can be this close to you and not be with you."

"Then be with me," she said as she breathed out.

Low moans escaped her mouth as Lorenzo kissed her delicate skin and he decided, in that moment, that being with her was the only thing that mattered.

He would do what he had to do to keep her safe. If that meant involving his family to make sure Evelyn was safe from the KKK, then that was what he would do.

Chapter Forty-One

Evelyn

Evelyn lay with her back against Lorenzo's chest. He'd taken her dress off and disrobed himself. He was warm... her body fit with his so perfectly.

He kissed her shoulder. "What are you thinking about?"

"You," Evelyn said sleepily.

"What about me?" He held her tighter.

"How wonderful you've been to me. You've helped me make my dream of being a professional singer come true. You've shown me that I can trust again. You're everything I thought didn't exist for me anymore."

"You're more than I deserve, Evelyn, but I promise to work hard to be worthy of you."

"There is something I want you to do for me," Evelyn said.

"Anything." Lorenzo kissed her shoulder again.

"I want you to stop being so hard on yourself. I want you to stop thinking I'm too good for you. We are right for each other and our pasts don't matter. All that matters is what is ahead for us."

"Okay."

Being held by Lorenzo in the soft linen of the bed lured Evelyn into a deep sleep...

Chapter Forty-Two

Lorenzo

The light cascaded into the room, lighting the chandelier above the bed as if it were on fire. Lorenzo rubbed his eyes. He hadn't felt happiness like this in so many years. He had to hold Evelyn tight just to make sure she was real.

Her hair was splayed across the pillow and over his chest. She had so much hair… Lorenzo just wanted to run his fingers through it all day. He kissed her neck and shoulders until she started to stir. They'd slept for several hours since their intimate encounter.

"Good morning." Evelyn turned on her back, smiling.

Lorenzo got up on his elbow and said, "Good morning to you too." He moved some hair out of her face.

"I guess we have to go back to reality now." Evelyn's long lashes brushed against her cheeks.

"I guess so. Are you ready to go back?"

"No, I'd rather stay here with you."

She pulled him to her and kissed him. He started to get excited again.

The knock at the door alarmed them both.

Lorenzo rolled his eyes. Why couldn't they just be left alone?

"Who is it?" Lorenzo called out.

The knock sounded again.

Lorenzo got out of the bed and Evelyn pulled the covers up around her. Lorenzo put on his pants and shirt. He walked to the door.

Opening the door, he sighed. "Mother, what are you doing here? How'd you know where to find me?"

"Son, you are one of the most important people in the world to me. I will always know how to find you."

She walked past Lorenzo into Evelyn's apartment.

Evelyn came in, She had quickly pinned her hair up and away from her face. She looked amazing in a pink lounge outfit.

Evelyn's eyebrows arched and her lips pursed. "Good morning, Mrs. De Luca. It is nice to meet you."

Lorenzo ran his hands through his hair, frustrated that his mother and his father had shown up unannounced. He loved his mother dearly, but he needed this time to be with Evelyn alone.

Evelyn's phone rang and Lorenzo answered. "Hello."

"Where the hell have you been?" Dred's anger exploded through the phone.

"Where did you look? What do you need?"

"We need you here—now. Unless you no longer care that the KKK is on the fence about whether to trust you or kill you. The cross-burning last night was their final warning."

"Of course I care, but I needed one night away. I'm coming down now. Meet me in my office in an hour." Lorenzo hung up. Then he called Cook and ordered food for Evelyn.

"Lorenzo, can we talk?" his mother said.

Evelyn said, "I'm going to go get dressed. Take all the time you need." She left Lorenzo alone with his mother.

"Have a seat, Mamma."

Lorenzo sat next to his mother on the sofa.

"I came to tell you that I think you should take Evelyn and leave the city. Your father is on a rampage against the Ricci family again, after hearing what almost happened the other night. Now the KKK are ramping themselves up to come against you too, if you don't follow through and join them. I worry for you. I worry for Evelyn."

"Thank you, Mamma. Evelyn's safety is the only thing that matters. And I have a plan. I'm going to call Father later, to let him know how we're going to handle this. Now, you have to go. I'll call you later."

Lorenzo ushered his mother to the door, kissing her on both cheeks before she left.

When Evelyn had finished in the bathroom and opened the door, the smell of lavender and fresh laundry wafted through the air. Evelyn's hair was now pinned into loose waves that fell to her shoulders, and her camel sweater and pants looked elegant on her. Her cheeks had the slightest rose-colored tint to match her full lips. Her lashes looked as long and curly as ever.

Lorenzo couldn't believe how gorgeous this dame was. She had a glow about her…like she was always bathed in sunlight.

"Something wrong?" Her brows creased.

"No, I'm sorry. You're just…beautiful. And I can't believe I got to wake up next to you this morning." The words fell from Lorenzo's lips before he could think better of them. He shouldn't show all his cards, or she'd have him wrapped around her finger.

"Thank you."

Lorenzo picked up the pants and dress shirt that had Jerry delivered while Evelyn got dressed. He had carefully folded Lorenzo's clothes, so they wouldn't be wrinkled.

"I'll be right back," Lorenzo said, and walked into the bathroom. He wanted to kiss Evelyn, but feared he wouldn't be able to stop.

Their food arrived while Lorenzo was showering. When he opened the door to the bathroom, the smell of bacon hit him like the most delicious pile of bricks.

"You clean up nicely yourself, Mr. De Luca. I mean, Lorenzo." Evelyn's smile lit the room.

"Thank you." Lorenzo walked over to the table by the window, where Evelyn sat, and picked up a piece of bacon. "About last night, Evelyn... You aren't having regrets now that the sun is shining, are you?"

"No—are you?"

Lorenzo knelt in front of her and took her gloved hands in his. "No, last night was amazing. The best nights of my life have been with you. I don't want this to end, but..."

"But what?" Evelyn said.

Chapter Forty-Three

Evelyn

After several more seconds of silence, Lorenzo said, "I want to be with you, Evelyn, but I think it would be too dangerous for us to be together. I'm not good for you—not like that. You'll get hurt being around me, and now that your singing career is taking off maybe you should consider leaving Blues Moon."

Evelyn wasn't sure what she'd expected Lorenzo to say, wanted him to say, but that was not it.

"Are you ill? I hardly call being asked to sing at one baseball game my career taking off. Blues Moon is what's made this possible. If you ask me to leave, I'll have to start completely over."

"I'll give you a great reference. I know other speakeasy owners. There's a club on the other side of West Eden in Colorado. I think you would like it. The owner and I went to school together. He's a good guy."

"It sounds like you've been thinking about this for a while."

Evelyn feared the worst—that all her thoughts about him using her to live out a fantasy of being with a Black woman were true. That she'd managed to let another White man steal something from her.

The pain of Greenwood rushed forward like it never had before.

"No, I just think you getting as far away from me as you can would be best."

Lorenzo was clasping his hands in his lap so hard, his veins showed through his light skin. Evelyn could tell he was hiding something.

"Lorenzo, you can't do this to me again." Tears clouded Evelyn's vision.

"I'm just trying to…to do what's right."

"What's right? You make love to me and then you send me away? You can't think that's right."

Lorenzo didn't respond. He swallowed hard and stared straight ahead.

A sob escaped Evelyn's throat. She covered her face with her hands. He'd done exactly what she'd feared. He'd played her…used her. Her grand was right. Evelyn was nothing more than an exotic fantasy for Lorenzo. He'd got what he wanted and now he was disposing of her, hiding his little secret.

"How could you?" she said, barely above a whisper.

Chapter Forty-Four

Lorenzo

The words burned like acid in Lorenzo's throat. He didn't want to tell Evelyn to leave, but he loved her too much to let her get hurt. He couldn't be honest with her about the KKK because he knew she would stay. She was stubborn, and fearless, and if she knew what was really going on she would insist on staying by his side. That simple fact made Lorenzo love her even more.

He was torn up inside, listening to her cry and being the reason for her tears. He'd hurt her so much. He should have exhibited more self-control with her. He shouldn't have allowed himself to believe for a moment that he could be with her. He'd been selfish, and now she was hurting because of his inability to stay away from her.

He stood just as the sun shone brightly through the windows of her apartment. It was the perfect metaphor for their relationship. It had shone so brightly, if only for a moment in time, and now it would fall behind the clouds of time… the inevitable fate of their burning romance.

Lorenzo walked toward the door. "I want you to know that I care about you, and I just want you to be happy. I think it would be best for you to visit the club in Colorado as soon as possible. I know my friend will hire you on the spot."

Evelyn stared at Lorenzo in a way that made his heart

stop. Anger shadowed her features, but something else was there…the pain that she always carried with her. Lorenzo hadn't seen it in a while, but it was back in the downcast shadows of her eyes and the dimming of her gold irises.

"I'll figure out where to go. I just need a few days, and then I'll be gone forever. You won't have to worry about me any longer."

She tried to move past him. Lorenzo grabbed her arm, barely holding on to his resolve to go through with this. It was killing him. A piece of his heart was being ripped from his chest with each word he said to push her away. If he hadn't worked so hard for so many years to use restraint where his emotions were concerned, he would have broken down right in front of her.

But he fought against the burning sensation behind his eyes. He swallowed the desire to ask her to stay. Because she was more important to him than anything ever had been.

She turned her fiery gaze on him and he let her go immediately. "Don't touch me. Never touch me again."

She ran to her bedroom and slammed the door behind her.

Lorenzo let himself out.

Lorenzo hoped Evelyn would leave the city, as he had advised her to do. There weren't any safe clubs for her in this city. She'd be in danger in Kansas City no matter what. She had to leave. He would have a train ticket to Colorado purchased this morning…

Rummaging through the drawers in his office, Lorenzo chucked a pen across the room in frustration.

"Ouch, that hurt," Jeb said, walking into the room.

Lorenzo looked up. "Sorry, I'm just…"

"Upset again about Evelyn?" Jeb said. His large figure filled the room.

Lorenzo sat at his desk. "Yes. I just don't know what to do about her. I feel like she's the one I'm meant to be with—like she walked into Blues Moon because of fate. But how ridiculous does that sound?"

"Very ridiculous." Jeb smiled.

"Shut up, man. I'm just saying... I want to be with her so badly, but anyone being with me is like a death sentence."

"When are you going to let what happened to Holly go? You can't keep dragging her ghost around with you. It wasn't your fault."

"Of course it was my fault!" Lorenzo erupted, throwing his hands up. He took a deep breath and looked at his friend. Calmly this time, he said, "It *was* my fault. If she hadn't been in love with me she wouldn't have been a target for the Ricci family's retaliation. If Evelyn hadn't been in my club, she wouldn't have been almost killed."

"Lorenzo," Jeb said, putting his hands on Lorenzo's desk. "Your father has made a lot of enemies. Those enemies are after you not because of you, but because of your family. You are as much a victim as Holly was. You have to forgive yourself. Because that means you can start to accept the family you were born into and make choices that are wholly yours. You can't predict the future. Yes, you have some enemies now, but you also have the means to protect anyone you care about. And you have to give Evelyn some credit. I don't know her well, but being a Black woman in this world...she's a survivor already. Let her show you who she is. Then decide what to do."

Lorenzo took a deep breath. It was probably too late for him to change his mind. Evelyn was beyond furious with him—as she should be. He'd made love to her, knowing he was her first, then pushed her away and fired her.

Lorenzo shook his head. He'd dug a hole. Now he had no way to get out of it.

"I don't want to add to everything she already has to

deal with. I don't want to be another burden for her to carry," he said.

"You should let her decide that. Taking a woman's choices away is not the way to show her you care for her."

Lorenzo got up and started to pace.

"This is what we're going to do. The new governor is on board with cleaning up the city. He plans to be there at the ambush, to let the members of the KKK who hold positions with the city know that they will be fired immediately if they continue to organize. The KKK is planning to leave the Avalon music club on the other side of town and come here to try and intimidate me again. Tommy just confirmed this, like I hoped. So the ambush is set up. Now we have to make sure they understand the choice they have to make. They can continue with this racist crap or they can live their lives. Seems like an easy choice to me. That should take care of all the issues we're having with the liquor as well. They'll be behind bars if they make the wrong choice."

Jeb nodded.

"Now I need you to go to the winery and the distillery and see how much we need to make to build our supplies back up. You need to keep on your guard. Dred is making sure Tommy doesn't get in too deep with the Klan. I'll be here to protect the club."

"I got it." Jeb walked to the door. "Stay safe."

"You too."

Chapter Forty-Five

Evelyn

Evelyn pulled her cloche hat down over her ears. She'd only walked about twenty minutes to get to the Avalon. The speakeasy in the east end of the city was much smaller than Blues Moon, but Evelyn wanted to stay in the city.

Carmichael had told her about this place. He'd sold some vegetables to the Avalon cook, who had mentioned he'd heard about Evelyn. The cook had told Carmichael that the owner of the club would hire Evelyn for a good salary as she would be able to build up his clientele.

The club was segregated, though, so Evelyn planned to ask about that during her meeting with the owner.

The Avalon was red on the outside, like a barn in the middle of the city. Evelyn pulled her coat closed as the bitter wind hit her. A chill ran down her spine as she stepped over the threshold into the club. She'd thought the red on the outside of the building was bad. Everything was red on the inside too—the floor, walls, tables. The color reminded her of blood, which sent another chill up her spine that settled into a knot in her neck.

"Can I help you?"

There was no warmth or kindness in the woman's voice as she approached Evelyn from behind the bar.

"Hello, yes. I'm Evelyn Laroque. I'm here to meet with Mr. Martin about the singing job."

"Oh, so *you're* who everyone is fussing about. I didn't know you were one of those coloreds."

The big woman shook her head. Her greasy hair clung to her head, so even the movement didn't disturb the matted-down mess.

"I'm sorry."

"Follow me."

The woman smacked her lips over whatever was in her mouth and brushed past Evelyn, walking toward the back of the club.

Evelyn took a deep breath and followed. If this wasn't motivation for her to save up enough money to start her own club, she didn't know what would be.

As much as she was grateful to Lorenzo, for giving her a chance and helping her become known as a singer, she now hated him. For forcing her to find work in another club where she wouldn't be treated kindly because of the color of her skin. She hated him for taking something from her and then throwing her away. He'd even tried to refuse her on multiple occasions, but she'd kept pushing. She'd been so stupid.

Mr. Martin was a heavyset short man with a cigar hanging from his mouth. "You must be the singer everybody keeps talking about. You're a looker—especially for a colored girl."

Evelyn lost her words. She'd been going to say *Nice to meet you*, or some other pleasantry, but nothing came out.

"Well, you do talk, don't you?"

Snapping out of her outrage, she held a gloved hand out to the man. She'd opted for short pale pink gloves that matched her pale pink knee-length dress. "Yes, I'm Evelyn. It is...um...nice to meet you. Thank you for seeing me on such short notice."

"I'm a businessman—and I hear you're good for business."

His hand tightened around hers and the look in his eyes sent chills down Evelyn's spine. She took her hand from his grasp. "I'm looking for a lead singing position for three nights a week. I only wish to work part time. Would that work for you?"

"You need to learn when to talk and when to be quiet. I'll give you your schedule, and you'll either work it or be fired. That's how I run things around here. Now, does that work for *you*?"

His beady eyes slid over Evelyn, making her skin tingle as if at tiny little spider legs.

"Um…sure."

"Sure?"

"Yes, that should be fine." *For now*, she thought.

Every second she was in Mr. Martin's presence, she hated Lorenzo a little more.

"You'll start tonight. Be back here by eight and wear something more revealing."

"Yes, I have show dresses that are very different from what I have on."

"Good, I don't need you looking like a church lady. We're in the business of selling. Remember that."

Mr. Martin turned his back on Evelyn.

"Mr. Martin, there's just one more thing."

Mr. Martin turned to face her. The ash on his cigar fell to the ground.

"What?"

"This club is segregated, and I was hoping if you hired me, you would consider desegregating it. I don't feel right singing in a club that doesn't serve everyone."

"I'm not paying you to feel. All you need to do is show up and sing. Don't worry about who you're singing for. Let me handle that."

He walked away.

"I think it's time for you to leave—and when you come back tonight, come through the back door."

It was the woman from earlier. She must have been watching the entire horrifying encounter.

Evelyn's eyes burned from the smoke, and tears that were starting to form. She walked quickly out of the club and back down the street toward Blues Moon. The sun shone brightly, as if to magnify her mortification.

How could she agree to sing for a man like him in a place like that? What was she doing? Proving a point to Lorenzo?

She stopped and took off her gloves, rubbed her eyes. She took a few deep breaths before she started back walking.

She'd successfully avoided Lorenzo all this week. He'd come by her apartment a couple of times, but she'd ignored his knocking.

She missed Benny and the band. She hadn't had the courage to go back inside the club since she'd been fired. After she saved some money working at the Avalon, she would rent another apartment. Her heart sank because she knew it wouldn't be nearly as nice, and she wouldn't be able to afford to furnish it with the kind of modern furniture that Lorenzo had purchased for her current place. But it would be hers. She wouldn't owe anyone for anything.

She got on the elevator, greeting the attendant. She was looking for her keys when the gates opened to her floor. Distracted, she almost tripped.

She didn't regret that she'd been intimate with Lorenzo. She'd known what she was getting into, and she didn't blame him for her decisions. She could have stayed away from him, but she hadn't. Now she had to live with the fact that he filled her dreams every night.

She took her time opening her door. She was trying to calm down.

Inside, she placed her pocketbook and gloves on the counter.

Tears clouded her vision as she picked up the phone to call the club downstairs. "Um…hello, yes, this is Evelyn. I need someone to bring me a few boxes. Yes, as soon as possible. Thank you."

She put the phone back on the receiver and went to the bathroom to wash her face and look presentable for whoever came up with the boxes.

A few minutes later someone knocked at her door. She opened the door without even looking at the person who stood there. She turned to walk back toward the living room, distracted with her own thoughts.

"Hello, come in. You can place the boxes in the living room. Thank you so much for coming so fast."

When the person didn't respond, she turned to see who it was.

"Lorenzo…" she breathed.

"Evelyn. You're packing up?" Lorenzo looked around. He stood so close to her that Evelyn could barely move.

"Lorenzo, what are you doing here?"

"Tommy told me you called and wanted someone to bring boxes. I came to say… I don't know… Goodbye, I guess."

"I… We've already said our goodbyes."

"I know, but I guess I'm just…"

"You're what?" she asked. "I'm not doing this back and forth with you any longer."

Lorenzo looked confused.

"The first time I could understand your hesitation— even the second time. But after the last time we made love I thought for sure my dreams had come true."

Evelyn looked away, embarrassed by her own honesty. She hadn't wanted him to know how much he'd meant to her.

"Evelyn, I—"

"You should go—and please do not come back until I'm gone." She walked to the door and held the handle, indicating he should leave. She blinked back tears. "You need to go. Please don't show up here again. I'm moving out as soon as I can, and then I will be out of your life. Just as you wanted."

Chapter Forty-Six

Lorenzo

Lorenzo stood frozen. He desperately wanted to say the right thing. He wanted Evelyn to forgive him. But he still wanted to send her away for her own safety.

"So you're leaving for Colorado?"

Lorenzo's heart skipped and a pain coursed just under his skin. He wanted her to be safe, but he hated that it meant he wouldn't see her again. This was goodbye.

"Where I go is no longer your concern. Just know that I will be out of here by tomorrow."

Evelyn took a deep breath. Tears glistened in her golden eyes.

"You're not safe here," he said. "Even though the KKK is being handled, I'm learning that Simmens poses a threat of his own. He is after you, and no amount of compromise from me is going to satiate his obsession with you. Leaving Kansas City is the only thing for you to do. You're not safe here."

"Neither are you."

Evelyn's hand tightened on the handle of the door. She didn't look at him.

"Listen, I know you're upset with me—"

Evelyn turned her fiery gaze on him.

He blinked slowly, but continued. "But everything I've done, I've done because I care about you."

He walked closer to Evelyn. He could smell the lavender in the air around her. Tears glittered in her beautiful eyes. He tried to take her hand.

She yanked away like his hand was electrified. "Don't touch me."

"Okay, okay…" Lorenzo backed up.

He wanted to hold her. Take her into his arms and let her know how much she meant to him, how he would die if something happened to her.

"What can I do?" he asked. "I want us to be friends. I want you to have all the opportunities you deserve. I talked to my friend in Denver. I can drive you there tomorrow. He's prepared to pay you twice what you made at Blues Moon."

"Why? He doesn't even know me."

"No, but he knows me, and he knows I know talent. If I say a singer is one of the best, he believes it."

"If I'm 'one of the best,' why exactly did you fire me? Why are you pushing me away?"

"The KKK is going to kill you if they get to you. I can't let that happen. Just know that I wouldn't ask you to do this if I didn't think it was for the best. I'm just looking out for you."

"I can look out for myself. Wherever I go from here is up to me. Please leave."

She looked at him. The tears had disappeared and been replaced with palpable anger. He had failed to communicate with this woman he'd grown so attached to in such a short time. He saw in her eyes the hurt and anguish, and decided it was time for him to go.

He walked toward the door. At least she was going. He hoped that meant she was leaving town. Even going back to West Eden would be much better than staying in Kansas City.

He looked at her. At her face, so beautiful and so void of emotion. She looked at him like he was a stranger to her.

His heart clenched. He left without another word.

He went into his club. Once inside, he heard Dred and Jeb before he saw them. They were arguing—as usual. Lorenzo wondered when they were going to stop pretending they didn't like each other and get together, already. Their attraction toward each other was so blatantly obvious even hard-of-seeing Benny knew about it.

Lorenzo opened the door to his office to see Dred sitting on his antique desk and Jeb pacing, throwing his hands in the air. Jeb was only ever theatrical around Dred.

"To what do I owe this honor?" Lorenzo said.

"You're acting like we don't have a huge problem that's only getting worse with time," said Dred. "While you're around playing the love-sick puppy, we're here trying to keep you alive."

Dred pushed off from the desk and stood, folding her arms in front of her. She'd used to do that all the time when they were kids, and Lorenzo would tease her about how she pouted like a girl. She'd punched him in the nose enough that he knew better than to say that now.

"I've already spoken to the governor," he told them. "The boys should be on their way here for the meeting, and we will ambush them when they leave their favorite place, the Avalon. I've realized I have no choice—we need more muscle power—so I've told my father to have the family there as well, just for added force to ensure that my message is clear. Evelyn and any other woman in this city that Simmens has his eye on are not to be touched."

"I know it must have been hard for you to go back on your word not to get involved with your family," Dred said.

"It was, but I won't let anything happen to Evelyn. I'll do whatever it takes to keep her safe."

"I know you will."

Dred turned and walked out.

"Not going to say goodbye?"

Lorenzo laughed to himself. Dred was so socially awkward. She ignored him and kept walking.

Jeb, who'd been silent since Lorenzo had walked in the room, finally stood still, staring at Lorenzo. "Is there anything you need me to do?"

"Just keep your eyes open."

Lorenzo poured himself a full glass of whiskey and drank it in three gulps.

Then Tommy walked into Lorenzo's office. "There's a problem."

"Of course there is," Lorenzo said with a sigh.

"I think Evelyn is in some serious danger. You shouldn't let her leave."

"There's nothing I can do. You've met her. She's very determined."

"Hire her back, then."

"I can't do that either." Lorenzo ran his hand through his hair. "She's leaving town, Tommy. She'll be safe as long as she's away from me."

"I hope you don't regret this."

Tommy left and slammed the door behind him.

Lorenzo would let that breach of respect go. He could tell Tommy was really worried about Evelyn.

And Lorenzo already regretted pushing her away.

Chapter Forty-Seven

Evelyn

Evelyn paced in her living room after Lorenzo left. Her nerves were on end and she couldn't sit still. She had to sing at the Avalon in an hour, and she really didn't know what to do about the fact that the owner was a racist. She hoped she wouldn't have much interaction with him or his customers. She just wanted to go, sing and get paid.

The club in Denver sounded tempting. Lorenzo had paid her very well, and to think she could make twice that was enticing, but she didn't want to leave Kansas City. Her grand needed her to be close, and the music scene was larger in Kansas City. She had more of a chance of meeting the right people if she stayed.

She wouldn't let Lorenzo run her out of town. She would get to the bottom of the secrets he was keeping and show him that she wasn't some damsel in distress. She could and would take care of herself.

With that fire in her heart, she went to her wardrobe and pulled out her most seductive dress. She needed to feel strong, and the dress with the red fringe and beading down the bodice made her feel like she was already a star. She'd been saving it to wear on a special night at Blues Moon. That night would never come.

She stopped her thoughts before tears filled her eyes

again. She couldn't believe she'd almost let Lorenzo see her cry. Never again.

She decided she didn't want walk to the Avalon knowing the KKK was after her, so she went downstairs to hail a cab. She had a little extra money, thanks to working at Blues Moon.

The night air chilled her face, but her coat kept her warm. Cars honked, and the city throbbed with excitement. People bustled about in beautiful coats, hats and gloves. Evelyn loved the winter because everyone wore gloves and she didn't stand out as much with her gloves always in place.

"Miss Evelyn, what are you doing?" Jerry stood on the sidewalk, gawking at her.

"I'm going to catch a taxi to the Avalon. That's where I work now."

"I'll run and get the car. I'll take you. Mr. De Luca would have my head if he knew I'd let you get in a taxi."

"No, Jerry, really."

"Miss Evelyn, I must insist. I know the boss, and he won't like this one bit."

Jerry ran off in the direction of the garage where Lorenzo kept his cars. Evelyn sighed and walked back inside, glad for the warmth. She hoped Lorenzo wouldn't come out of the club at that moment. She couldn't bear another painful conversation with him. She needed to conserve her energy to sing.

She tapped her fingers on the glass door, waiting for Jerry to pull up. She wondered what car he would drive. She hoped Lorenzo had something less ostentatious than what she'd seen of his cars so far.

Her heart dropped when Jerry pulled out front in the Rolls.

Rolling her eyes, Evelyn walked outside. "Jerry, I don't think I should pull up to the Avalon in this car."

"Miss, this is the kind of car a star like you should be in. Besides, I'm technically off tonight, so I'm at your service."

"I don't know when my set will be over."

"Then I'll wait."

"Jerry, that is not necessary…really."

"It is my pleasure to ensure you arrive safely—and not just because I know the boss would want me to, but because I consider you to be a good person, and you need to keep yourself safe. I can help you do that."

Evelyn squeezed Jerry's hand. He opened the door for her and she slid in. She rubbed her hand across the red interior and took a deep breath. The car smelled of spices, just like Lorenzo.

Her heart sank at that realization. Perhaps going to Denver wasn't the worst idea. If she stayed in Kansas City she would never truly escape Lorenzo. Maybe she could convince her grand to come with her.

Trapped in an automobile that was filled with Lorenzo's scent, his laughter, his captivating eyes and perfect hair, Evelyn didn't notice when Jerry pulled up in front of the Avalon.

"We're here." He got out of the car to open her door.

The parking lot was filled with trucks. This was a very different club than Blues Moon. There were no fancy cars or fur coats here.

Evelyn looked at Jerry. He had concern etched in the lines between his brows.

"I'll be fine," Evelyn said, and gave Jerry a big smile.

She walked into the club, clutching her knife in her coat pocket. The cold steel of the handle pressed into her palm.

The smoky air hit Evelyn like a slap in the face. She cleared her throat, which immediately burned from the tobacco and sweat-thick scent. Bodies pushed together on the dance floor, music blared and glasses clanged. This club was so different. Where Blues Moon was all elegance and prestige, the Avalon was crude and sticky.

She hadn't been dropped off in the back, like she'd been told. She refused to act as a second-class citizen when she'd arrived in a Rolls Royce and was obviously the best dressed person in the place.

She held her head high and walked to the stage. There was a pianist and a microphone.

"Hello," Evelyn said to a man with a cigarette hanging from his mouth. He was the only other brown-skinned person in the speakeasy. "I'm Evelyn, the new singer."

"Pleased to meet you, miss. I'm Ezequiel. You can call me Eazy. You ready to get started?"

Evelyn nodded. "Is there somewhere I can put my coat and pocketbook?"

"I'd keep 'em as close as you can in this place. They don't like to see colored folks have nice things."

"Thank you for the tip."

Evelyn climbed onto the stage and put her coat and purse on top of a box right by the piano. She was determined to prove her strength. She wouldn't allow anyone to tell her where she belonged.

Walking over to the piano, she placed her glove-covered hands on its black shiny top. "Do you know any Mammy Smith songs?"

"*Do* I?"

The older gentleman changed songs with such precision Evelyn was impressed.

She decided that when she opened her own club—and she would—Eazy would be a part of her entertainment. She wanted Benny and the band at Blues Moon too, but she wouldn't steal them from Lorenzo.

She walked over to the microphone and cleared her throat. The dancers stopped to look at her. Some glared,

some smiled, but she didn't care about any of that. This
was about her proving her talent and her worth to herself.

The first note came out stronger than she could have
hoped, with her nerves on edge like they were. And after
the first note, the second and third followed easily. Before
she knew it the crowd had started moving again, and once
the song was over some people cheered. Music had the
power to bring people together, and she held that power
in her voice.

Looking back at Eazy, she laughed.

His smile filled the stage with brightness. "Let's keep
going," he said, transitioning to another song.

He did that so well. She stared at him for a moment, before turning back to the crowd. She could make out some
of the faces closest to the stage, but in the back by the bar
everyone was blurred together. The small club was dark,
with spotlights throughout over the tables and the bar area.
She hoped she would get used to the smell of the place…
Her stomach churned a little.

After Evelyn had sung another ten or so songs she
looked at Eazy, and he announced that they would take a
break. She and Eazy worked well together already. Just a
look and he knew she was getting tired.

"Where do you go to rest?" Evelyn picked up her coat
and pocketbook.

Eazy laughed. "You must come from a nicer club than
this one, miss. There ain't nowhere for us to go except
out back."

"What? What about when it's too cold to be outside?"

"I usually just play through the night, so I can stay in the
warmth, but you looked really tired so I called for a break.
I don't mind going outside with you, though. I wouldn't
want you out there by yourself anyway."

Evelyn sighed and followed Eazy to the back door. She'd

got about five steps when someone grabbed her arm. She turned to see the blotchy red-faced owner, Mr. Martin.

"Where d'you think you going, girl? My customers don't want you to take a break."

"I'm sorry," Evelyn said, yanking her arm from his sweaty grasp. "But I have to rest my voice. You want me to be able to sing again, don't you?"

"You better be quick about it."

"I need at least thirty minutes, Mr. Martin. At Blues Moon—"

"This ain't Blues Moon. Remember that." He spat on the floor and walked away.

Evelyn fought the urge to throw something at the man's retreating figure. She turned to see Eazy eyeing her.

"You handle yourself well, miss. Let's get outta here. I'll walk outside with you. Where you from?" Eazy held the door for her.

"I'm originally from Louisiana, but I live in a small town not too far away."

Once she was outside, the chill in the air whipped across Evelyn's face.

"Wow, it's getting cold already. It's early."

"Oh, you mean West Eden? Yeah, I've been trying to get there, but they ain't opened a club yet, so I gotta stay where the money is. Yeah, seems like fall is fading away. It goes straight from summer to winter around here."

As they stood on the steps outside of the Avalon. Evelyn felt a wave of nausea overtake her and she stumbled a little.

"Miss Evelyn, are you all right?" Eazy grabbed Evelyn's arm to steady her.

"We need to get back in there, but I'm feeling a little dizzy."

Eazy directed Evelyn to sit on the steps. He took his coat off for her to sit on. The cool air hit her once she was seated, and she immediately felt better. Her heart had raced unexpectedly, which had made it hard for her to breathe. But now she took several long, deep breaths and her head cleared.

Eazy stared, with concern etched in his gaze. "You want to go back into the Avalon?"

"Not right away. I'm just going to sit here for a moment longer. I'll be right in. You should go in, since I'm using your coat. It's too cold out here."

"I don't want to leave you by yourself."

"I just need a moment. Please, go inside. You'll catch your death out here without a coat."

Eazy looked up and down the street. It was empty. "Are you sure you want to be alone?"

Evelyn nodded. "I'm okay. I'll be right in." Evelyn had her fur and gloves.

Eazy hesitantly walked away. He looked back at Evelyn several times before disappearing through the back door to the Avalon.

Evelyn blew out a sigh of relief. She needed just a moment alone before going back in to finish singing. She would tell Mr. Martin over the phone tomorrow that she wouldn't be back. She was probably forfeiting her pay for the night, but she didn't care.

She was about to stand when out of the darkness appeared a figure, covered in shadows. It looked like the person could manipulate the light and stay hidden.

"Who's there?" Evelyn asked, getting to her feet, gripping the knife in her pocket. "Let me see your face now." Her voice sounded fearless, but she was terrified.

Mr. Simmens spat tobacco on the street as he emerged into the light of the streetlamp. "You really should be more careful, Miss Laroque. Being in this part of town all by yourself...well, that's just not smart. We don't take kindly to colored folks over on this side of town—but you might not have known that."

Evelyn took a step back, trying to get closer to the door. "You stay away from me."

"But you're so pretty… I just want a taste. I'll save the rest for my boys back in the truck. We got mighty plans for you and that mouth of yours."

Evelyn gripped the knife in her pocket more tightly.

"Now, come here so I can see what that mouth feels like when it's put to good use."

Simmens kept advancing, until he was only a foot or so from Evelyn. She needed him close enough so he wouldn't see her pull the knife out of her pocket.

"I haven't done anything to you. You need to leave me alone."

"It's because of you that some of my boys are sick. Whatever happened to them in Blues Moon still ain't worn off completely."

Simmens grabbed Evelyn's neck.

She shoved the knife into his stomach. She had to push hard to get through the layers of clothes, but she knew the moment she broke his skin and the knife plunged into the soft tissue of his abdomen.

He stumbled back and looked at her. He put his hand to his stomach. It came away covered in fire-engine-red blood. He staggered back into the street.

A figure somersaulted into Mr. Simmens, kicking him to the ground, forcing the knife in deeper as his body fell face forward to the concrete. Dred.

"Are you okay?" she asked, stepping on Mr. Simmens's back.

Evelyn couldn't tell if the force from the kick had knocked him out, or if the knife wound had killed him. She hadn't meant to seriously injure him. She'd just wanted to protect herself.

Dred, not appearing at all fazed by the possibility that the man was dead, looked back at Evelyn. "Are you okay?"

Evelyn nodded.

Dred turned Simmens over on his back, pulling Evelyn's knife free. "We have to get out of here," she said, with urgency sharpening every word.

Evelyn nodded. "What are you doing here?"

"I came to make sure you were okay, and I need to talk to you about Lorenzo before it's too late. Come with me."

Evelyn followed Dred, staring at the bloody knife in her hand as they headed away from Avalon toward the alley.

Chapter Forty-Eight

Lorenzo

Lorenzo drove slowly as he approached the Avalon. The Klan would be sauced and easy prey. They needed to know how powerful the mob was and that it wasn't worth losing their lives. Not to mention Lorenzo's own power, which was starting to become solid outside of the influence of his father. Lorenzo had networked and made some pretty serious connections that would shape the future of the city. His father's ways were of the past.

Lorenzo had already demanded that no one was to die tonight, but he couldn't ensure what would come in the future if the KKK continued to terrorize the city. All he knew was that he would protect Evelyn no matter what.

His roadster led the line of fancy cars driven by members of the De Luca family. There were twenty cars in all. He pulled around the back of the club and saw, as promised, that the governor had the street blocked so there would be no escape for the Klan.

The governor had brought with him the police officers he trusted, and was putting them into places of power to ensure the city got clean of dirty cops. Lorenzo's father wasn't exactly pleased with that idea.

To his horror, Evelyn stood in the middle of the alley, flanked by Dred and surrounded by at least ten Klansmen.

"What the hell is going on?" Jeb asked, exiting his car seconds after Lorenzo.

"I'm about to find out."

Lorenzo led the massive group of De Lucas, along with Tommy and Jeb. He had asked Dred to go ahead and make sure the street was cleared of everyone with the exception of the Klansmen who were planning to destroy Blues Moon.

The Klansmen were so consumed with whatever was going on with Evelyn and Dred they barely noticed Lorenzo and the men approaching. The few who had noticed started backing away.

Lorenzo cleared his throat when he was about a few feet away and a number of the Klansmen started at the sight. The De Lucas, Tommy and Jeb were all dressed in black. They probably looked terrifying to these backwoods country bigots.

"I'm going to give you an opportunity to turn your back on the Klan," Lorenzo began. "It might just save your life. If you walk away now, you won't be hurt. If you choose to stay, then I'm sorry to inform you but the city will know all of your names by morning, and the governor has assured me that anyone involved in harming young women will be promptly fired from his position and arrested. That would be a shame, as I know some of you are doctors and police officers. Oh, and, hey—a detective. Nice to see you again. How much will your family suffer if you are in prison? How about those criminals you've put behind bars? Will they be happy to see you in a cell with them?"

"This whore killed Simmens!" one of the men shouted.

Lorenzo looked at Evelyn. She stood tall, but he could tell she was frightened. On the ground in front of her was Simmens.

Lorenzo sighed. "And I'm sure he deserved it. If he attacked her, like he's done multiple times before, then what she did was self-defense. He caused his own death. Do you really want to die for a man who couldn't have cared less what happened to any of you?"

"We don't have to listen to you Italian dogs," another man shouted, with spittle flying from his mouth. He was obviously drunk.

A man stepped from the shadows. It was a Ricci boss—a young one. "Is that what you think of all of us?"

Upon closer inspection, Lorenzo realized that this Ricci was the same man who had shot Holly all those years ago. The man still walked with a slight limp.

"No, of course not, Mr. Ricci," one of the younger Klansmen said quickly.

The Ricci boss laughed, and without hesitation punched a Klansman in the face.

The fight started quickly.

Lorenzo pushed his way to Evelyn, who was being protected by Dred. She stood defiant in the face of danger once again.

Lorenzo grabbed her hand and dragged her from the melee. To his surprise, she followed him without hesitation, although her dress prevented her from running fast. He just wanted to get her to the roadster so she could get out of there.

A Klansmen blocked their path and pulled a knife. Lorenzo kicked the knife out of the man's hand and punched him in the face. Out of the corner of his eye Lorenzo saw the barrel of a shotgun, pointed at him at point-blank range. Evelyn tried to push him out of the way but he was able to pivot, putting his body between her and the gun.

The hot, searing bullet tore through Lorenzo's flesh. He was knocked to the ground by the force of the shot, falling on top of Evelyn. Darkness crept in from the edges of his vision. But he saw the man with the shotgun tackled by the young Ricci boss. That shocked Lorenzo. It appeared the young man was fighting *with* the De Lucas instead of against them.

Lorenzo had a moment of déjà-vu. And for just a second he wanted to wrap his hands around the young Ricci's throat and pay him back for what he did to Holly. But looking at Evelyn under him, safe, he realized that death wasn't the closure he needed. This Ricci boss had helped Lorenzo save Evelyn.

The gunpowder in the air was making Lorenzo cough. "Are you okay?" he asked, trying to roll off Evelyn so she could get to safety.

But he never did hear her response.

Chapter Forty-Nine

Evelyn

The night sky was filled with billowing black smoke and the taste of soot was heavy in the air. Sirens blared as the fire engines zipped down the street.

The scene had sent memories sliding over her like a rushing river. The banks of her pain had overflowed.

She had endured it with the weight of Lorenzo's lifeless body on top of her, anchoring her to the moment.

She'd survived. But he hadn't.

Evelyn rubbed her eyes, squinting against the bright lights of the hospital room. Her head throbbed and her sides ached from sleeping in the chair all night.

She walked over to where Lorenzo lay unconscious in the bed. He hadn't opened his eyes. He hadn't even flinched after they'd brought him in from surgery. The doctors had told her that they wouldn't know his chances of survival until he woke up.

"Please wake up," she said, placing a soft kiss on his brow.

He'd saved her, and she wouldn't even consider that he wasn't going to survive.

A groan startled Evelyn and she looked at Lorenzo.

"He's awake!" she shouted.

Suddenly there was a rush of movement. Several people rushed in and fussed over him. They took his vitals and flashed more lights in his eyes, which Evelyn imagined was painful.

She wasn't sure what showed on her face, but her emotions roared inside of her. All she wanted was to see that Lorenzo was okay.

After everyone had left, she went to him. Her scars were on full display because she hadn't left his side since he was admitted. She had no idea where her gloves were.

Seeming to hear her thoughts, he kissed her scars. "I tried, Evelyn, but I just couldn't do it." His eyes looked so sincere.

"Do what?" she said.

"I tried to stay away from you, but I… I can't. I know you deserve a life of peace and safety, but I can't stop loving you. When you tried to push me out of the way of that bullet… I don't know what I'd do if I lost you. I just can't be without you Evelyn."

"I know you live a dangerous life, Lorenzo, but so do I. Being Black in this country is no walk in the park. Either way, danger or not, you're worth it. I want to be with you too."

"I have a way for us to be as safe as we can. You've brought so much light into my life. You're like the sun shining, scaring away the darkness inside of me. So I'm leaving my family here in the city and I'm hoping to move to West Eden with you, where we'll be safe. I love you, and I want you to marry me. Be my wife and open a new club with me. Help me fight for political change against Prohibition. I want to give you the life you deserve, and I think we can have that in West Eden—if you'll have me."

Chapter Fifty

Lorenzo

Lorenzo waited to hear Evelyn's answer. He'd only known her a short time, but there was no doubt in his mind that she was the one he was meant to be with. He wanted to spend the rest of his life with her. She'd proved that she could handle dangerous situations, and not only keep herself safe, but protect those around her. She was talented, beautiful and selfless. She was more than he thought he deserved, but he would work to make her happy.

"Yes," she said with tears in her eyes. "I will marry you."

She reached out to him and he wrapped her in his arms. He'd been dreaming of this moment. It was the most beautiful dream he'd ever had. He envisioned their children, her gift of music to the world, their happiness at seventy years old.

He'd go completely legit, get out of the bootlegging business until Prohibition could be repealed and start a music publishing company. And the only reason any of this would be possible was because she'd helped him see the good in himself.

He ran his hand in circles along her back. He winced as sudden movement hurt.

"Are you okay?" she said.

"I'm better than I've ever been. Thank you for...for being here," he said.

"I wouldn't be anywhere else," she said, kissing him, careful not to touch his side.

"When are they going to let me out of here?" Lorenzo asked, staring up into Evelyn's eyes.

"They said as soon as you woke up they would assess your progress after the surgery. Then you'll need to stay here and recover for four weeks at a minimum."

Lorenzo sighed. "As long as you're here with me, I don't care where I am."

Epilogue

Lorenzo admired the freshly painted club. Evelyn had decided on light gray walls with a feature wall behind the bar painted gold. He loved the theme of gold and silver that she'd chosen. It gave the club a regal feel, which was so appropriate for Evelyn's style. She was royalty.

The arched dome ceiling had an intricately painted mural from an artist who'd moved to West Eden from Harlem. The style of the mural was fragmented, with bold colors and a nod to Senegalese culture. The mural was Lorenzo's favorite part of the club.

The opening night for Gold Sun was just a week away, and Lorenzo and Evelyn had a lot of work left to do. The easy part had been picking the band. Evelyn had hired Eazy, the pianist from the Avalon, and Benny and the band had come from Blues Moon.

Lorenzo would reopen Blues Moon eventually, but he wanted a break from the city until things cooled down. He wanted to focus on being the best husband to Evelyn. They'd set a date for next year to have their wedding.

"Boss, where do you want these?" Tommy rolled a couple of tables through the front door.

"Put them along the perimeter of the dance floor. Thanks, Tommy."

Lorenzo was happy that Tommy, Jeb and Dred had wanted to join him and Evelyn in West Eden. He had purchased a building with apartments for each of them. Evelyn said that until they were married, she thought it would be best for them to have separate places. He couldn't wait until they bought their first home together.

Gold Sun was on the first floor of the building, and the apartments were on the third, fourth and fifth floors. Lorenzo had given Evelyn the top-floor apartment. She was the star after all. He didn't really care where he lived, as long as he could be close to her.

"Lorenzo, stop daydreaming and help," Dred said.

It had been hard for her to walk away from Kansas City, but when Evelyn had asked her to join them, Dred had surprisingly agreed. And, of course, when Dred agreed, Jeb agreed.

The only person Lorenzo worried about was his father. He'd decided to take matters into his own hands with the Ricci family, but Lorenzo wanted to find an amicable resolution to the long-held feud between the families, especially after the young Ricci boss had taken down the Klansman who'd tried to shoot him.

It would take both families to be willing to put their differences and their long history of murdering each other aside. Lorenzo wasn't sure that it would ever happen...

Picking up a box, Lorenzo unpacked it and put away the brand-new glasses he'd ordered. Then the door opened, and Evelyn stood at the threshold. She paused, and Lorenzo marveled at her beauty—as he had done since the first moment he saw her at Blues Moon. She wore wool white pants with her fur coat and hat. Lorenzo put down the box he held and walked from behind the bar.

Evelyn's skin was the color of wet sand. Her beautiful midnight-black hair fell in waves around her shoulders and down her back. She'd stopped wearing gloves and her hands were delicate and beautifully scarred. Lorenzo stared at her, remembering where his life had been just a few months ago.

He'd never thought he'd find someone to share his life. The reality of his family and his choices as a businessman had always created a barrier to his happiness. He'd feared for Evelyn's life more than his own, only to learn that she was resilient and capable of protecting herself. He knew he would always worry for her, but he respected her ability to navigate the complexities of his world and her own. He still had a lot to learn about her world, but he wanted to learn with her and from her.

He'd never imagined that finding the woman he was to spend the rest of his life with would mean he would be entering into a relationship that would require so much of him, but he couldn't wait to show her how much he loved her.

"Lorenzo, how's it coming?" She glided over to him.

He put his hand on her cheek, staring into her golden eyes. "Everything is fine—and even better now that you're here."

He kissed her, softly at first, and then he released the heat of his passion, holding her to him. They had similar scars from their pasts, but she had healed Lorenzo from within.

"Can I see you in your office?" Lorenzo said. He'd made sure he and Evelyn both had offices, and Evelyn also had a dressing room.

Evelyn smiled, her eyes sparkling with mischief. "Of course, Mr. De Luca."

Lorenzo laughed. "That's my dad's name."

"Oh, gross," Dred said, rolling her eyes.

Evelyn took Lorenzo's hand and led him to her office. She closed the blinds and locked the door.

He'd waited for weeks to make love to her again. His side had had to heal because he wanted to be able to caress her and explore her entirely. He pinned Evelyn against the door. He moved her thick black hair away from her face and kissed her cheek, moving slowly down to her neck. Her skin warmed his lips. She tasted like the sweetest dessert. He licked her delicate skin, lingering in the sensual curve of her slender neck.

"Lorenzo, everyone is just on the other side of the door..." Evelyn breathed.

"You belong to me and I belong to you. We've both waited a long time to have our happiness. We don't have to wait any longer."

Lorenzo kissed her lips. He would savor her for the rest of their lives, with the fire of their love forever burning.

* * * * *

"Are you alright?" he said.

She didn't respond right away. Lorenzo worried she was in shock from the near assault.

"I'm fine, and I don't need you acting like a Neanderthal for my benefit." Her hands were balled into fists. Lorenzo wondered if she'd planned to hit Simmens herself.

Lorenzo couldn't understand why this woman would get sore when his gesture was nothing less than chivalrous. It seemed like she had been offended by his defending her.

"I...I was just... He was going to say..." No one had made Lorenzo stutter in his entire life.

"I know what he was going to say, Mr...."

"De Luca. Lorenzo De Luca." Lorenzo tried to regain some semblance of control over the situation.

"Mr. De Luca. And it wouldn't be the first time, and it won't be the last. I don't need your help."

Lorenzo, aghast at her words, couldn't think of anything to say, partly because of her harsh tone and partly because of how beautiful she was. The demure dress couldn't hide her womanly figure. With her high cheekbones and sharp chin, brown skin and pink lips, she should have been a movie star; maybe she was.

"I'm looking for the owner of this club."

"I'm the owner," Lorenzo said, still confused by her reaction. He realized everyone in the club was looking at him, this woman and the unconscious man on the floor.

Author Note

This book was created out of a need—a need to see the beauty in diversity, hear the untold stories of our history and uncover the ugliness of the truth. In my pursuit of truth, I realized the depth of human interaction that takes place in life. Good and evil can live simultaneously within us. We are all a combination of things. That's what makes us human.

Yes, this is a work of fiction, but fiction is a reflection of so many truths. The inspiration for this story evolved over time. I'd recently learned about the Tulsa Race Massacre, and shortly after that, the characters came together in a whirlwind of unimaginable sadness, anger, love, beauty, cruelty and hope.